Also by Susan Gabriel

Fiction

The Secret Sense of Wildflower
(a Best Book of 2012 – Kirkus Reviews)

Lily's Song
(sequel to *The Secret Sense of Wildflower*)

Grace, Grits and Ghosts:
Southern Short Stories

Temple Secrets

Seeking Sara Summers

Circle of the Ancestors

Quentin & the Cave Boy

Nonfiction

Fearless Writing for Women:
Extreme Encouragement & Writing Inspiration

Available at all booksellers
in print, ebook and audio formats.

Trueluck Summer

Susan Gabriel

Wild Lily Arts

Trueluck Summer

ISBN 978-0-9981050-0-0

Cover design by Lizzie Gardiner, lizziegardiner.co.uk

Wild Lily Arts, Inc.

Printed in the United States of America.

To Mary Jane
Who has known me since I was a "pup"

I have a dream that my four little children will one day live in a nation where they will not be judged by the color of their skin, but by the content of their character.

—Martin Luther King, Jr.

Chapter One

Ida Trueluck

Losing a lifetime's collection of belongings is like taking away all your mirrors and no longer knowing what you look like. Three weeks ago, I moved in with my son and his family on Queen Street in downtown Charleston, South Carolina. I now inhabit a lovely room on the second floor overlooking the backyard, with only enough space for a handful of my favorite things. The rest I had to sell or give away. Something that was much harder to do than I imagined.

From my bedroom door, my granddaughter Trudy studies me as though she is an archaeologist, and I am an artifact unearthed from another time. Ancient. Yet not quite mummified. I reach for the shoes I took off the evening before. At least nothing ever gets lost in this small space. Not even my glasses, which I managed to displace at least once a day in my spacious old house.

In the corner of my bedroom, I sit in my favorite armchair, the one with the magnolia print that used to be in our living room—Ted's and mine—next to a fig tree whose growth exceeded my expectations. After forty years together,

Ted and I had refined a sense of comfort, like me and this old chair, at times feeling like one person instead of two.

"Are you thinking about Grandpa again?" Trudy asks.

My granddaughter is curious and observant, and I am convinced that someday she will do great things. Of course all grandmothers think their grandchildren are special. That's part of the job, isn't it?

The last time she caught me sniffling, I confessed to thinking about her grandfather. Will I ever stop grieving? It has been over a year since he passed, and I still expect him to walk in the door any minute and ask me what's for dinner.

"Actually, I was thinking about how your Grandpa Trueluck and I met. Have I ever told you that story?"

With the effortlessness only possessed by someone twelve years of age, Trudy dives onto my four-poster bed and props her head up on one arm, ready to listen. We have already had several heartfelt talks over the last three weeks with her in this same position. If not for Trudy, my moving here would present a much harder transition.

"Tell me," she says. Trudy wears a summertime outfit: shorts and sleeveless blouse, her sneakered feet not touching the bed.

"It was at the Mayberry Club," I begin. "It doesn't exist now, but back then it was a place downtown where you could go and listen to music and dance. It was where I first learned to dance the Charleston."

I look over, expecting her to be impressed, but my reference appears lost on her.

"Our city had a famous dance named after it," I say to educate her. "It was a craze back in the twenties."

To Trudy, forty-years ago must seem like the Middle Ages, but to my relief, her interest doesn't appear to wane.

"When I saw your grandpa that first time, goosebumps danced up my arms," I continue.

She sits up and rubs her arms as though inheriting the goosebumps.

"Oh, Trudy, I'd never seen such a handsome man in my entire life," I continue. "Tall. A sparkling smile. A twinkle in his eye." A sigh, filled with history, escapes me. "We were married a year later," I add.

Trudy lays back, her arms folded underneath her head as though imagining our meeting. She was really quite close to her Grandpa Trueluck.

"We never stopped dancing," I begin again. "Over the years we slowed down a great deal, but we never stopped. Every evening before we went to bed, we danced cheek-to-cheek in our living room. A slow rendition of 'Tea for Two,' with your grandpa singing the words softly in my ear."

Cross-legged now, she says in a half-whisper, "I saw you two dance once. I was spending the night, and you thought I was sleeping."

"You saw us?" I smile.

She nods.

I stand and close my eyes, swaying to imaginary music. I feel my husband's breath tickling my ear. When I open my eyes and realize that I am not in my home of forty years, but in an upstairs bedroom in my son's house, my eyes mist. Trudy crosses the room and puts her arms around me.

"Everything will be okay, Nana Trueluck," she whispers, sounding older than her years. She always adds the Trueluck to my name as though I am one of a dozen grandmothers she possesses and needs to keep them all straight. But perhaps she simply likes the way it sounds.

"I'm supposed to comfort you, not the other way around." My voice wobbles over the words.

"We'll take turns," she says.

A voice yells upstairs, causing us to part.

Abigail—Trudy's mother, my daughter-in-law—isn't exactly pleased with the new living situation, even though she pretends everything is fine. A behavior practiced by southern women from birth until the grave. This morning at breakfast, Trudy and I were asked to deliver one of Abigail's pies to Callie's Diner where she sells them. A plot, I believe, to get us both out from underfoot so she can watch *As the World Turns* in peace. Yet Trudy and I are not ones to have to be coaxed out of the house.

Trudy leads the way downstairs, and we enter the kitchen, steamy from baking. Charleston in summertime can reach oven temperatures. At least it feels that way. To not have my own kitchen anymore is strange. And as far as I can tell, Abigail's domain is not to be shared. At least not yet.

A small vase of summer roses sits on the kitchen table. It reminds me of my plan to pick up flowers while on our errand. Flowers on the table in front of my bedroom window might make me feel more at home. I miss my garden's display: my beloved tea roses, hyacinths, moonflowers, and star jasmine. A flowering that extends six months of the year.

"Trudy, please don't slouch," Abigail says.

My granddaughter straightens her spine long enough for her mother to approve and then resumes her usual position. Abigail's posture is as straight as a Charleston lamppost. She wears a dress, though it is a weekday, just in case someone drops by. The only time I have ever seen her wear pedal pushers or the occasional pair of shorts is at the beach, and even then she looked dressed up.

Abigail gives me a sideways glance as though she has heard my thoughts. "Are you going out like that?" A smile is attached to the question as though to camouflage the criticism. A comment I doubt she would have shared if my son, Ted Junior, weren't already at work.

To Abigail, appearances are everything. They used to be important to me, too. But after Ted Senior passed, I got tired of wearing black. I wanted more color. The latest addition to my wardrobe is what I call my gypsy skirts. Skirts of my own creation, made with special order fabrics that are airy and have a flower pattern to remind me I still have some life left in me.

For Abigail's benefit, I give a geriatric twirl to show off the complete outfit: gypsy skirt with large purple and green flowers, a short-sleeved white blouse, and white high-top sneakers to accentuate my skinny legs.

She doesn't look amused and hands Trudy a lemon meringue pie, one of Abigail's specialties, boxed and tied with twine. She makes spectacular pies—apple, peach, and lemon meringue—but if baking and child-rearing hadn't called her, Abigail would have made a good nun. The kind that carries rulers and occasionally raps knuckles.

"Please, get it there in one piece," Abigail says to Trudy, tossing a glance at both of us.

"We will," I say in a sing-song voice, sounding more jovial than I feel, though I doubt I have fooled anyone.

Once Trudy and I leave the house, the smell of salt water overtakes us. A reminder that not only Charleston Harbor, but the Atlantic Ocean is nearby. Trudy and I walk down Queen Street and take a right onto East Bay. Callie's Diner is a few blocks away on Broad Street. Mid-morning, the June day is already sticky. If I hadn't lived in the Lowcountry my entire life, I might find it oppressive, but this June heat is nothing compared to what will come in July and August.

It is the first day of Trudy's summer vacation, and she has a lightness to her step, full of possibility.

"Any big plans this summer?" I ask.

She grins in my direction. "Not yet," she says as though confident something will present itself.

I think of my summers as a girl and wonder what happened to my adventurous spirit. My family lived near a coastal waterway. With Maisie—my best friend throughout grammar school—I made forts, treehouses, and driftwood rafts that sunk as quickly as we released them onto the marsh. Entire days were spent on Sullivan's Island or Folly Beach building sandcastles while my family's maid, Sweeney, watched us from under an umbrella—barefoot, yet still wearing her uniform.

My mother's properness makes Abigail's seem tame in comparison. I remind myself to give Abigail a chance. After all, she did let me move into her home—although I imagine Ted Junior had to do a great deal of convincing before she agreed.

As Trudy and I walk east toward Broad Street, the sun rises above the buildings. Trudy holds her head high as though open to anything the world has to offer. I wonder if I ever possessed the confidence she has. At my age, it feels like I am closing instead of opening, a flower near the end of its bloom, its sweet aroma threatening to turn bitter in the sun.

At least I haven't lost all of my color, I think to myself, glancing at my skirt.

Imitating my granddaughter I lift my chin with renewed hope. Perhaps it isn't too late for this old broad to have an adventure, too.

Chapter Two

Trudy Trueluck

While Nana Trueluck stops to buy flowers from one of the colored women who sits on the corner of Broad and Meeting Streets, I continue on past the post office to Callie's Diner. Until my grandmother started living with us, I didn't spend that much time with her. Mama always came up with reasons why I couldn't go visit, not to mention that Nana and Grandpa Trueluck did a lot of traveling before he died.

A huge crowd gathered at his funeral. Daddy said that Grandpa Trueluck was well loved. He was certainly well loved by me. I still miss him. He smelled of Ivory soap and pipe tobacco and his mustache tickled when he kissed me on the cheek. Without fail, every time I saw him, he slipped a Brach's caramel into my hand when Nana Trueluck wasn't looking.

Nana Trueluck still misses him, too. Since she moved in, she stays in her room a lot, and sometimes I find piles of tissues in the corner of her armchair. I do my best to take her mind off how sad she is.

At the corner of King Street, I wait for the traffic light to change, tapping my foot on the sidewalk. The pie is heavy and my fingers ache from the twine. Callie's Diner is less than a block away. A dark cloud covers the sun and momentarily softens the heat. For about the hundredth time that day I wish for a summer adventure.

In the next second, a Sunbeam Bread truck barrels down Broad Street from the opposite direction. Something about it seems off. The truck weaves into the other lane, and a car veers out of the way. The driver of the car sits on his horn. A moment later the truck comes straight for me. I freeze, my legs refusing to move as danger prickles up my spine. Brakes squeal, and I hold my breath. An instant before I am smashed flatter than one of Nana Trueluck's pralines that she always makes at Christmas, a brown hand jerks me out of the way and the truck crashes into a streetlamp right where I was standing. The engine sizzles, and a cloud of steam rises from the hood.

"Are you okay?" the boy asks.

In that moment, I realize I have never seen a colored boy up close. He is about my age, though shorter and skinnier, and is much stronger than he appears, given he just pulled me out of the path of a runaway truck.

"You saved my life," I say.

He blinks like he is as surprised as I am.

"My name is Trudy Trueluck." I extend my hand.

He hesitates, like maybe he has never touched a white girl before. But then he shakes my hand.

"Paris Moses," he says. "No relation."

"No relation?" I ask.

"No relation to the guy in the Bible," he says.

"Oh," I say.

The lemon meringue pie I was to deliver to Callie's Diner is a gooey mess on the sidewalk.

"That could have been me," I say to Paris, "except there would be blood and guts instead of yellow filling."

He offers a quick grimace followed by a smile. At that moment I know that Paris Moses and I will become friends.

People gather around us, and the driver of the truck asks me if I am sure I am okay. Evidently, he spilled hot coffee onto himself and lost control of the truck. His white shirt is stained with the evidence. Over the mumblings of the crowd, I hear Nana Trueluck call my name as she runs down the street. She divides the crowd with her arms like she is parting the Red Sea.

Nana Trueluck's hair is solid white, and she wears it pulled up in a bun on the top of her head. Everybody loves her, with the exception of my mother. For one thing, she has a fondness for Doris Day songs and sings sometimes when you least expect it. The same fondness extends to Broadway show tunes. According to Daddy, she wanted to be a nightclub singer someday but never got around to it. On more than one occasion, she has burst into song at the dinner table and made my entire family jump. Last Sunday, she belted out "Everything's

Coming Up Roses" over pot roast because pot roast was always a favorite of Grandpa Trueluck's. Once we got over the shock of her singing, all but Mama joined her on the chorus.

However, Nana Trueluck isn't singing now.

"Are you sure you're okay, sweetheart? I would never forgive myself if anything happened to you." Her brow creased, she searches my knees and elbows for cuts and bruises.

I insist I am fine, which I am. For one thing, if this didn't happen I don't think I would have ever met Paris. I take Nana's hand to introduce her to my new friend, the boy who saved my life. But when I turn around, Paris Moses has disappeared.

The next morning when I go into the kitchen, the newspaper is on the table. The headline of *The Charleston Post* reads:

Mayor's Daughter Saved by Negro Boy

In the newspaper article, Daddy calls Paris a hero and later that night some cowardly white folks throw rocks through the windows at City Hall where his office is. It is 1964, and I am twelve years old.

Chapter Three

Ida

Abigail and I stand side by side in front of the kitchen window overlooking the small backyard. As she washes dishes at the sink, I dry them and sit them on the counter. My daughter-in-law has been wound tighter than a yoyo after the call last night that windows were broken at the courthouse. My son, Ted Junior, went with the Charleston police to survey the damage. I overheard him tell Abigail that this incident was bound to happen after the article appeared in yesterday's paper.

"Did that boy really save her life?" Abigail asks.

"That's what Trudy said." I put away three cups and saucers while Abigail watches to make sure I put them in the right place.

"Why didn't you watch out for her?" she asks, as though wanting to say this all morning.

This is something I have asked myself many times already. Trudy is quite independent, even at twelve, and is growing up fast. Sometimes I think she acts more grown up than I do. Also, television has matured us all, bringing the world into our living rooms, the news delivered every evening by Walter Cronkite—an exciting, sometimes alarming world, and one that is evolving with every passing day.

From what I gather, Abigail would prefer to stop everything: the wheels of time, the wheels of progress, anything to do with forward movement. Forward is the unknown. Yet as a culture, forward movement appears to be exactly what we need. Of course no one asks my opinion, and I don't offer it. Not even to Ted Junior. A mother must choose her battles carefully with a grown son—especially if she lives in an upstairs bedroom of his house.

Abigail tells me that helping with the dishes isn't necessary, but I don't believe her for a second. A person knows when someone is trying too hard to make something work. If I had another option rather than living here, I would have chosen it.

How did I know that Ted Senior and I had depleted our nest egg with all those trips? At least this arrangement has given me a chance to get to know my grandchildren more than I would have. Especially Trudy. My grandson, Teddy, doesn't sit still long enough to get to know. At least not yet. He is six and in constant motion from sunrise to sunset. I am lucky if I see him streak through the house from time to time.

"Did people see her talk to that Negro boy?" Abigail asks.

My hackles rise from the disapproval in Abigail's voice.

"Just so you know, I was raised by a Negro woman named Sweeney," I say, surprised by my outburst. "She was the most honorable woman I have ever known. And I imagine the boy who saved Trudy's life is just as honorable."

Abigail turns off the water faucet with an extra hard twist, as if to turn off our conversation. Then she removes her apron and hangs it on the hook on the back of the kitchen door, all calm, like I am the disagreeable one in this scenario.

"I imagine Trudy did talk to the boy," I say, in an effort to regain the peace. "You know how Trudy is." But I wonder if she does.

As far as I can tell, Trudy challenges Abigail's sense of propriety. No matter how much she insists that Trudy remember who she is—the daughter of the mayor—Trudy appears to see no point. She makes a friend of anyone she chooses, not giving a moment's thought to who their family is, much less hers. She is brave in ways none of the other Truelucks are brave. Including me. If I had to guess, I'd say she inherited some of her great-great-great-grandmother's courage. A woman who gets a footnote in the Charleston history books as an abolitionist. Not that I inherited an ounce of my ancestor's bravery.

"If you're out together in public, I expect you to keep Trudy out of trouble," Abigail says to me. "Is that too much to ask?"

"Not at all," I say. I have to resist adding a "ma'am" at the end. Sweeney knew how to deal with uppity white women. I watched her do it. She did exactly what they asked but with a twinkle in her eye that said in no uncertain terms that it was by choice she did these things, not victimhood.

Abigail sits at the kitchen table and begins to read the newspaper while I dry the remaining dishes until they squeak. I carefully stack things in the cupboard and think about Charleston culture and about how your importance is measured by whether your money is old or new—old being the most preferred. Status is determined by who your family is and how long you've lived here. Ancestry is central to identity.

The Trueluck family came to Charleston in the 1820s and my family—surname Rutherford—has been here even longer than that. When I moved in with my son and his family, I also moved into the attic an old steamer trunk full of my great-grandmother's memorabilia. And when it is my turn to pass from this life, I will leave that old steamer trunk with Trudy.

Just the other day, I was at the Piggly Wiggly, and some-one in the check-out line asked me if my family had been here since The War. And by war, she didn't mean the First or the Second World War, or the Korean, or what is happening in Vietnam right now. The War referred to in these parts is al-ways the Civil War. A war that has never ended and plays out in the shadows on every street corner in our fair city.

Abigail puts the newspaper aside as though distracted. "You don't think Trudy will befriend the boy, do you?" she asks.

"Trudy is her own person," I say, to avoid telling truth or lie.

"Speak to her, Ida," she says. "Tell her it's not a good idea."

But it is too late for talks. Last evening, I overheard Trudy call people in the telephone book with the last name of Moses, asking for Paris a dozen times before finally finding him. She has probably already arranged a meeting or perhaps is meeting with him right now.

"She's got a good head on her shoulders," I say. "She won't do anything foolish."

Abigail elicits a short laugh, as though *foolish* is Trudy's middle name. But perhaps fools are the bravest souls of all.

The front door slams, and Ted Junior's heavy footsteps approach. I can only guess his frustration. He has been mayor less than a year and already people are calling for his resignation. If Ted Junior had been a horse at the racetrack the odds would have him guaranteed to lose, but he won anyway. In fact, it was a landslide victory because of the colored vote. News that made it into the national newspapers.

Yet it seems that any time progress inches forward, the past pulls us right back into what was before. It is a tug-of-war that has been going on for centuries. Charleston is slow to change the way things have always been. Come to think of it, I haven't been that quick to embrace the big changes in my life, either, like moving in with Ted Junior and his family; however, I am willing to learn. Even if I don't have a clue how to begin.

Chapter Four

Trudy

My oldest friend Vel and I walk the dirt road along the marsh and share a banana Popsicle. Vel's full name is Velvet Ogilvie. She shortened it to Vel in third grade. Her hair is straight, the color of straw, and looks like someone put a broom on her head and removed the handle, leaving a space for her face.

We are on our way to meet my new friend, Paris, the boy who saved my life. It is a secret meeting on account of two white girls aren't allowed to be friends with a colored boy. But I have never been especially good at following rules. Especially stupid ones. Mama says not caring what people think is Nana Trueluck's influence, which she doesn't see as a good thing.

Nana Trueluck is an honest-to-god descendent of a famous Charleston abolitionist. Evidently, I come from a long line of rule-breakers and secret-keepers. And according to Nana, I should be proud of that.

Giant oaks tower over us, sprinkling a patchwork of sun and shadow at our feet. We lick the last sweet juices of the

Popsicle from our fingers and avoid a yellow jacket that circles like we are two petals of a sticky flower. Then we take turns jumping from one piece of shade to the next as if they are hopscotch squares.

Frogs croak and the cicadas hum along in the heat. It is already blue blazes hot on the coast as it is every summer. By July the heat will be like a fire-breathing dragon shooting flames in our faces. Sweat is plentiful and serves to cool us when the breeze blows, at least a little bit.

The air is heavy with the smell of Charleston Harbor—a cross between stinky feet and a conch shell that rots on a back porch with the animal still inside. Yet it is the smell of home, and I love it.

"I'll catch h-e-double-hockey-sticks, if my parents find out we are meeting a colored boy," Vel says.

"Mama wouldn't be thrilled about it, either," I say. "That's why we're keeping it a secret, remember?"

Vel looks at me as though this is the first she has heard of secrets.

"If they find out, they probably won't let me hang around with you anymore, even if your father is the mayor," she says.

Vel is not a rule-breaker. Nor is she good at keeping secrets. All of a sudden I wonder why I asked her along, except that she is my oldest friend, and Nana Trueluck plays bridge on Tuesday afternoons.

"If not for Paris, I might not be standing here, Vel. He saved my life. The least I can do is be his friend."

She rolls her eyes but then leans her shoulder into me. Vel and I have gone through everything together. Kindergarten. Head lice. We even caught German measles at the same time and connected the raised red bumps with black magic marker until we looked like we were dressed as Spiderman for Halloween.

"We could get in big trouble for this," Vel says, like this is something I don't know.

I could forgive Vel for almost anything, but I don't like how closed she is to having Paris as a friend.

"Are you jealous?" I narrow my eyes.

"No," she says, as though offended. "I've just never had a colored friend," she whispers.

"What about Rosemary?" I ask.

"Rosemary's our housekeeper. That's different."

"How is it different?" I ask.

Vel's face turns a light shade of pink to match her blouse. I know she loves Rosemary practically as much as she loves her mama.

"Look, I've never had a colored friend, either, but there's a first time for everything." I sound like Nana Trueluck.

Vel pulls a book from her pink purse and opens it like it is some kind of secret room she can escape into. Vel is what some people call a bookworm. She devours books as if they were M&M's. She is also the only person I know who can walk and read at the same time without tripping or falling over things.

"What are you reading?" I ask.

"Nancy Drew." She licks her lips like the story is delicious.

Nancy Drew is Vel's latest hero. In case a mystery needs solving, she now carries a pad of paper and a Bic pen in her purse to take notes. She looks over at me like I am her latest case.

Vel always wears pink from head to toe: pink sneakers, pink bobby socks, pink shorts, pink tops, and even pink ribbons in her hair. Except for her skin, she looks like a bottle of Pepto-Bismol. She is more girly than I am and wears dresses even when she doesn't have to. Sometimes, she even squeals when boys chase her on the playground at school. These are rituals I have never understood.

"Why are you always trying to rescue things, Trudy?" Vel looks at me as though intent on cracking her latest case. "You'd be a friend to every three-legged dog in town if you could."

"Paris isn't a three-legged dog." This time I roll my eyes at her. These days we spend a great deal of time communicating with our eyes.

"You know what I mean," she says.

"Actually, I don't know what you mean. Besides, I'm tired of talking about it."

"That little colored boy is just another one of your projects," she says.

"Don't talk about him that way!" I snap.

This shuts her up fast.

It is true that our family has four cats from me bringing home strays, and we almost had a three-legged dog if he hadn't outrun me. But this has nothing to do with Paris. He is the one who saved *me*!

Paris waits behind a live oak at the corner wearing light blue shorts and a matching shirt with white socks and white sneakers. He dresses better than any kid I have ever known, colored or white.

We all look around to make sure nobody sees us. But I chose this road to meet because on most days it is deserted.

"Good afternoon, ladies," Paris says, his voice formal. He sounds twenty instead of twelve. He then offers us a big smile. Paris goes to the colored school across town and could win a contest for the boy with the whitest teeth in Charleston. Not to mention that he does a southern drawl better than people born and bred here. Better even than that actress in *Gone with the Wind* who played Scarlett O'Hara. Considering he told me on the telephone last night that he moved from Detroit to Charleston six months ago, this doesn't make sense.

We walk on and the three of us settle into a nice mosey, as if it is the most natural thing in the world for two white girls and a colored boy to spend time together. At the same time something about walking with Paris feels as though we are standing on the beach during a thunderstorm, the lightning crackling all around.

Vel does her bookworm imitation and periodically steals looks at Paris to study him.

Meanwhile Paris is quiet and I wonder if he might be shy. Or maybe he is questioning why in the world he is hanging out with two white girls.

"I've been meaning to ask you, Paris, how it is that you speak with a southern accent even though you grew up in Detroit?"

"It's my strategy," he says.

Strategy is a word I heard Daddy use when he first wanted to get elected mayor. After that he said in a speech that we should judge people on their merit, not by the color of their skin. As a result, more colored people voted in the city election than ever before. Mama said he attracted some new voters, but also an equal number of enemies.

"What do you mean about having a strategy?" I ask Paris.

"Well, you see, Northerners aren't trusted in the South," Paris begins. "It doesn't even matter if my kin are here. So I'm just trying to fit in."

"Being colored probably doesn't help, either," Vel says, turning a page.

They exchange a quick look.

"Vel needs a *strategy* to keep her mouth shut," I say to Paris.

Paris and I laugh, while Vel gives us the evil eye, which makes it feel like the three of us are actually friends and not just strangers on our best behavior.

Even though the Civil War ended a hundred years ago, colored people still cross the street to avoid walking past white people. Anybody with half a brain could see that somebody needs to apologize and make this thing right.

"Tell us more about your accent," I say to Paris. "Is it hard to do?"

"Well, in Detroit I talked fast." To demonstrate, he speeds up his words like some kooky cartoon character. "But to speak Southern, I have to slow every word way down, like every syllable is going out on the front porch to sun themselves for a while."

The way he says this makes me laugh, and out of the corner of my eye I see Vel smile a little. I learned a long time ago that just because Vel is reading doesn't mean she is not paying attention.

"You could be an actor, Paris," I say.

"That's exactly what I want to be when I grow up." His words come out in a mixture of slow and fast. "Someday I want to be like the actor, Sidney Poitier. But I also want to be a civil rights leader like Martin Luther King Junior."

Saying those two names makes him stand taller.

"When I get famous, I'm going to change my last name to France," he says. "Then I can say that I am Paris France—the person, not the country—and then nobody will ever forget my name."

"A lot of actors have made up names," I say. "Nana Trueluck told me that Doris Day's real name is Doris Kappelhoff."

Vel looks up and grins, and Paris offers a short laugh before we turn serious again.

"Daddy has read us stories from the newspaper about Dr. King," I say. "He thinks he's a very brave man."

Paris smiles, as though happy I understand.

I am proud that my family isn't like a lot of other people's. Nana Trueluck likes to say that we are rare birds here in the South. Birds who think everybody should be equal. But we are not to talk about it in certain circles or people might aim buckshot at us.

A red pickup truck rounds the corner, and Paris dives into some nearby bushes as though he has been shot out of one of those historic cannons at the Battery. Did the people in the pickup see us talking? Vel puts away her book, and her wide eyes ask me what we should do now. I tell her to stay calm.

Seconds later the driver comes right up behind us and guns the engine. It is the second time in two days a truck has almost mowed me down. We stop walking to let it pass, but it pulls up right next to us and slows to a stop. Two teenage white guys stare out the open windows like they have never seen girls before. The closest one wears a dirty baseball cap and a white undershirt just as filthy.

"What are you looking at?" I ask, even though Mama has told me more than once that my big mouth will get me in trouble someday. But my main concern is whether or not they saw Paris. They don't appear to since they are looking at us and not the bushes.

The driver guns the engine again, and the passenger guy sneers at us as though we are escaped convicts or worse. Then he leans out the window and spits a giant hocker right next to my sandal.

"What do you think you're doing?" I yell.

"You girls shouldn't be walking out here alone," the driver guy says. "You might run into some unsavory characters."

The spitting guy nudges the driver guy and winks. "Hey, aren't you the mayor's kid?" the spitting guy asks. "The girl that little colored boy saved?"

I nod.

"Your daddy shouldn't have called him a hero," the driver guy says.

"But he *was* a hero," I say.

"I don't care who he saved," the spitting guy says. "It's best for his kind to not get any ideas and stay in their place."

Then the driver turns to me and Vel as though he is all of a sudden our Sunday school teacher. "You girls shouldn't walk out here. It's where the coloreds come to catch crawfish. If your parents knew, they'd tan your hides."

"My parents do know, and they don't mind one bit," I say, though this is actually a lie.

They exchange a glance.

"Let's get out of here," the spitting guy tells the driver. He reaches behind his seat and pulls out a rebel flag to drape from his window. He shakes it in my face as though wanting to scare us. Then both guys laugh, and the driver speeds off spraying sand and dirt all over us. The flag snaps in the wind as he drives away.

Speechless, Vel and I watch the dust settle for a few seconds. The pool of spit sinks into the sand by my foot. My scalp tingles as though I have just avoided a lightning strike. Paris comes out of the bushes, brushing sand and dirt from his nice clothes.

"Are you okay, Paris?" I ask.

He walks over and buries the spit in the sand, as if to bury the insult. Then he lifts his chin, and I wonder if he is thinking about Sidney Poitier and Martin Luther King Junior. If so, it appears to give him courage.

"I'm okay, Trudy, but we almost got caught. Maybe we shouldn't do this again. I don't want anybody to get in trouble." His head remains high.

"That's the most intelligent thing I've heard him say," Vel chimes in.

Paris walks ahead, and I shoot Vel a look that could stop a charging armadillo in its tracks. She tightens her lips, and we catch up with Paris.

"I can't imagine what it's like to be a colored person," I say to Paris. "Especially in a place where every other pickup truck has a rebel flag hanging in its back window. It must be like living in *The Twilight Zone*—one of those episodes where the past plays out over and over again."

Paris agrees. "I like the thought of becoming your friend, Trudy. But, seriously, we could both get in a lot of trouble for this."

"Nothing bad is going to happen, Paris," I say.

He doesn't look convinced, and I am not so sure I believe it myself.

We meander toward home next to one of the many waterways along the Charleston coastline. But something has changed from when we first started our walk. For one thing, we take turns looking over our shoulders.

To help us forget the two guys in the pickup I decide to tell a story. Nana Trueluck loves my stories, and I mostly collect them to tell her. But they are good for telling new friends, too.

"An alligator ate a dog along this road last summer," I tell Paris.

He gasps like a girl, and his shock at my opening line pleases me. It has the opposite effect on Vel, who yawns. She has heard this story before.

"It was Miss Myrtle Page's white poodle," I say, getting on with my tale. "Miss Myrtle Page always wears white dresses with a white belt cinched up on her waist just under her tiny bosoms that are the size of two concord grapes."

Paris laughs when I say the word *bosoms*, and I think that maybe he is a boy after all.

"Miss Myrtle Page is an original member of the Daughters of the Confederacy," I continue. "At least she looks that old, and her hair is the same shade of white as her unfortunate poodle's. His name is Chester."

I lower my head and place a hand over my heart in honor of Chester's memory. Paris does the same, and I take note of how white his nails are compared to his skin.

"Chester, may he rest in peace, was the most obnoxious dog who ever lived," I begin again. "He yapped nonstop at everyone who passed Miss Myrtle's house." I pause long enough to swallow and whet the appetite of my audience. "Most dogs like me fine, but Chester never warmed to me in all the years I knew him," I continue. "Nonetheless, I was sorry that Chester met his end that way. The only thing left of him was a piece of fur the size of a cotton ball."

For a second it looks like Paris might faint, and I wonder how someone brave enough to pull me out of the path of a runaway bread truck could also be squeamish.

"Are there really alligators here?" Paris looks around like one of those poodle-eating gators might jump right out of the marsh to grab one of his scrawny limbs.

"Trudy's pulling your leg, Paris," Vel says, looking up from Nancy Drew. "Alligators are common in the marsh but they rarely show themselves," she adds as if reading a book about reptiles now makes her an expert.

I appreciate that she is trying to be nice to Paris, but she is also ruining my story.

"This particular gator must have been desperately hungry," I continue with added drama. "Either that or he was tired of Chester's yapping."

Vel shakes her head like she is tired of *my* yapping. Meanwhile, Paris' eyes are as wide as two white jawbreakers.

"Relax," I say to him. "You're too skinny. Alligators like critters with meat on their bones."

I don't know this for a fact, but it serves its purpose, and Paris' eyes return to normal size. The truth is that stupid rednecks in pickup trucks are probably more dangerous than any alligator you will find in the swamp. But I don't tell Paris that.

Vel sighs. Alligators don't faze her on account of her being too busy reading to notice. In the meantime, Paris has moved as far away from the marsh as possible while still being able to walk with us.

Vel closes her book and turns her back to Paris as though he no longer exists.

"What are we going to do this summer?" she asks me.

"Beats me," I say. "Any ideas, Paris?"

"You mean you still want to be my friend?" he asks, like he hoped I forgot.

"Of course," I say, now wanting it more than ever.

As Vel and Paris and I walk along the marsh road, I imagine we look like the inside of a carton of Neapolitan ice cream: the chocolate, vanilla, and strawberry side by side. Truth be told, just like Nana Trueluck I have always preferred Neapolitan ice cream to a carton of plain vanilla.

Chapter Five

Ida

The Tuesday afternoon bridge game is one of the few places where I rub elbows with old Charleston society. The truth is, not even my elbows would be invited if Ted Junior wasn't mayor. With the exception of Madison Chambers, who was an old friend of Ted Senior's, I have nothing in common with this haughty gaggle of gossipers. I am only here because it gets me out of Abigail's hair for a few hours—and her out of mine.

We gather in the foyer of an elegant mansion along the South Battery. "You look lovely today," Madison says to me.

Madison is a retired attorney and known advocate for the marginalized. When I extend my hand, he kisses it, his mustache tickling my age-spotted skin. We do this with each other, making a play of old manners and bygone days. Like me, he has a head of solid white hair, but all resemblance ends there. Madison is much more formal in his attire—he is one of the few men alive who still wears spats on his polished shoes—and his tickling mustache rises up at the ends in a smile. To be honest, he looks a bit like the photographs of Mark Twain in his old age.

Dapper would be the word to describe him, but it is his eyes that draw me in. Eyes that are quick to wink or twinkle and reveal that he is not who he seems.

"Is your granddaughter all right?" he asks. "I saw the story in the newspaper."

"She's fine," I say. "None the worse for wear. Not a scratch on her."

"Thanks to her rescuer, no doubt." He pets his mustache.

"Yes, he was very brave," I say.

I like being reminded that I am not only a grandmother, but also someone who enjoys spending time with a person my own age. Though I adore Trudy and even look up to her in some ways, she is busy with her own life. As for her brother, Teddy, he is an altogether different breed of grandchild. Someone who is often called a *handful*. A handful of what, I am not sure, but a grandmother isn't to judge.

Card tables are set up in the sunroom, a room resplendent with marble floors and large plants that reach their arms toward the domed ceiling. We are invited to take our places by the mistress of the house, a Ravenel, one of the old Charleston families.

"I wonder who we'll skewer today," I whisper to Madison, who sits to my left.

He leans in to whisper back. "To hear them tell it, Charleston is worse than Peyton Place."

"Oh my," I say, whispering again. "How scandalous."

"Indeed," he says with another wink.

Madison's wife died two summers ago, and since then the Charleston widows have circled like scavengers, to use his word. According to him, he is invited to so many social events he has to turn down half of them. Since Ted Senior's passing, there certainly haven't been any old men in line to court me.

As bridge begins, the gossip grows as thick as the Charleston humidity. Madison and I exchange periodic looks and the occasional grin, the closest I have come to flirting in the last forty years. Servants fill our iced tea glasses, and after the first game we are all given a small slice of peach pie. Pie I recognize as coming from Callie's Diner and baked by none other than my daughter-in-law, Abigail, who I can't seem to get away from. I thank the older black woman who slips in and out between tables, a substantial woman who goes unnoticed by most everyone here. And a woman who has probably waited on this same Ravenel family her entire life, as did her mother, and perhaps her grandmother.

Charleston is a grand stage on which history has played. The actors may change with every generation, but the same lines are read and the same stage directions followed. Our only hope is that behind the scenes, white and black children are rewriting the script and becoming friends this very minute.

"What are you thinking about?" Madison discards a six of clubs.

"I am thinking about change," I say.

He raises an eyebrow. "That's an odd statement to make in the midst of one of Old Charleston's finest homes," he says. "I doubt this place has changed in a century."

"To change." I raise my crystal iced tea glass.

We clink glasses as the others at our table exchange glances. I take a sip of iced tea and silently toast my granddaughter. The thought of Trudy on the side of change gives me more optimism than I have felt in a long time. Nonetheless, the dangers that surround changing times are nothing to celebrate.

Chapter Six

Trudy

Vel and Paris and I walk in silence, as if getting used to the idea of becoming friends.

"Paris is a weird name," Vel says.

"So is Vel," he answers. They exchange a quick look that reminds me of alligators.

"Trudy Trueluck is pretty silly, too," I offer. "Who has a name like that?"

Paris shrugs, and I notice how skinny his shoulders are. "It sounds like a perfectly good name to me," he says.

"Well, my name is okay, but my birthday is unfortunate," I say, perfectly serious.

Paris' confusion rises to meet Vel's boredom.

"You see I was born on the first day of April—April Fool's Day," I begin. "So every year on April Fool's day, people make lame jokes and tell me Happy Birthday and then say *'April Fools!'* right after. Or they ask me what it's like to be an April Fool. As you can imagine, the jokes get old." I appreciate how carefully Paris listens.

"When my brother came along six years later, he was born on Abraham Lincoln's birthday," I begin again. "A much more respectable holiday. His real name is Theodore Trueluck the Third, but everybody calls him Teddy."

"What I want to know is why girls can't have numbers after their names, too?" Vel says.

Every now and again Vel says something that surprises me.

I agree with her that it makes no sense and wonder what it would be like to be the fourth Trudy Trueluck in my family. Actually, I wouldn't mind if Nana was a Trudy, too, but her real name is Ida.

"My name is Paris because my mother wanted to go there." His accent is as thick as one of Mama's apple pies. He kicks a pebble that ricochets off a tree, and the sweat on his brown skin glistens. The day is warming up.

A few steps later, Paris takes a big breath like he is about to recite Shakespeare in a southern drawl.

"Didn't you say you were looking for a summer adventure?" he asks.

"I did. You got an idea?"

"I do," he says.

"Well, out with it." Vel sounds just like her mother.

Paris hesitates. "Never mind," he says.

"No, Paris. You can't do that," I say. "You can't bring something up and then drop it."

"Well, you probably won't like it because it's something really big," he says. "Maybe too big."

Nothing gets my attention more than a big idea. Vel and I stop walking and turn to wait. Boredom is usually our big summer pastime. Boredom with an extra scoop of monotony on the side, though having a new friend has already changed that—even if we do have to keep it a secret.

"Tell us, Paris," I say.

"Well, I had a dream last night that I went to Columbia and took down that rebel flag that flies over the State House," he begins. "Dr. Martin Luther King Junior was in the dream, too. He even shook my hand afterward."

Paris puts a hand over his heart like this is the highest honor he can imagine.

"I know the flag you're talking about," I say. "It flies over the State House in Columbia. Two months ago our class went there on a school field trip, and we saw it for ourselves."

Vel was on the same field trip, though she read her way through most of it and probably doesn't remember a thing.

"Our school doesn't go on field trips," Paris says, "but my Uncle Freddie told me about it."

"You really dreamed that?" Vel asks Paris, looking skeptical.

Paris makes a cross over his heart with his finger like it is a solemn swear, and he hopes to die if it isn't true. I wonder if Vel even knows who Martin Luther King Junior is. Just yesterday Nana Trueluck was talking about him in the kitchen because he won the Nobel Peace Prize and was *Time* magazine's Man of the Year.

I think about Paris' idea. I have to admit it intrigues me. It also sounds impossible. The three of us can't even take a walk together in downtown Charleston without getting in trouble. How in the world are we going to get to Columbia and take down a flag in broad daylight?

"I think we should do it," I say, taking a giant eraser to my doubts.

"Do what?" Vel asks.

"Take down that rebel flag," I answer. "It's been a hundred years since that war, and it is darn well time to move on."

I am struck by how much I sound like Nana Trueluck, but it doesn't bother me one bit. Maybe I can even talk her into helping us take it down. She needs something to take her mind off of how much she misses Grandpa Trueluck.

"Let's do it," I say. "Let's take that flag down."

Vel looks over at me like I suggested we fly to Mars and hang out with Martians.

"I have to admit it's the boldest idea for a summer adventure we've ever had," I say, "but at least we won't end up counting freckles like we did last summer." I look at Vel, who has 344 freckles as of our last count.

"What's a freckle?" Paris asks.

I laugh until I realize he is serious. It occurs to me that white people are foreigners to him in some ways, like he is a foreigner to us. I show him the crop of freckles on my arms that always get darker in the summer. It feels like show and tell.

In the next second something rustles in the marsh and the three of us take off running like the ghost of Chester is chasing us. After the length of about two football fields we stop, gasping for breath.

Between breaths, Paris and I laugh about how scared we were. Vel doesn't see the humor and puts her hands on her hips like she was simply pretending to be scared. It dawns on me that even brave people are cowards sometimes, even the ones who save people's lives. I imagine most people are a mixture of both.

A few steps later, Paris and I collapse into the arms of one of the live oaks and sit on a low limb that creaks like a rickety porch swing. Vel leans against the wide trunk and begins to read again. Then Paris grabs a long strand of the gray Spanish moss hanging in the branches and puts it on his head like it is a wig. Before long he is singing and stroking an imaginary guitar, pretending he is Elvis Presley singing "All Shook Up." I laugh so hard I hold my sides and beg him to stop. All Vel manages to do is tap her foot.

"You are a piece of cake, Paris Moses," I say between laughs.

"What kind of cake?" Paris asks as though enjoying the idea of being a dessert.

"Chocolate, of course," I answer. "Maybe devil's food if we pull off this dream of yours."

He strums his make-believe guitar one last time and bows. Vel refuses to clap, but I applaud enough for both of us. The live oak holds Paris and me, and its massive limbs sag down to touch its roots.

In the heat of the day my imagination revs up. "I bet Rebel soldiers rested under this tree during the Civil War," I say. "I bet their guns leaned against that branch." I point to a branch about waist high that is as thick as Paris and me put together.

Paris shudders. Vel turns another page but briefly looks at me as if it is one of my more interesting made-up stories. Living in Charleston means there is a ghost story that goes along with nearly every mansion, church, and bridge. Nana Trueluck has told me a bunch of them.

A hot breeze shakes the leaves. Sun and shade dance on the ground underneath us.

"Y'all want to hear a secret?" Paris asks.

I nod, glad I am not the only one with secrets. I didn't tell either of them how scared I was when that guy spat at my feet.

Vel looks up from her book and closes it. Secrets always get her attention.

Paris lowers his voice like he is going to tell us the most delicious confidence ever. Even Vel licks her lips.

"My great-great-great-grandmother was a slave," he whispers.

Vel and I look at each other and then back at Paris. "Your great-great-great-grandmother was a slave?" I whisper back, like maybe I didn't hear it right the first time. "I've never known anybody who was related to a slave," I add.

"Miss Josie told me about it."

"Miss Josie?" I ask.

"She's my grandmother. Everybody calls her Miss Josie, colored and white folks alike. Even I call her that."

I wonder briefly if Nana Trueluck would prefer I call her Miss Ida. Then I shake the thought away.

"My great-great-great-grandmother was a house slave at Magnolia Plantation." Paris' voice remains soft.

"Don't joke about things like that, Paris."

"I'm not joking," he says.

I pause to imagine it. "I went there with my family once," I say. "Somehow it never occurred to me that slaves worked there." I wonder what else has never occurred to me just because I am white. I try to connect the dots in my brain and get nowhere. Then I realize that maybe Martin Luther King Junior is carrying on the work of Abraham Lincoln. Maybe that's why Paris admires him so much.

Nana Trueluck is a big fan of Abraham Lincoln. An old photograph of him is in a trunk in the attic that belonged to my great-great-great-grandmother. It was given to her by President Lincoln himself for the work she did as an abolitionist. It occurs to me how different Paris' ancestors had it than mine, and I wonder if maybe they ever ran into each other on the streets of Charleston, not knowing that someday their great-great-grandchildren—one black and one white—would become friends.

"Miss Josie said my great-great-great-grandmother was finally freed, but she died thirty-six days afterward."

"Oh my, that's awful," I say to him.

Hearing about Paris' great-great-great-grandmother makes me regret all my complaints about having to clean my room. What must it be like to clean up an entire plantation every day of your life? Not to mention being owned by somebody and not having a choice over what kind of life you have.

I hug the massive arm of the tree; its rough bark scrapes against my arms.

"Miss Josie also said that as long as that flag flies anywhere in the country, it is a reminder from the masters to the slaves about who is boss."

Vel stops reading, her eyes wide.

Being around our new friend Paris is an eye-opener for sure.

"I never thought of it that way," I say.

Truth is, until today, I never thought about that flag at all. I just thought it was something from the past that didn't mean anything.

For the longest time we are silent, as though holding a private memorial for Paris' great-great-great-grandmother. I think about how lucky I am that I wasn't born with darker skin and about how we don't have any choice about who our parents are.

The smell of the ocean mingles with our salty sweat, and the sadness feels as thick as the trunk of the live oak. I am thirsty and have the urge for lemonade. Lemonade always makes me feel better no matter what is going on. Not knowing what else to do I suggest we head toward home for lunch.

The three of us turn and go back in the direction of town. At the end of the sandy road along the marsh, we say our goodbyes, knowing we have to part. I hate that I don't have the courage to walk down the streets of Charleston with my new friend. Instead, Vel and I walk several steps ahead pretending we don't know Paris, while he hangs back, pretending he doesn't know us.

A few minutes later we arrive at the Esso station at the corner of Mary Street and wait in the shade. This is the dividing line in town between the whites and the coloreds. Even though it is invisible, everybody knows that line is there. It has been this way for as long as I can remember. This is where Paris will go one way and Vel and I will go another.

He passes us without even glancing in our direction. Ahead, a man and a woman pull out of the Esso station in their Ford Fairlane with Georgia license plates. They stare at Paris like he is doing something wrong simply by walking on the sidewalk.

To the side of the Esso station is the pickup truck that passed us earlier. Paris walks faster, as if to avoid the truck.

"Not so fast, boy!" somebody yells.

Hoot Macklehaney walks out of the gas station. Hoot used to ride my bus until he dropped out of school. Now he hangs out in front of the gas station all day drinking RC colas and bumming cigarettes off the mechanics who work there—apparently one of whom is the guy who spat near my foot.

In the distance, the spitting guy walks out and stands next to Hoot. They must be brothers because they both have pointed noses, and when they smile they have small, uniform teeth that look like a row of yellow corn kernels.

"What should we do?" Vel whispers to me.

"Just ignore him," I whisper back.

Vel ducks behind her book.

"You some kind of hero, boy?" Hoot says to Paris.

Hoot's brother smiles at Hoot like he is proud and then puts a quick elbow to his ribs that makes Hoot flinch.

Paris looks over his shoulder as though wishing Martin Luther King Junior would all of a sudden appear and help him out.

"Leave him alone, Hoot," I call out.

Vel takes a swipe at me with Nancy Drew and warns me to keep my mouth shut.

Hoot used to brag on the bus about how his uncles wore white sheets from time to time. When I asked Nana Trueluck what he meant, she said that the Ku Klux Klan hates colored people and burns crosses in their yards if they do anything they don't like. They wear white hoods when they do mean things so nobody will recognize their faces. Nana Trueluck says they know they are doing something wrong or they wouldn't hide behind sheets. She also says the Klan is one of those things that white people pretend doesn't exist or they would have to do something about it.

"Let's walk away." Vel's voice sounds urgent.

"But that's wrong," I say. "What if Paris had just walked away when that Sunbeam Bread truck was coming straight for me?"

I leave Vel in the shade of a crepe myrtle tree and walk toward Paris. I stand close enough to hear his shallow breathing.

"Does your daddy know you have a little colored boyfriend?" Hoot asks me.

Hoot and his brother laugh, and I want to knock their corn-kernel teeth right out of their heads. Hoot has the worst case of chin pimples I have ever seen. They look like tiny volcanoes ready to erupt.

"Does your daddy know you are the most disgusting human being alive?" I say to him.

Shock registers on their faces like they never expected a girl to stand up to them. Hoot aims his volcanic pimples in my direction, but then a police car drives up to the pump to get gas. Hoot's brother goes to the pump.

"Go home, Trudy," Paris whispers.

Sweat glistens on Paris' forehead and upper lip, and I don't think it is from the heat.

"I can't," I say.

"What do you mean, you can't? You've got to. This is my business, not yours."

"How is this not my business, Paris Moses? You saved my life. I owe you."

"Well, now you can save my life by walking away," Paris says.

We exchange a brief look, and his eyes beg me to stay out of it. I let out a long sigh and join up with Vel again. We walk down the invisible line that divides our city. Paris is on the other side, and I can feel the wall between us. My life isn't any more valuable than Paris' is, yet he is treated totally different than I am. The unfairness of this makes me want to kick something, and I look at Vel's leg before thinking better of it. In the distance, we see Paris make it safely past Hoot and his brother, and my relief comes out in a sigh.

On the way home, I feel a growing determination to rid the State House of that Confederate flag, a glaring symbol of an invisible barrier between me and Paris. And I want to talk Nana Trueluck into helping us.

Chapter Seven

Ida

Like I do on every Tuesday, I swear off ever playing bridge again with Charleston's upper crust mainly because bridge isn't the only game played. A subtle competition is dealt in with every hand alongside the finger sandwiches. A comparison of clothes, homes, travels, and overall largesse. Spending time with Madison is the only redeeming part of the gatherings. We are two odd ducks in a sea of squawking geese, pretending that we belong and at the same time taking pride that we don't.

Home again, I sit at the picnic table under the big maple tree in the backyard that provides bountiful shade. A box of stationery sits on the table that I retrieved from my room. After remembering the adventures Maisie and I used to have as girls, I want to write my old friend a letter. Yet I wonder what to write about. At this point, my life is about as exciting as liver spots.

The fence gate squeaks open, and Trudy enters the backyard. The expression on her face is one I haven't seen before.

She sits at the picnic table across from me. Her forehead is creased like it gets when she is thinking hard about something.

I place my fountain pen on the stacked linen sheets of white stationery and scoot forward to put my warm hands on hers. I catch sight of the waddle underneath my arms that comes with age. Who knew that skin could be like underwear and lose its elastic? I jiggle the waddle, thinking how interesting aging is. I have been alive seventy years, though in some ways I still feel like a girl.

"What is it, honey?" I ask. Trudy is like her father when something bothers her. To get her to talk is like pulling a heavy bucket out of a deep well.

"Nana Trueluck, I want to ask you something, and I don't want you to say 'no' automatically. Think about it first, okay?"

"Okay," I say.

Am I one of those people who always says "no" to things? That sounds more like Abigail than me. Or does it? In the last year I have done my fair share of grieving and soul-searching. I have to admit there was a part of me, right after Ted Senior died, that was ready to go, too. I didn't know how to continue on without him.

Also, it has taken some doing to figure out who I am without Ted Senior. When you've been married to someone your entire adult life, it is hard to remember how to be single again. Sometimes I wonder if I ever knew.

However, if given a choice of whether to be the kind of person who says "no" to life or "yes," I want to choose "yes."

I am not dead yet, after all, and as a grandmother I want to be a good example to my grandchildren.

In the next instant, Teddy runs through the backyard with another boy his size. Each of them brandish toy six-shooters and use Trudy and me as human shields. I cover my ears when Teddy shoots the cap pistol, and in a flash the two boys are gone again.

"Oh, to have the energy of a six year old with six-shooters," I say, more to myself than to Trudy.

The backyard quiet again, I remind her that she was about to ask a question. Instead, she tells me the story of her day. About how she, Vel, and Paris walked along the marsh road. About how Paris had to dive into the bushes to avoid being seen by some delinquents in a red pickup truck. About how one of the delinquents stopped and spat at her feet. She even tells me about a boy named Hoot with a case of what sounds like nightmarish acne. I nod and listen, wishing I'd had a grandmother when I was a girl who had done the same for me. Perhaps I would have grown up with more gumption.

"Vel acted weird the whole time, like we were doing something wrong by talking to Paris," she says. "Mama and Daddy probably wouldn't want me to be friends with him, either," she concludes.

"It's because they're protective, Trudy. They don't want anything bad to happen to you." *Nor do I*, I want to say. But protection doesn't seem to be what Trudy wants right now.

"Like what bad thing could happen?" she asks.

"You'd be surprised," I say, my words soft. I look off into the backyard thinking of examples that I am not about to tell her. She has a right to her innocence for a while longer.

"Did people really throw rocks through Daddy's office windows because he called Paris a hero in the newspaper?"

"It looks that way."

"But why?" she asks.

"*Why* is such a big word, Trudy."

"Tell me," she says. "I need to know."

I pause to admire her youthful passion and wonder how to put something so complex into simple language. Not that I fully understand it, either. The world is a complicated place.

"It's just that people want to keep the old ways alive. It feels safer to them. Change frightens people."

It frightens me, too, I want to say.

"Not changing is also scary," she says, sounding wiser than her years, something she does quite often.

In some ways, losing my comfortable life with Ted Senior has allowed me to see who I am without the role of wife to define me. Not that I wouldn't return to that role in a heartbeat if he were to come back. But even then I think I would try to keep more of myself in the relationship and not always default to meeting his needs without considering my own.

"Why can't I be friends with anyone I want?" Trudy asks.

"Good question," I say, not having any answers.

The screen door slams, and Abigail walks into the backyard carrying a tray.

"You missed your lunch," she says to Trudy. "Where have you been all day?"

"Just around," Trudy says.

Abigail puts a plate in front of her with a sandwich and a scoop of fruit cocktail on the side, the cherry carefully placed on the top. Trudy thanks her. Manners are a prized possession here in the South.

When Trudy takes a bite of a peanut butter and banana sandwich on Sunbeam Bread, I recall the scene from yesterday. The screech of tires in the distance. The bread truck heading straight for her. A picture on the side of the truck of that smiling blond girl with dimples. I never realized how totally white that picture was until now. White girl. Blond curls. Blue eyes. White bread. I can't imagine what it would be like to be a person of color and have all this whiteness around them.

However, the main thing I remember was my heart lurching into my throat. Then how strange it was to run at my age. A kind of half-run, half-walk accompanied by the fear of broken hips and Trudy being hurt.

If not for the boy who saved her, Trudy might be in the hospital, or worse yet at the funeral parlor with our whole family crying over her like we did Ted Senior. I hope to never feel that devastated again.

"You want anything, Ida?" Abigail asks.

I thank her and say no, not wanting to give her anything to complain to Ted Junior about.

"Why don't you join us?" I say to her. "No need to work so hard on such a beautiful afternoon."

Abigail laughs like the world might stop spinning if she sat in the shade for five minutes. She leaves, telling me to enjoy my *lazy* afternoon, letting a tiny bit of resentment sneak out in the way she says it.

Meanwhile, Trudy pokes a finger into the sandwich, making two eyes and a mouth, before licking off the peanut butter and smashed banana. At moments like this I remember she is still a child even though she acts like an adult sometimes.

"What did you want to ask me that I shouldn't say 'no' to right away?" I ask again.

She hesitates. "We need your help."

"Who is 'we'?"

"Paris and Vel and I."

"And what kind of help do you need?"

She hesitates again. I settle in to wait for more.

"We want to go to Columbia and take down that rebel flag that flies on top of the State House." Her eyes glisten as though a passion is on the verge of igniting.

"You what?" I ask, my shock evident.

She starts to repeat what she said, and I touch her hand to stop her. I want to say "no" on many levels, ranging from shouts to whispers. But I can't seem to say anything.

"How do you plan to take it down?" I pretend to be calm.

"We have no idea," she says. "But we're meeting at the cemetery tonight to talk about it."

The Trueluck family has been members of Circular Church for over a century. The church was founded in 1681, the cemetery in the 1700s, though there has been no room for new residents for quite some time.

Is Trudy seriously considering such a bold move? How does a child even think to do something that audacious? Something that dangerous? While I don't know Trudy's new friend, I am surprised Velvet Ogilvie is included in on her plan. She is not the type to spark a revolution unless it involves the mistreatment of books.

"I'm not so sure—" I stop myself. Trudy counts on me to not be like her parents. I don't want to discourage her, but I don't want to encourage her, either. Nor can I even begin to imagine a scenario where I might be helpful.

"Don't tell Mama and Daddy," she says. "They wouldn't understand."

I agree to keep her confidence, but I am not so sure I understand. When I dared to support her summer adventure, I never dreamed it would be one of this magnitude. Befriending someone of another race would have been big enough. Besides, how are three children going to take down a flag that flies at the State House a hundred miles away? I guess that's where I come in. I tell her I will think about it. That's the best I can do. I haven't said "no" automatically, and I haven't said "yes," either.

Trudy excuses herself to go make plans for her secret meeting scheduled for later tonight. A meeting I feel I have no choice but to attend, at least from a safe distance, hiding in the shadows of the churchyard.

Chapter Eight

Trudy

The sound of crickets in full chorus greets me when I open the black iron gate to the cemetery. Paris and Vel and I will have our secret meeting here. Nana Trueluck couldn't hide how worried she was when I told her about what we want to do, and she probably doesn't want to be involved with any part of it. At least she is willing to keep it a secret.

Earlier today when Paris told us about his dream and about his great-great-great-grandmother being a slave, it felt like the right thing to do—for him if for no other reason. What surprised me most was that Vel went along with it. But I will see if she actually shows up tonight.

Darkness falls quickly. A full moon rises behind the clouds. Circular's cemetery is one of the most haunted in Charleston, second only to St. Philip's Church, two blocks away. According to Nana Trueluck, one of the ghosts that haunts this place is a captain in the Confederate army who lost his life at Gettysburg. I have never seen him, but if he overhears what we want to do this summer, he might try to talk us out of it. That flag means something totally different to him.

Instead of masters and slaves it probably means honor and loyalty. Something worth dying for and ending up in the cemetery. Is this what Nana Trueluck means when she says things are complicated?

One of the grave markers lies on the ground like a low bench. The stone is so old you can only read the dates, 1813 – 1823 and the words *Beloved Daughter.* A crumbling carving of a lamb sits at the head of the stone. Even though the temperature is boiling, a shiver of coldness taps me on the back. I wish Vel and Paris would hurry up. I hear a rustle in the bushes behind me. Is it the captain? I shiver a second time.

"Is somebody there?" I call out.

The crickets answer, and I decide it is probably my imagination. Mama thinks my imagination gets overexcited. But I'd rather have an *over* excited imagination than an *under* excited one. Otherwise, I'd be like everybody else.

While I wait, I contemplate the dead girl whose grave I am sitting on. She was dead by the time she was my age. My imagination conjures up a scenario that ended her life: a runaway horse, influenza, malaria, or maybe a hurricane or an earthquake. From what I can tell from the markers in the cemetery, people didn't live that long. It occurs to me that I could be dead, too, if Paris hadn't saved my life.

I lay down on the flat slab of stone, cross my arms in front of me, and imagine my death. My eyes closed, I hold my breath like I do when I float underwater. I start to feel the peacefulness of it when a voice startles me. "Trudy Trueluck, what in blue blazes are you doing?"

With a lurch I sit up and gasp for the sweet air of life. "You shouldn't sneak up on a person," I say to Vel. At the same time, I am glad she came.

"I can sneak up on whoever I please," she says, like she is practicing being surly.

"Whomever," I say, sounding like Nana Trueluck.

As usual, Vel carries a book. Given it is practically dark, I am not sure how she intends to read out here.

"Paris isn't here yet," I tell her.

She shrugs like she could care less.

"I'm indebted to Paris for saving my life, Vel, so I want to do this thing in Columbia."

"You don't owe him anything, Trudy."

In the distance, the gate at the side entrance squeaks open. We turn toward the sound to make out shapes in the darkness.

We hear Paris before we see him. "This place is downright creepy," he drawls.

The streetlights from Meeting Street send an eerie glow through the trees, a kaleidoscope of shadow and light.

"We're lucky we don't have company," I say.

"Company?" Paris joins us in the shadows.

"She means the ghosts," Vel says. "Charleston is full of them."

Paris' eyes widen to where the whites can be seen. It is getting darker by the minute, and a hot breeze shakes the leaves of the giant oak that guards the back of the cemetery.

"We never had alligators or ghosts in Detroit," Paris says.

I invite Paris to sit next to me on the grave of the unknown girl.

"This girl was our age when she died." I pat the cool stone underneath us.

"We're sitting on a dead girl?" He stands straight up.

I pull him back down.

"Do you know what killed her?" I ask in a low voice.

He says he doesn't.

"A Sunbeam Bread truck hit her," I say to be funny.

Paris moans, and Vel lets out a short laugh that sounds more like a snort.

"Actually, this girl was recovering from influenza," I begin, making up the story as I go. "A lot of people died of influenza back then. It's what we call the flu today, and doctors didn't have a cure for it. But this poor girl miraculously recovered and was riding her beloved horse, Mirabelle, when the famous Charleston earthquake hit in 1886. The earthquake spooked Mirabelle, and she reared up and the girl fell off and broke her neck."

Vel laughs full out this time, like I have a lot of nerve rewriting history. "Paris, don't believe a word of it. Trudy's making up that whole story to tease you." She looks pleased to tattle on me, even if it is just to Paris.

"You've got to admit, it held your attention," I say to him.

He agrees that it did. "This is good practice for when I'm an actor and play parts where I need to act scared," he tells us. "I get plenty of practice now that I live in South Carolina."

"But you've had practice at being brave, too," I say, thinking of the day we met.

He thanks me for saying that. "By the way, Miss Josie says I need to be home by nine thirty."

According to Nana Trueluck, Paris' grandmother, Miss Josie, sells flowers on the corner of Meeting and Broad. She weaves sweetgrass baskets, too. Miss Josie is who Nana was buying flowers from when Paris saved my life. She told me later that she took off running so fast she had to go back and pay Miss Josie afterward.

I check my Barbie watch in one of the slivers of light from the lamppost. "It's nine o'clock. I guess we'd better hurry."

Paris looks relieved. Maybe he has had his fill of gators and ghosts for one day.

"So let's talk about how to get that flag down," I say.

"Are you serious about going to Columbia?" Vel asks, her hands on her hips. "Your idea doesn't hold spit much less water."

Paris and I look at each other like we are both thinking: *Who invited her?*

"Okay, if you two are so smart, how will we get there?" Vel asks.

Before looking at her again, we lower our heads as though prayer is called for. Nana Trueluck said she would think about it, and that's definitely not a definite anything.

"We haven't thought that far ahead, Vel. But there's bound to be somebody that we know who drives to Columbia sometimes."

Paris smiles. "My Uncle Freddie drives melons to Columbia every Saturday for the farmer's market," he says.

I remember how it was Paris' Uncle Freddie who told him about the flag in the first place.

"See, Vel, it won't be as hard as you think."

Vel scoffs.

"Okay, Paris, tell me more about your Uncle Freddie. When does he go to Columbia?" I ask.

"Every Saturday, except in the winter. He takes produce to a farmer's market there."

Vel pulls out a notepad and pen from the pink purse that is permanently adhered to her shoulder.

"Can you see to write?" I ask her.

"Not really," she says.

Now it is my turn to scoff. At the same time, I wonder what in the world she has to write about. We haven't even started our adventure yet.

"What kind of truck does your uncle have, Paris? Is there room for us to hide in the back?" I ask.

"There's no way I'm going to hide in the back of a colored man's truck," Vel says, her backbone straight. "Or any truck, for that matter," she adds, giving her hair a poof.

"Then I guess we'll have to go separately," I say. "Maybe Vel and I can find someone to take us, and Paris can get a ride with his uncle."

My thoughts return to Nana Trueluck. She didn't seem too thrilled with our idea, but maybe she would drive me and Vel to Columbia. Of course, we might have to listen to Doris Day songs all the way. She likes to sing in the car.

Vel stops writing like she just thought of something. "Is what we're doing illegal?" She whispers the word *illegal*. "Nancy Drew would never do anything illegal," she adds, all serious.

"Of course it's not," I say, pretending to know what I am talking about.

Vel jots something in her notepad. Is she reminding herself to consult an attorney?

"The next thing we need to figure out is when to go," I say. "Then after that I guess we need a plan to get that flag down from the top of the State House."

We sit in silence as the crickets laugh at us. It is one thing to get from Charleston to Columbia. It is quite another to figure out how three kids—who aren't even supposed to be friends—are going to: get into the State House, figure out how to get to the top of dome, and remove that flag.

"What would Martin Luther King Junior do?" Paris says thoughtfully.

An owl hoots, and Vel grabs my arm. "What was that?" she asks.

"Just an old hoot owl," I say to her.

Someone laughs, and then Hoot Macklehaney steps out of the shadows.

"Y'all thought I was an owl." Hoot snickers. The only thing uglier than Hoot's face in the daylight is his face at night.

"What are you doing here?" I look around to see if Hoot's brother is with him, but it appears he is alone. Two Macklehaneys seem a lot more threatening than one. "Did you follow us?" I ask.

"I didn't follow you girls. I saw the little colored boy come in here and followed him. Y'all aren't supposed to hang out with his kind. Don't you know that?" Hoot sounds almost concerned.

"Go away," I say to Hoot, sounding braver than I feel.

"Make me," Hoot says. The concern leaves his voice as quickly as it came.

"You do not scare me, Hoot Macklehaney," I say, hands on my hips. A sound from behind makes me turn. Did someone sneeze?

Paris taps me on the shoulder and I jump. "Is it nine thirty yet?" he asks.

I position the pink dial of my Barbie watch in a splotch of light. "It's nine fifteen," I say.

"You better hope I don't tell a soul you were here with these white girls," Hoot says to Paris. "You could get in big trouble for that."

Hoot's meanness is tamer without his brother around.

Paris announces that he has to go and says a quick good-bye to me and Vel. He makes his way to the other side of the cemetery, stepping around every tombstone like the bodies are above the ground instead of below.

Vel and I follow Paris and leave Hoot throwing rocks at one of the tombstones. If we weren't in the middle of town I would be more afraid of Hoot. But a loud scream will bring all sorts of people running. At least I hope this is the case.

We stop at the gate. "I sure hope Hoot didn't hear our secret," I say to Vel.

"I think he would have said something," Vel says.

Paris steps out of the shadows again, and we both jump.

"I thought you'd gone," Vel says, her arm reared back like she might slap him.

Paris ignores her and turns toward me. "I know I dreamed about taking down that flag, Trudy, but maybe we shouldn't put that much stock in dreams."

"Dreams are the most important thing you can have," I say to Paris, wondering when I started sounding so much like Nana Trueluck.

"Ask your Uncle Freddie if he can take you to Columbia next Saturday," I say to him. "And I'll ask Nana Trueluck if she can give me and Vel a ride."

Paris hesitates but then gives me a salute as though I am the captain in charge.

"Between now and then we need to come up with a good, solid plan to pull it off," I say. "You two be thinking about it."

Paris heads home to Miss Josie's, the gate closing at his heels. Before Vel and I have time to leave Hoot shows up again.

"Are you trying to get that colored boy killed?" he says to me.

"Mind your own business, Hoot," I say.

"I'll mind it once you keep it out of my face," he says. "Y'all have something up your sleeve."

"No we don't," I say, which is the lie of the century.

The truth is we have something big up our sleeves, and we need Hoot Macklehaney to keep his pimply nose out of it.

In the distance I think I hear the little ghost girl laugh. But maybe that's my imagination getting overexcited again.

My next thought surprises me and never would have entered my mind before that Sunbeam Bread truck swerved in my direction. Could taking down that flag actually be dangerous?

Chapter Nine

Ida

Even with my car parked the next block over from Circular Church, it is all I can do to beat Trudy home. The plan I overheard in that graveyard, or the beginnings of a plan, made me both frightened and proud. That three children would see an injustice and want to make it right gave me hope. Hope is something in short supply these days after the shocking assassination of President John Fitzgerald Kennedy the world witnessed on November 22nd of last year. Killed by a man named Lee Harvey Oswald who hid with a high-powered rifle in a book depository.

When I enter the kitchen, Abigail is busy making pies and isn't in a talkative mood. For this I am grateful. She slides the last apple pie into the oven to cook. She sometimes cooks her pies in the evenings so the kitchen can cool down by morning. It is hot as royal blue blazes in here. Only the tiniest of breezes comes in through the open kitchen door. A mayor's salary isn't much. Abigail sells pies to Callie at the diner to make extra money. Before becoming mayor Ted Junior worked at the post office like Ted Senior did before he retired.

Apple, peach, and lemon meringue pies are Abigail's specialty, and at Christmas she makes pecan, too. She bakes pies every day, except on major holidays when Callie's Diner is closed. On holidays, the family rarely has dessert because it is Abigail's day off from baking. Although I knew enough that my family didn't starve, I was never the greatest cook, and I only baked at Thanksgiving and Christmas.

I settle at the kitchen table and open the newspaper to the crossword puzzle so it will look like I have been sitting here a while. Five minutes later Trudy walks in the kitchen door. In the summer she can stay out from morning till night as long as she is in the vicinity of the house by ten o'clock, which is still early for a night owl like her. Trudy and I are both night owls. Sometimes she sneaks into my bedroom after everybody else has gone to sleep and we have our best talks.

When she sits at the kitchen table, I nudge her knee to ask how her secret meeting went. She gives me a wink. I wink back. I won't tell her that I hid in the shadows and overheard every word. Or that Paris was someone I liked instantly.

"Is Daddy here?" Trudy asks.

I motion toward the attic. Ted Junior has been writing a novel since the mid-50s. None of us have read a word of it, though he works on it every evening and weekend. It must be a thousand pages long by now, but he refuses to show it to us no matter how much we ask.

"Can Vel spend the night?" Trudy asks her mother.

Abigail swats a fly before agreeing. Trudy grabs the kitchen telephone and pulls the cord out into the hallway like she always does. I hear her muffled excitement. Maisie and I did the same thing. We could spend all day together and then have a sleepover the same night.

"Vel's mother is giving her a Toni perm, but she'll be over when it's finished," Trudy says, returning to the kitchen.

"How can that straight hair of hers even hold a curl?" Abigail asks.

"You'd be surprised what strong chemicals can do," I say.

My own curls are captured in a bun on the top of my head. I tuck in stray pieces and reassert the bobby pins. Will Trudy and Vel still be friends after they grow up? Childhood friends are hard to keep unless something special bonds you together.

"I think I'll wait for Vel on the porch," Trudy says. "You want to join me?"

I nod my acceptance and excuse myself, head lowered. More than once I have picked up on Abigail's subtle jealousy of my closeness with Trudy. Abigail's agenda is to make Trudy into a miniature version of herself. But even at twelve, Trudy is like a tree that needs not to be planted too close to anything else. Abigail's life is too confining for her, and as soon as Abigail realizes Trudy isn't like her, the better their relationship will be.

But who am I to judge? I tell myself. *Perhaps Abigail isn't the only one with a chip on her shoulder.*

When I go outside, Trudy is sitting on the top step, looking out over the small front yard and street. Four cats congregate on the porch and take turns rubbing their whiskers against her legs—a calico, two tabbies, and a solid gray. Ted Junior and Abigail have forbidden her to bring home any more strays.

I sit next to her. It seems like a long time since we talked, although it was only this afternoon that she asked me for my help. Moths gather around the porch light and the two tabbies leap after the moths. The night air is not much cooler than the daytime air. A trail of sweat travels from the crease in my knees down the side of my leg into my high-tops. I inch up my skirt to study it; something that Trudy has been known to do.

"Let's time it," Trudy says.

With her prized Timex, a present from her parents last Christmas, Trudy counts the seconds it takes the sweat to trickle down my leg. The watch has a picture of a blond, perfect Barbie on the face, the Sunbeam Bread girl all grown up.

"Do you think colored kids have watches with brown Barbie dolls on them?" Trudy asks. This is the kind of question I have come to expect from her.

"I don't know," I say. "If they don't, they should."

"I've never liked pink or Barbie dolls," Trudy says. "But I like the second hand. I can get an accurate timing of things."

"Timing is important," I say.

"Seventeen seconds is my world record for sweat traveling from knee to heel," she says, matter of fact. "But it looks like you could break that record."

"Interesting," I say, "I've never broken a world record."

Ever since the Beatles were on Ed Sullivan last February, Trudy hums Beatles songs. I bought her their first album for her birthday last April. Whenever we have the house to ourselves, Trudy and I put the album on the phonograph and dance.

A curtain moves in the house across the street, and I give a wave to Widow Wilson. Trudy and I begin to sing "I Want to Hold Your Hand" really softly. We are all smiles, tapping our feet and singing in our loudest whisper, *Oh please, say to me* . . . I have been known to belt out a show tune on occasion, but that is only in front of family.

The telephone rings in the kitchen, stopping us mid chorus, and Abigail answers. Seconds later she shows up at the door, drying her hands on her dishtowel. Like a knight never without a sword, Abigail Trueluck is never without a dishtowel. She uses this same dishtowel to take pies out of the oven, chase away flies, as well as flip Trudy and Teddy on the legs if they irritate her. I half expect her to take a swipe at me one of these days.

"Someone's on the telephone for you," she says to Trudy.

Trudy disappears into the house. When she stretches the telephone cord around the kitchen corner and into the hallway, I can hear her clearly.

"Hoot Macklehaney, what are you doing calling my house?" she says in the same half-whisper we were singing in.

She listens for a long time and then says, "I don't care what people like or don't like. It's none of their business." Trudy sounds angry. She goes back into the kitchen and hangs up the telephone so hard it bounces out of the cradle onto the floor cracking against the linoleum. She makes a sound that's a huff with a scream mixed in. Then Abigail asks her why she is so upset. Trudy makes up a story about someone from school selling raffle tickets.

"Raffle tickets for what?" Abigail asks, like she might buy one.

Trudy tells her never mind, and the house gets quiet again.

It is amazing how much I overhear in this old house without even wanting to.

Trudy comes outside and lets the screen door slam. My sweat has started a new race, but our lightheartedness from earlier is lost. The cats return as soon as she sits down again.

"My guess is that telephone call wasn't about raffle tickets," I say.

"Hoot needs to keep his pimply nose out of my business," she says.

"What did he say?" I ask.

Trudy picks at a scab on her ankle, and when it starts to bleed I hand her a tissue from the pocket of my skirt.

"He was calling to warn me," she says. "He said I needed to quit hanging around Paris. That if people get wind of it, it won't be pretty. And that people already hate Daddy, and that I'm making it worse for him."

Her eyes tear up. I put an arm around her shoulder and hug her close.

"First of all," I begin, "you are not making it worse for your father. Ted Junior can take care of himself. If he doesn't get reelected, it will have nothing to do with you. It is the inevitable backlash that happens throughout time. The world progresses for a while, then like a rubber band, things snap back to the way they were. That has nothing to do with you, Trudy, and everything to do with how the world is set up."

She takes a deep breath, and I know she has heard me.

"Second of all," I continue, "the fact that this Hoot knows about Paris means you aren't being careful enough. I know you want to be Paris' friend, but you have to think of Paris. The people Hoot is warning you about will blame him instead of you. So you have to protect your friend. I wish this wasn't the case, but unfortunately it is."

I pause with the hope that Trudy will give up on taking down that flag. The more I think about it the riskier it feels.

"Is there a third thing?" Trudy raises her head.

"Yes, there is," I say. "Third of all, I love you very much, and I am here for you whenever you need me." I squeeze her shoulder in case she has any doubts.

"Does this mean you'll help us?" she asks.

"You and Vel come to my room later tonight, and we can talk about it," I say. "I'll give you my answer then."

Emotion rises in my throat, a combination of pride, love, and protection. I can't imagine being twelve years old and dealing with such big issues. All I want is to keep my granddaughter safe. But I also want to encourage her to follow her passion, whatever that might be. Passions are so easy to lose once you get a certain age—though I wonder sometimes if I ever had any. When I think about Ted Senior dying, and my coming to live here with Ted Junior and his family, I have to believe that part of the reason I am here is to encourage Trudy. For that, I would not mind being famous or winning a world record. The big question is if I have the courage to join her. I am not so sure I do.

Chapter Ten

Trudy

After Mama sets her last pie to cool on the counter, she gives me a look like I am a character in an Alfred Hitchcock movie who is guilty of something. She loves Alfred Hitchcock. She can always figure out who committed the crime before everybody else does.

"Please go tell your father I need him in the kitchen," she tells me.

"But Vel's coming soon. Tell Teddy to do it." But I know my brother must have been sent to his room. Otherwise, the house wouldn't be so quiet.

I think of Hoot Macklehaney again and open the refrigerator and get a sip of orange juice right from the bottle. Mama has told me a million and one times not to do this, but Daddy does it all the time. She aims her dishtowel toward me, but I jump out of the way, and it barely grazes me. That dishtowel has taught me to have quick reflexes.

Mama tells me to go get Daddy again, and I stomp out of the room even though I am not actually upset about it. I don't see him that much on account of him writing the great American novel and being mayor at the same time.

At the bottom of the steps I check my Barbie watch to time how many seconds it takes to get to the attic. Anything to get my mind off of stupid Hoot Macklehaney and how history is like a rubber band. Twelve seconds is my best time for running up the steps so far, and I am intent on another Trudy Trueluck world record.

As soon as the second-hand reaches the top of Barbie's head, I take off like a sprinter in the Olympics. Two flights of steps, two stairs at a time. At the top, I check my watch again: twenty-one steps in ten seconds. I smile, having shaved two seconds off my previous time. Daddy will be proud.

When I open the attic door a wall of hot air hits me in the face. An oscillating fan rattles as it throws the heat around. A roll top desk, belonging to my Grandpa Trueluck, sits next to the small window with a view of the street. Ted Trueluck—part-time novelist, full-time mayor of Charleston, South Carolina—sits at the desk. He is dwarfed by the large chair with wooden arms worn from years of his ambition resting against them. The chair has rollers on its feet and swivels. If we crammed in it would be big enough to hold Paris, Vel, and me all at the same time.

Daddy clacks away at the Royal typewriter Mama got him for Christmas the same year I got my Timex. He wears his lucky shorts—an old pair of Bermudas he wears every time he writes, even in winter—and is without a shirt. Since he has never sold a thing he has ever written, I don't know why they are called his "lucky shorts." Mama calls Daddy an eternal optimist and says that he gets it from Nana Trueluck.

"How can you stand working up here?" I ask him.

A single lamp sits on the desk-top while the rest of the attic is in shadow.

"An artist must make sacrifices," he says, all serious. He slows down long enough to turn to look at me and smile. But then he keeps typing.

The attic has the smell of memories. A single window in the eave of the roof shoots squares of moonlight onto the dusty wooden floor highlighting footprints leading to the desk. Old trunks, as well as boxes that are older than I am, line one wall. Lamps without shades share space with chairs with broken legs like a hospital for the past.

On the other side of the attic is a stack of boxes that are Nana Trueluck's. Next winter she promises to bring me up here to show me things from her past including Daddy's baby pictures and baby shoes as an only child, and photographs from when she was a girl.

In the past, I played up here in the cooler months. Revisiting toys long since outgrown: an old rocking horse, boxes of building blocks. Toys that at one time I could not bear to part with are now orphaned with the passing of time.

My old crib is stored to the left of the window. It is hard to imagine that I was ever small enough to fit into it. Now it would break into splinters with my weight.

"Is your mother looking for me?" Daddy asks.

"Yes, sir," I say.

"Let me finish this paragraph." His fingers rest on the keys as if he is about to play the piano.

I walk over next to him and press my fingerprints into the dust that covers the surface of the desk. The old typewriter begins again as he creates the longest paragraph in the history of words. Or at least it feels that way.

Hoot Macklehaney's call is still upsetting me, but I don't want my parents to know. Parents stop a lot of perfectly good adventures in the name of safety, and I'd bet a year's allowance that they will never agree to us taking down that flag. Nana Trueluck has to agree to it, or I don't see how we can pull it off. Later tonight, I will tell her what Paris and Vel and I discussed at the cemetery.

I rest an arm on the back of the desk chair and inhale my father's summertime smell—the remnants of Old Spice and overworked deodorant. Since I fall asleep to the click, click, clicking of the keys nearly every night, the sound of the typewriter makes me yawn.

"Daddy, what's a person supposed to do if they see something that's wrong?" I ask.

The heat must be getting to me. I usually don't ask him these kinds of questions. Or maybe that telephone call from Hoot is still haunting me.

He stops typing, swivels around in his chair and looks over his glasses at me like he has seen plenty of wrongness in his life. "Like what, sweetheart?"

"Like if people are treated badly because of something they can't help," I say. "Like the color of their skin."

He pauses and takes off his glasses. "I think we have to be a part of the solution instead of the problem, and practice the golden rule."

"But what if it gets you in trouble?" I ask.

He sits back in his chair as if giving his answer extra thought.

"Doing the right thing isn't always popular, Trudy, and it's never easy. But I think you have to do it anyway."

At that moment, Daddy sounds like Nana Trueluck, too. What would he think about our plan to go to Columbia? I have a sneaking suspicion that once he got over being scared for me he'd be proud. Just like I am proud of him for writing this novel even if nobody ever reads it.

I hear Vel's voice in the kitchen and kiss Daddy on his warm cheek. "Don't forget Mama wants you."

He smiles and swivels back around to the typewriter.

I return to the kitchen. Another fan whirls in the corner, moving the humid, fruity air from one side of the room to the other. Nana Trueluck is at the table finishing up her daily crossword puzzle. With every pass, the fan on the countertop blows loose strands of her white hair.

Mama cleans flour off the countertops as she talks to Vel. When Vel sees me, she gives a wide smile and points to the tight blonde curls that now cover her head, compliments of the Toni perm. I swallow a gasp.

"Tell me the truth. Is it hideous?" she asks me.

In the South we are taught to spare people the truth, especially if it guarantees to end a friendship. I avert my eyes to the disaster that sits on her head. A compliment is called for, and I search my brain for one.

How do I tell my best friend that she looks more like a poodle than the unfortunate alligator-eaten Chester ever did? In fact, I should warn her to stay away from the marsh or she might be that gator's next victim.

"Your hair is . . . unlike anything I've ever seen," I say finally.

Nana Trueluck looks up from her crossword as though the next clue is a four-letter word for someone who doesn't tell the truth.

Vel tests the buoyancy of the curls, apparently pleased. She reeks of Toni perm, and the smell makes me sneeze. She says, "bless you," and then pets her perky ringlets again as if they are a new poodle puppy she has brought home from the pound.

Mama gives us each a peach turnover made from the leftover filling from her pie and a tall glass of milk. Vel sits across from me at the kitchen table, and I try my level best not to stare at her head. Nana Trueluck gives my leg another nudge under the table to remind me to be kind. Meanwhile Mama hovers in the background with her dishtowel poised in case I take a notion to tell the truth about Vel's hair. But I already know better.

"I hope this heat doesn't destroy my perm," Vel gives her curls another pet.

If a dog catcher shows up I will be out one best friend. Loud footsteps descend the stairs—too loud for Daddy, unless he has suddenly taken up stomping.

Teddy, who I prefer to forget exists, speeds into the room. Before I can stop him, he takes the last bite of my turnover. I yell, and Mama tells him to go back to bed. He starts to finish the last of my milk but stops mid-gulp.

He gives Vel's head the once-over and swallows. "Jiminy Cricket!" Teddy says.

"Come on, Vel, let's go to my room," I say before he has a chance to say more. She agrees and follows me out of the kitchen, her curls swirling like a hula-hoop.

Teddy follows us into the hallway and stares at Vel's hair like he wonders what breed of dog it is. With a look, I warn him not to say a word. Meanwhile, Teddy mounts the bottom rail of the staircase like it is a wild bull in a rodeo, throwing up his arm in a dramatic arc. I grab his shirt to pull him off, causing him to exaggerate a fall and tumble into a heap on the wooden floor.

When he grows up, Teddy wants to be a stunt man in Hollywood. At six years of age, he is already an expert at falling.

As a result of his constant practice, he has an impressive number of bruises of various shapes and sizes that cover every exposed area of his skin. When he heard about my incident with the Sunbeam Bread truck, he was envious of the experience and asked to go with me next time when I deliver one of Mama's pies.

Mama shows up and swats the back of Teddy's leg with her dishtowel to signal that this time she means business. He scrambles up the stairs like King Kong is chasing him to the top of the Empire State Building.

Vel has a brother, too. He is older and wants to be a horse vet someday. This makes a lot more sense to me than becoming a stuntman. I wonder if Paris and Teddy might get along since they both want to go into the movie business—unless Paris decides to follow in the footsteps of Dr. King instead.

At the top of the landing, Teddy pretends to crash against the banister and then bounces across the landing and hits the wall with a dull thud like in the old cowboy westerns. He does this every few steps until he finally lands in a heap in front of his door. His tongue hangs to one side of his mouth, a stricken look on his face. Vel and I step over him.

Once we get to my room, I shove my window open as wide as it will go to let in fresh air. This time of day you can smell the ocean if the breeze comes from the east. Unfortunately, it hasn't cooled down much yet.

Typing sounds come from the attic and the theme song of *The Dick Van Dyke Show* wafts up from the living room. Nana

Trueluck never misses an episode. She loves Mary Tyler
Moore, who plays Laura Petrie, and loves it when she says,
"Oh, Rob," in that exasperated way that she does. If Vel
wasn't here, I'd be watching with her.

Vel sits on my bed, and I force myself to think of serious
things so I won't laugh at her hair.

"Hoot Macklehaney called here tonight," I say.

"Hoot called your house?"

Vel's wide eyes and her permed hair make her look like a
poodle struck by lightning. I hide my laugh inside a cough.

"How'd he find your number?" she asks.

"We're the only Truelucks in the old telephone book," I
answer. I don't mention to Vel that we aren't listed in the new
telephone book because Daddy kept getting so many mean
calls.

"Well, what did Hoot say?"

"He warned me again to quit hanging around with Paris."

Vel twists her curls. "I know he saved your life," she says,
"but that doesn't mean you have to hang out together."

"Nobody saw us, Vel. It was a secret meeting, remember?"

"Hoot saw it."

I pause, thinking about what Nana Trueluck said about
me being more careful. Even though nobody saw us along the
marsh road, I did step up to defend Paris at the Esso station.

"It must be weird to be chocolate cake among all this vanilla," I say.

"Vanilla goes best with vanilla, Trudy, and chocolate goes best with chocolate. You're not supposed to mix them."

"That sounds boring," I say.

Vel pulls two pieces of Bazooka bubble gum from her shorts pocket and tosses me one. "I still can't believe that stupid jerk spit at us yesterday," she says.

"Don't forget that rebel flag he waved in our faces like it was a gun or something."

"What is it with that flag?" Vel asks. "I don't understand why it's so important to people."

"Nana Trueluck says it's because we lost the Civil War, and Union troops burned down Atlanta and a bunch of other places to rub it in. She says hanging onto that flag is a way to hang onto pride for some folks."

"Your nana sure does have a lot to say about things," Vel says, petting her hair again. "My grandmother doesn't talk about anything interesting. She just wears smelly perfume."

The bubble gum is rock hard and makes my jaws hurt to chew it. Neither of us talks as we work up enough saliva to soften the gum.

"We need to take down that flag for Paris, Vel. If it was the other way around, I bet he would do it for us," I say.

Vel pauses as if having a hard time imagining it the other way around. Then she takes a book from her pink purse and puts it on my nightstand. I guess it is in case she gets the urge to read in the middle of the night.

"So why would we take something down that helps folks hang onto some pride?" she asks.

"It's more complicated than that," I say. "By the way, I think this bubble gum has been around since the Civil War, too."

"I think you're right." Vel holds her jaw while she chews, and her curls tremble with every bite.

I think about Vel's question. "Maybe pride isn't good if it makes one set of people think they're better than another set of people, or if they use it to boss them around."

I give up on the gum and toss it into my metal trash can. It makes a loud thud. But I am not willing to give up on Vel yet. We've been best friends forever for a reason, even if I can't remember that reason right now.

"People will know we're up to something if Paris is with us." She spits her gum out, too.

"He won't be with us," I say. "Not really. He'll have to tag along like he did this morning, or we'll draw attention to ourselves. Unless Nana Trueluck has a better idea."

I suggest we go talk to her, and Vel follows me down the hall. We find Nana Trueluck on her bed rubbing Jergens lotion into her hands. She wears a white night-gown that looks too hot for summer, but as she has told me before, old people tend to run cold. Nana's bed is an antique and was evidently made for very tall people because it requires a jump to get on it. Vel's hair bounces higher than she does.

Nana Trueluck's white hair is down and draped over her shoulders. In a way she looks beautiful. She motions for me to give her my hands so she can rub the excess Jergens from hers to mine.

"So will you drive us to Columbia?" I ask.

"Are you still planning to take down that flag?"

"Yes, ma'am," I say. Nana Trueluck has never required me to use my manners like Mama has and for some reason it makes me want to do it more.

"Is your new friend Paris coming?" she asks.

"He's going to ask his Uncle Freddie to take him," I say.

"What about you, Vel? Are you in on this, too?" She knows Vel is not that easy to convince of anything, but Vel nods, her hair much more enthusiastic than the rest of her.

However, Nana Trueluck is the one who doesn't look convinced, and she still hasn't agreed to take us.

"Do you have any ideas of how we can take down that flag?" I ask her. "When our class went there it was flying on top of the dome. Surely they don't make ladders that high."

"They had to get it up there somehow," Nana says. "I imagine there's a way to get to the dome from inside." She pauses, a thoughtful look on her wrinkled face. "You'll have to be very careful," she continues. "If anyone gets wind of what you want to do you won't be able to get near the building."

"You mean you'll take us?"

For a few seconds she looks like she might back out, but then she agrees.

All of a sudden, the possibility of Paris' dream becoming a reality gets me to bounce on Nana Trueluck's bed. Then Vel jumps up and down, too, her curls in a tizzy. And then to my further surprise, Nana Trueluck starts to bounce, too, and the three of us get a major case of giggles.

A voice yells up the stairs that it is time to go to bed and turn out the lights. Nana Trueluck puts a finger to her lips so Mama won't know she is in on it, too.

"If we're going to pull this off, it needs to be kept a secret," Nana whispers. She holds out her little finger for a pinkie swear. "Secret?"

"You mean grandmothers know what pinkie swears are, too?" I ask.

"Of course," she says.

I lock my pinkie in hers. "Secret," I repeat.

Then Vel and Nana do the same.

When we get back to my room, Vel takes her book and hugs it to her chest like it is the book version of a teddy bear. Her hair has expanded in the nighttime heat.

"Do you really think we can do this?" she asks.

"As long as Paris can get to Columbia, too," I say.

For the first time in my life I am relieved to turn out the light so I won't have to look at Vel's hair anymore. I hear Nana Trueluck walk into the hall bathroom humming a Doris Day

song and feel grateful to have her in on our plan. While un-
dertaking a rebellion, everybody needs at least one grandmother.

Chapter Eleven

Ida

Loud noises startle me awake in the middle of the night. At first I think it is my grandson Teddy doing one of his stunts downstairs, but then I hear Ted Junior and Abigail outside my door, their voices raised. I join them in my robe and slippers.

"What's going on?" I ask.

Ted Junior is wearing only his pajama bottoms, and Abigail cinches her peach colored robe tighter around her waist. "Something's going on outside," Ted Junior says.

"You've got to go see what it is," Abigail insists.

"Maybe we could all go," I say. "Safety in numbers and all that."

Trudy and Vel come out into the hallway yawning and wiping their eyes. Poor Vel's hair looks worse than before. One side sticks straight up in the shape of her pillow. I put an arm around Trudy while Abigail and Ted Junior debate whether the police should be called. Abigail holds Teddy, who wears his Batman underwear, to keep him from going downstairs first.

A decision is made to investigate, and we follow Ted Junior down the stairs in single file.

When we go onto the porch, my first thought is that it is too early for the sun to come up. Then I remember the house faces west, not east. The bright light isn't the sun at all but a fire burning in the yard near the front gate.

We stand on the porch, holding hands, unmoving. A cross—as tall as Ted Junior and about three feet across—crackles its message. The smell of gasoline and burning wood fills the air. Ted Junior sprints into action and stretches the garden hose across the yard. He yells at Abigail to turn on the water. I take charge of Teddy as white smoke billows into the black sky, and the flames are extinguished. Vel and Trudy are still holding hands, their friendship the only lifeline to be found.

All my life I have heard of burning crosses but I have never seen one, and never felt the utter fear inherent in the message: *We can get to you anytime we want. We are watching you.*

Ash assaults my nose and throat, and I spit into the yard. I don't want to swallow any of this. It is bad enough to see, smell and taste it. How can people do this to their fellow humans? Deliberately invoke fear. Terror. In someone's own yard. A place we count on as sanctuary. My hands begin to tremble, and I rub them together to get them to stop.

Neighbors show up to help, an army in housecoats. After the sizzling stops, two charred pieces of smoldering lumber remain. The cross is planted in the front yard like the dozens of bulbs I planted along the fence the weekend after I arrived here to make this place feel a little more like home.

"Don't worry girls," I say, seeing fear in Trudy's eyes. *Let me worry for you,* I want to say. You are too young to know these things happen. Too young to joke about rebellions or even dream of them.

For some reason I feel the need to document the scene. I go inside and grab my Kodak camera and a package of flash bulbs from my closet. The camera I used on my last trip with Ted Senior, the film inside not yet developed because I haven't had the courage to look at them. I take a photograph of the cross and of the neighbors standing nearby looking out into the darkness. I only wish I had thought to take a photograph of the way things were before. Before everything changed.

Trudy takes my arm.

"You okay?" I ask, though I know okay-ness will probably take days to reach after something like this. Maybe weeks.

"I guess this is what Hoot was trying to warn me about," Trudy says. Her lips give a momentary quiver.

Who are these characters capable of burning a cross in somebody's yard? I have heard stories of the Ku Klux Klan, but mainly these stories took place outside of Charleston. Miles away. Thugs who wear white sheets, determined to keep things the way they are no matter how destructive.

Teddy finally breaks from Abigail's grasp. He leaps from the top step of the front porch and then runs and trips over the garden hose, making the scary moment feel a little more normal. Seconds later, Vel's parents stride toward us in their bathrobes, late to the party. They look as frantic as Abigail and Ted Junior. The parents stand together and talk in hushed tones. I go into the street now and get a photograph from the other side. I think of the perpetrators watching our house, waiting until all the lights are out to plant the cross.

A police car arrives, and a policeman gets out to talk to Ted Junior. The first month or two after he was elected mayor the police sat in front of our house at night. When I heard about this from Abigail, I thought it was an overreaction, but maybe not.

Trudy and Vel remain frozen on the porch. Just hours before, Trudy and I timed my sweat here. Cats danced around our ankles. Now life has taken a drastic turn.

"I hope Paris and Miss Josie are safe," Trudy says to me, when I return to the porch.

I have always liked Miss Josie, Paris' grandmother, the woman I now buy flowers from. I have often thought we could be friends if we lived during a different time. A culture imposes boundaries that we don't even think to cross. Now I wonder why I didn't pursue the friendship anyway.

"We should never have tried to make friends with that colored boy," Vel says to Trudy in a half whisper, like she has forgotten Paris' name. I think of rubber bands again, the snapping back to the old ways, the supposedly safer ways. Vel's parents motion for her to join them in the street.

"No, you were right to try," I say to her before she goes. "That's the only way anything will ever change."

I say this, but then wonder if I believe it. Both things are true. I also want to tell them to stay away from him. To never mention Paris again. What the cross burners intended has worked. I am afraid. Afraid enough to keep my life small. To suggest that Trudy keep her life small, as well, and not take any chances. And never do anything that might attract attention—especially not this kind of attention. But isn't that exactly what the bad guys want? Isn't that letting them win?

At that moment, I need an arm around me. I need Ted Senior to tell me everything will be all right. I wrap my arms around myself and imagine him there. His memory fortifies me.

"I don't have one ounce of hesitation about helping you take down that flag," I say quietly to Trudy.

"You don't?" she says, as though her hesitation can now be measured in pounds, not ounces.

"It isn't right to fly a flag that intimidates people," I say, "just like it isn't right to burn crosses in people's yards."

Something has ignited inside me. Something I don't have a name for yet. Maybe it is a spark my great-grandmother passed along to me. A spark I have felt many times before but never acted on. Action is called for. If we don't do something, we are like everybody else who pretends nothing is wrong.

After the policemen leave the small crowd on the street disperses. Trudy and I go back inside. Ted Junior and Abigail look like they have aged overnight. We say our goodnights again, and everyone returns to their rooms, not that sleeping after something like this is actually possible. A few minutes later, Trudy comes into my room.

"Will you still take us to Columbia?" she asks.

I look into her eyes. A spark is there, similar to mine.

"Trudy Trueluck, if it's the last thing I do on God's green earth, I will help you take down that flag."

We embrace, charged with our mission.

We stop to listen to something happening downstairs. Ted Junior is locking all the doors. Somehow this feels like the end of something precious. The only reason people lock doors is because they feel it is unsafe outside. After seventy years of life, this is the first time I have lived in a home where we felt we had to lock our doors.

From my bedroom, I smell the remains of the burnt wood outside as well as the faint fumes of Vel's perm. The crickets make their nighttime sounds, yet even they can't convince me that everything is normal. Something has changed forever. I can no longer stand by in the comfort of my cowardice and pretend that everything is fine anymore. It is time for me to do everything I can to help with our growing pains here in the South. I have no idea how we'll do it, but I will help Trudy and her friends take down that flag.

Chapter Twelve

Trudy

When I come downstairs the next morning, my parents and Nana Trueluck are huddled in the kitchen. I hear Teddy playing in the backyard and wonder if I will be banished, too. They stop talking when I come in.

"I wish you wouldn't do that," I say, grabbing a cereal bowl from the cabinet.

"Do what?" Mama asks.

"Stop talking when I come into a room," I say. "I was here last night, too, you know. It's not like you can hide what happened from me."

A long silence follows.

"Last night frightened us," Mama says.

Should I admit it scared me, too?

"When you came in, we were trying to decide what to do," Daddy says.

"It's not our battle," Mama says. "We need to stay out of it."

Daddy looks over at her, a hint of disappointment in his face. "Things are riled up all over the South," he says. "Innocent people are getting hurt in Alabama, Georgia, Tennessee. All over."

Nana Trueluck is quiet. Yet the determination in her blue eyes has not wavered since last night. Our secret sits between us, as tangible as the sugar bowl and creamer on the kitchen table.

"Why do you think it happened?" I ask.

"We're guessing it was the article in the newspaper," Daddy says.

Mama gets up and pours me a glass of orange juice. Nana Trueluck and I exchange a look that confirms the need to move forward with our plan.

After breakfast, I get dressed and go outside. The cross is down. The wood is out by the street for the trash men to pick up. A black outline is seared into our front lawn, a not-so-subtle reminder of the warning we received. If the people who burned it were wanting to make me stop being friends with Paris, they have failed.

In the light of morning, the night before feels like a dream. I walk to Vel's house. It is Saturday morning, and her parents sit at a white wicker table on the porch to have their coffee.

"Beautiful day, isn't it?" Vel's mother says. She looks like an older version of Vel but with makeup and minus the book.

Nobody talks about the cross burning we witnessed last night. Unpleasant things are never talked about in the South, at least not openly. It is one of those unspoken rules Nana Trueluck always talks about. Rules we need to start breaking, although I am not about to start with Vel's mother.

When I go inside I find Rosemary, the Ogilvies' maid, polishing the coffee table in the living room. Vel sits nearby on the light green sofa painting her toenails.

"Hi, Rosemary," I say, realizing how many times I have come in this house and not even noticed her.

"Hello, Miss Trudy," she says, kind of surprised.

I wonder if she has heard about the cross burning. How could she not?

When I get close, Vel's hair startles me again. Luckily she doesn't notice me take a step back. Leaning over, she puts a streak of hot pink nail polish on her big toenail. To Vel, painting toenails requires the same precision as brain surgery.

Rosemary lifts Vel's foot off the coffee table to clean underneath. Vel acts like Rosemary is totally invisible. When the kitchen timer goes off, Rosemary leaves to pull something out of the oven.

"Let's go visit Paris today," I say, wanting to send the cross-burning folks a message.

"In the colored section? Are you crazy?" Vel paints another toenail and then another, pursing her lips as though this somehow helps her be precise.

"What's the big deal?" I ask. But we both know what the big deal is.

Vel frowns for several seconds, giving my request serious thought. I drop to my knees and resort to dramatic begging, which always makes Vel laugh. Then I tell her that Paris will probably love her hair and that she could show it off on the way over.

"We can go as soon as they dry," she says, wiggling her toes at me.

She finishes one foot and starts on the other. With a huff, I collapse into the green wingback chair in the living room and resort to counting the freckles on my arms to see if I have any more than I did last summer. By the time Vel finally finishes, I have counted arm freckles and leg freckles for a total of 213 overall freckles. According to Barbie, completing the freckle-count takes exactly seven minutes and twenty-seven seconds.

After blowing on her toenails one last time, she touches them to make sure they are dry, making motions like she is touching a hot stove. She grabs a new Nancy Drew from the coffee table and tucks it in her waistband before sliding her feet into her pink flip-flops. Finally, she announces she is ready to go.

My 213 freckles jump up to join her.

"Do you know where he lives?" Vel poofs her hair.

"Across from the fire station, close to Calhoun."

We ride our bikes sixteen blocks to get to an address I memorized from the telephone book. On the way, we cross the dividing line into the colored neighborhood. Once we cross the line, there are a lot more people out on their porches and in their yards. They only wave if we raise our hands first. A few must realize I am the mayor's daughter because they actually smile. But most of them pretend we don't exist—something they probably learned from white people.

In our white neighborhood all the houses look alike, but here every house is painted a different color. Some need repairs. We lean our bikes against a green picket fence with Paris' house number on it and enter a yard full of flowers, some of them as tall as me and Vel. We find Paris lying on his grandmother's porch swing with his legs sticking up, reading a *Seventeen* magazine.

"What are you two doing here?" Paris is so surprised to see us he forgets to use his southern accent.

"That's a girl's magazine," Vel says, ignoring his question. "What are you doing reading a *girl's* magazine?"

When Paris sees Vel's hair, he doesn't even blink.

"When do you think you'll start plucking your eyebrows?" Paris sits up, and his southern accent has returned, dead-on perfect.

"I'm not allowed until I'm sixteen," Vel offers, as though counting the days. It is the first time Paris and Vel appear to have something in common.

"I find the whole idea of tweezing facial hair barbaric," I say.

"Someday you won't," Paris says with a wink of wisdom.

"Want to bet?" I say.

Paris turns to Vel. "There's a great article in here about how to do it." He pulls up his brow with two fingers and turns his head to imitate the photo in the magazine.

"Can I read it when you're done?" Vel asks.

"Of course," Paris says. He turns down the page corner and closes the magazine.

Since when did you two become so idiotic? I want to ask. Who cares about eyebrow plucking when idiots are burning crosses in people's yards? "Did you hear about what happened last night?" I ask instead.

When he says he hasn't, I tell Paris the story from beginning to end. By the time I finish he is sitting up ready to walk to Columbia this very minute.

Seconds later, a white-haired black woman comes onto the front porch with three lemonades with lemon slices floating on top. She is large and round and beautiful. Her white hair is thick and clipped short. I wonder if there is a magazine called *Seventy* that is like *Seventeen* and gives old ladies fashion tips. Nana Trueluck and Miss Josie could be models.

"Welcome to our home," Miss Josie says, her dark eyes sparkling. "Any friends of my Paris are friends of mine."

Her smile relaxes me instantly. She compliments Vel on her toenails before handing us the lemonades, my favorite drink of all time. Since I have just ridden 16 blocks on a hot day, I take several gulps.

"This is the sweetest, most delicious lemonade I have ever tasted in my life," I say, and Miss Josie smiles again.

Nana Trueluck always says you can attract more friends with honey than with vinegar, or with niceness instead of being rude. All of a sudden I understand what she means. Miss Josie is sweet, the same color as honey, and I could stay here forever drinking her lemonade and being her friend.

When she pulls a paper fan out of her apron, I stand close enough to get the tail winds of her efforts and lean in to catch more of the breeze. When she notices what I am doing she gives me a few swift waves of her fan that feel as sweet as the lemonade.

Evidently, the unspoken rule about not having friends of a different color does not apply in this household.

We sit in the shade of the porch, Paris in the swing, and Vel and me and Miss Josie in rockers. Miss Josie's house is the prettiest shade of yellow I have ever seen. Come to think of it, it is the same shade as the lemonade. The front door is painted green to match the shutters and the picket fence. I marvel at how colorful Paris' house is compared to the houses on our street, which are all a dull white.

"What are you girls going to do this summer?" Miss Josie asks.

I shoot Paris a look to discourage him from telling our secret plans to someone even as sweet as his grandmother.

"Paris and Vel and I haven't decided yet," I say to her. Then I turn up my glass and let the last of the sugar flow into my mouth to sweeten up the lie I just told.

When I include Paris in our summer plans, Miss Josie's face reminds me of Nana Trueluck's. She fans herself again and offers me an uneasy smile.

When we finish our lemonade, I ask her permission for Paris to come to my house for lunch.

The uneasy smile leaves Miss Josie's face and is replaced with something bordering on a frown. "Are you sure it's okay with your father?" she asks.

"I'm sure," I tell her, not the least bit sure since I didn't think to ask him or Mama. If that cross hadn't burned in our yard last night, I may not have even thought to invite Paris at all. But rebellions call for action.

"Is this outfit all right?" Paris asks. He obviously has never seen my daddy in his lucky writing shorts.

"You look fine, Paris," I say.

"Grandson, I'm not so sure this is a good idea," Miss Josie says.

Paris assures her that everything will be fine and promises to telephone her if he needs her. Before she can say anything else, I give Paris my bike and straddle the back of Vel's. Her bike is pink—no surprise—and has white plastic tassels coming out the ends of the handle bars.

On the way back I talk more about the cross burning from the night before. He agrees that it was probably the Macklehaneys and then gives me a worried look that suggests that lunch at my house might be a bad idea after all.

"Trudy's mother makes great grilled cheeses," Vel says from in front of me.

"Do you like grilled cheese, Paris?" I ask.

He says he does.

We cross the dividing line, and I keep looking over my shoulder to see if the cross burners are watching. I don't like to think that people might be out to get us, and for the first time I realize this must be what it is like to be Paris and Miss Josie.

Meanwhile, an old white couple stops their morning walk and looks at us as though we are breaking every law on the law books. Curtains open and close in some of the houses. This makes me want to suggest Paris move in with us to force them to get used to it. But I don't think Paris would want to give up Miss Josie or her lemonade.

We lean our bikes on the fence and step inside my front gate. I pause in front of the burned grass in our yard. A faint smell of gasoline rises from the ground. We bow our heads as if holding a memorial. But I think the only thing that died last night was my innocent way of thinking. Now I know how hateful people can be.

Vel squeezes my hand like she remembers how we held on tight the night before, thinking the world was ending. At that second I remember why Velvet Ogilvie is my best friend—after Nana Trueluck.

Mama comes out onto the porch, her dishtowel slung over one shoulder. Surprise registers in her eyes when she sees

Paris. The look she gives me is not of surprise but more a promise that we will talk about this later.

"It's so wonderful to have you here," she says to Paris. "I don't think I ever thanked you properly for saving my daughter's life."

Mama says this louder than her usual speaking voice, all the while looking across the street. Widow Wilson's house has a ghost of a figure behind her curtains. I can almost hear our neighbor cluck before picking up the telephone to dial her friends on the party line.

Widow Wilson has spied on us for as long as I can remember. Sometimes I wave at her when I come out of the house to let her know that I am onto her. She is getting an eyeful now, just like she must have gotten an eyeful last night, but I don't even care.

"I wish you'd told me such an important guest was coming over for lunch, Trudy." Mama swats me lightly with her dishtowel.

"Sorry," I say, "it kind of came up unexpected."

Mama asks if we'd like grilled cheese sandwiches, and when we say yes she goes inside to make them. Grilled cheese is what she always fixes when I have friends over. Otherwise, lunch would be a plain old peanut butter and banana sandwich. The three of us walk around the side of the house and sit at the picnic table in the shade of the big maple.

A few minutes later, Nana Trueluck comes out the back door, her head held high and wearing one of her church hats like it is Easter. Nana shakes Paris' hand and welcomes him to our home as though he is Jesus and has resurrected on the spot. Then she pats me on the back like I have more gumption than she realized.

While Vel admires her toenails again, Nana Trueluck asks Paris about his family. He tells her how he stays with his grandmother, Miss Josie.

"I know your grandmother," she says. "She makes those beautiful sweetgrass baskets on the corner of King and Meeting. Not to mention those lovely flowers of hers."

Nana Trueluck smiles, and I imagine Mama having conniptions in the kitchen worrying about what the neighbors will think while also on the telephone to Daddy asking him what she should do.

"Trudy told me you had a dream," Nana Trueluck says to Paris. "Would you like to tell me about it?"

He repeats what he told me and Vel the day before, about how in the dream he took down that rebel flag and the next thing he knew he was shaking hands with Dr. Martin Luther King Junior.

Nana nods, her eyes widening at times to take it all in. Then she looks at me as though the trip to Columbia will happen *come hell or high water*, to use one of her favorite phrases. Since we live in the Lowcountry, high water is always a possibility.

Mama steps outside with a tray in her hands, no sign of any conniptions. The grilled cheese sandwiches are on paper plates, with Fritos on the side. Paper cups are full of cherry Kool-Aid. The ice cubes in the cups run a race to see which can melt fastest. I have to resist timing them.

"Can you help me in the kitchen?" Mama says to Nana Trueluck.

Nana excuses herself and tosses me a glance. We both know what's coming. Meanwhile, Paris and Vel and I eat and drink until we are full and then have a contest to see who can make the best cherry mustache.

"Hey, y'all, let's go downtown," I suggest once our drink cups are empty.

"Why on earth would we do that?" Vel asks. "Haven't we gotten into enough trouble already?" The cherry Kool-Aid on her lips accents her pink clothes.

"We need to show whoever burned that cross that they didn't scare us," I say.

Vel looks at me as though I have pulled a pin from a live grenade. "Are you nuts?"

"Quite possibly," I say. "But you should know how I am, Vel. As soon as somebody tells me I can't do something, that's when I want to do it the most. To me, that cross last night was the same thing as a double-dog-dare."

"I'll do it, if you do it," Paris says to Vel.

Vel hesitates long enough for the Civil War to be fought and lost right here in the backyard. But then she finally agrees.

We hop on bikes to go to Battery Park by Charleston Harbor. Paris rides Teddy's bike this time so I can ride mine.

Teddy's bike is banged all to creation from Teddy's stunts, but it still rides fine. At the end of our street we take a right onto East Bay, which runs along the harbor. Riding bikes in the summer is like catching a breeze from Miss Josie's fan. But it is a hot breeze, as always.

Paris hangs back so maybe people won't realize we are together, and I keep slowing down so he can't help but catch up. I lead the way down one of the cobblestone streets Charleston still has. The bumps make us laugh, our voices hiccupping over every stone. When Paris starts to sing it sounds more like a yodel. Nana Trueluck says the cobblestones are a reminder of what came before. A reminder of history. All of a sudden I wish she were here. She would enjoy singing a Doris Day song while bumping across the cobblestones.

"This is shaking the fillings right out of my head," Vel says, her curls bouncing.

The three of us laugh until we can't stay upright any longer and fall over on the sidewalk in hysterics. Paris is a few feet away on the other side of the street pretending he doesn't know us, even though the three of us are laughing at the same joke.

An old lady stops and stares at us, her lips puckered in the message that we should be ashamed for having such a good time. I realize it is Miss Myrtle Page, whose white poodle, Chester, was lunch to that hungry alligator.

"Well, hello, Miss Page." I go from laughter to being dead serious in less than two seconds. "I want to offer my condolences about poor Chester," I add.

Her sour face sweetens a little.

"Don't you children know that it isn't proper to lounge around on the sidewalks like vagrants?" she says.

Paris and Vel look at me like being vagrants is nothing compared to trying to be friends with people who are a different color.

"We're sorry to bother you, Miss Page," I say. "We didn't realize you were still in mourning."

She scowls and walks off, but then I realize it wasn't the fact that Paris was a different color that made her angry but that we were having fun. Considering what happened last night, this feels like progress.

"Let's pinkie swear that when we get old we will never, ever, make kids feel bad for laughing," I say.

I hold up my pinkie, as does Paris, but Vel hesitates as though Paris hasn't washed his hands in a year. I look at her like I have X-ray vision and burn my disappointment into her skull. Finally she holds up her pinkie, too, and our three pinkies wrap around each other, two white and one brown.

We hop back on our bikes and take East Bay Street again going toward the Battery. Two old men turn and look at us as we pass. Then a woman about Mama's age drops her jaw like we are some circus freak show. If Paris is scared, he doesn't let on.

Vel drops back behind Paris and calls ahead for us to stop. We pull our bikes into the shade in an alleyway. "I need to go home. I think I hear my mom calling me," Vel says.

"We're blocks from your house," I say. "There's no way you could hear your mom."

Vel lowers her eyes.

"Leave her alone, Trudy." Paris' voice sounds sweet, like he understands.

"Come on, Paris," I say, turning my back on Vel. "Rebellions require bravery and not giving up."

We leave Vel reading in the shade and circle back and turn onto Broad, one of the main streets in town. As we come around the corner, Daddy comes out of Callie's Diner with my brother, Teddy.

When he sees Paris on his bike, Teddy barrels toward us like a locomotive that's jumped the tracks. He lets out a Tarzan yell. Whenever I see my brother coming, I usually brace, duck and get ready for a crash. I warn Paris to watch out. Then Teddy slides in front of our bikes, a runner sliding into home plate. Seconds later, swatches of pink and red rise on both his knees.

"Uh, oh," he says as though the bike is now forgotten.

Daddy's eyes widen, and I wonder if it is from seeing me with Paris or Teddy's latest injuries. He greets us and shakes Paris' hand before pulling out the antiseptic from his pants pocket and spraying Teddy's knees. Teddy grimaces. Then Daddy dabs the corners of the wound with his handkerchief and pulls two new Band-Aids from his wallet to add to the collection on Teddy's knees.

Despite the fact that Daddy dreams of being the next Hemingway, he is also very practical. He never goes anywhere without first-aid supplies. If I weren't afraid of getting in trouble, he'd be the perfect person to ask how to get that flag down from the top of the State House.

"Trudy, can I speak to you for a moment?" He smiles at Paris, who is a few feet away. I put down my bike, and we step into the shade of a crepe myrtle tree. I know from the tone of his voice that a lecture is coming, but he doesn't look mad.

"I understand what you're trying to do here, honey, but I also think you need to think of Paris. He could get in big trouble."

I wonder if he has been talking with Nana Trueluck because that's almost exactly what she said, too.

Daddy puts the spare Band-Aids back into his wallet. "You understand?"

"Yes, sir," I say.

He says a quick goodbye before chasing after Teddy, who is already hanging onto the limb of a large live oak tree behind City Hall.

When I turn around, Paris has disappeared again like that first day we met. He is the Invisible Man when he wants to be.

"Paris, where are you?" I say.

"Over here." His voice comes from a cluster of bushes near a park bench.

"Sorry about this," I say, sitting on the bench. "Daddy's afraid I'll get you in trouble."

"It's okay, Trudy," Paris says from the bushes.

"It's just the way the world is set up, I guess. Doesn't mean we have to like it."

"I know," he says.

It is one thing to hide how you're feeling, like when you're scared or thinking something mean. But it is not like you can hide the color of your skin. It is out in the open where every-body can judge you. And it is not like you can hide in the bushes your whole life, either.

"Paris, can I ask you something?"

"Sure," he says.

"Where are your parents?"

He pauses, and I wonder if I have asked something I shouldn't have.

His voice comes out soft. "My dad died in Vietnam."

A warm breeze trembles in the live oaks. "Oh, Paris, I'm so sorry," I say, my voice matching his softness.

I have never known anyone who died in Vietnam. Nana Trueluck watches the news and gets upset about the war all the time, but I don't even know why we are over there.

"My dad saved a bunch of his buddies in a battle," Paris continues. "His sergeant told us that he was a hero."

I get up and walk over to the bushes. This is not some-thing to discuss from a park bench while your friend hides in the underbrush.

"You're a hero just like your dad, Paris. You saved my life, too."

In the middle of the bushes, I find Paris sitting on the ground cross-legged. I stand nearby.

"So where's your mom, Paris?"

I am almost afraid of the answer. What if she is dead, too?

"She's still in Detroit," he says. "She works twelve-hour shifts as a nurse's assistant. I live with Miss Josie because she didn't like me spending so much time alone. As soon as she gets enough money saved she's going to move here, too."

I am relieved he still has a mother.

A family walks by—parents with two boys who look like their father. I wonder if Paris looks like his father, too. The boys wear Confederate hats, the kind bought in tourist shops. They look at me like a girl who talks to bushes might be dangerous.

"Do you miss your mom?" I ask after they leave.

"All the time," he says from the bushes, "and I miss my dad, too."

I wish Vel could hear this and get to know Paris better. We are so lucky to have parents living with us, and I am extra lucky to have Nana Trueluck down the hall from me. I will have to tell her about Paris' dad. She will be sad, too.

Paris motions toward the entrance to the park.

Hoot Macklehaney walks in, hands in his pockets, as though simply moseying around. But I have a feeling it isn't by accident that he has found me. I return to the park bench, leaving Paris in his hiding place.

"Look what the cat drug in," Hoot says to me.

I think of my cat, Hazel, who is an expert hunter and sometimes leaves gifts on the front porch. Every chipmunk in South Carolina must be on the lookout for Hazel. In fact, if chipmunks had tiny post offices, I imagine her picture would be taped to the wall as America's Most Wanted.

Meanwhile, Hoot Macklehaney slinks toward the bench like I am a chipmunk and he is a cat. I want to believe he is harmless, but evidence to the contrary is burned onto our front yard. Another war is going on right here in Charleston, and Paris and I are on the front lines. Nobody talks about it, and it stays mostly hidden, but it is there. Right now we need to make sure that we don't become casualties.

Chapter Thirteen

Ida

Later that afternoon, Ted Junior sends Teddy to his room to play while the grownups meet in the kitchen. Abigail has that look she wears whenever she thinks someone will judge her.

"Where is she now?" Abigail asks. "Sitting in the back of a Charleston bus in protest?"

"She's not trying to make your life harder, Abigail. She's trying to be true to her convictions."

My comment surprises me. Since when do I offer what is on my mind?

"What kind of convictions does a twelve year old have?" she asks me, her voice shaking.

I think the shaking is more from fear than anger. If I had to guess, I'd say Abigail is proud of Trudy, and at the same time Trudy scares her.

"I saw Trudy at the park earlier today with Paris," Ted Junior says. "I had to suggest to her that people wouldn't understand."

"How are things supposed to change?" I ask my son. "How do things change if no one is willing to question the current situation?"

"You know how dangerous this is," he says to me. "In case you've forgotten, we had a cross burned in our yard last night."

"All the more reason to—"

"Stop," he says to me. "You've done enough."

"Are you suggesting I'm behind all this?" I ask, even though the "suggestion" is already loud and clear. "Paris saved Trudy's life, if you'll remember. That makes an impression on a person. I never suggested that she be friends with him or bring him to the house for lunch. Though I wish now that I had."

"It's okay, Mother," Ted Junior says to me.

He only calls me *mother* when he is upset with me.

"All I know is, in a matter of days, our life has turned . . ." Abigail searches for a word. "Unpredictable," she concludes.

"I would have gone with dangerous instead of unpredictable," I say, "but that doesn't mean we desert our principles."

"This is Charleston," Ted Junior says, as if I need a reminder of how history prevails.

"I know Charleston," I say. "I've lived here my entire life and much longer than you have, by the way." I was thirty-three when Ted Junior was born. Ted Senior and I had given up on having children.

My son and I exchange looks, and I remember the defiant little boy he used to be. A defiance I encouraged, even though it wasn't something I possessed myself. But I am getting nowhere by questioning their parenting.

I turn to look at Abigail who appears to be holding back tears. "I can't say I disagree with you," I say. "But do we want to crush Trudy's enthusiasm? Our only hope for change is her generation and the generations to come."

Abigail pauses. "Our first priority is to protect Trudy from getting hurt," she says.

"But are you wanting to protect Trudy or yourself?" I ask, knowing I've stepped over a line I promised myself I would never cross. I want to retrieve the words. Erase them. "Sorry," I add, but it is too late.

Abigail tosses her dishtowel onto the counter and looks at Ted Junior as though to remind him that she knew this setup would never work. "Talk to her," she says, leaving the kitchen in tears.

My son and I are now alone, sitting across from each other at the kitchen table. My outspokenness has surprised us both.

"Overprotection will stifle Trudy," I say to him, my words soft. "You know what a special child she is."

"But this isn't overprotection, Mom. She doesn't know the way the world works yet."

"But what better way to—" I stop myself.

Ted Senior always said that we must choose our battles carefully. And Trudy is my son's child, not mine.

How will I tell Trudy and Paris that, in the name of safety, the dream they have will have to wait for another day? How will I tell them that the old ways win again? And again. And again. Making us all losers.

"I appreciate how much time you spend with her," Ted Junior says. "She really loves you and respects you. You've made a strong impression on her, too. You've inspired her to do things she may not be ready for yet. She's only twelve."

"But I didn't mean to inspire anybody," I say. "You know what a coward I am. I've just encouraged her to question things, like I never took the time to do myself. Trudy is more mature at twelve than I was at twenty," I continue, and wonder if this is a good thing. There is something to be said for having a childhood. I think of growing up in the early part of this century. There were still physical reminders of the Charleston earthquake of 1886 that practically leveled the town to rubble. My mother, who was ten years old at the time, never got over it. A thunderstorm made her physically quake. I grew up with the knowledge that disaster could strike at any moment. I was twenty when World War I broke out in Europe. Wars make life unpredictable, always dangerous.

I stare at the crossword puzzle I abandoned earlier that morning. Life is a puzzle, too. Or perhaps it is something else entirely. I don't know what it is anymore. I am fresh out of metaphors.

"Tell Abigail I'm sorry," I say.

"Will you behave?" Ted Junior places a hand on mine. The irony isn't lost on either of us. Until now I was always the most behaved person in the room. What is bringing on this change?

When I look up I suddenly see how much he looks like his father. My eyes mist. Before leaving the room, he gives my shoulder a quick squeeze and promises to give Abigail my message. We are all doing the best we can given the circumstances. Including Abigail.

In the empty kitchen, I let myself feel a familiar sadness. Sadness for people no longer here and the ones left behind. Sadness for the peace this world can't seem to negotiate. Despite the voice inside me that insists we don't have time to waste, I contemplate how I will break the news to Trudy that taking down that flag is never going to happen.

Chapter Fourteen

Trudy

In the park, with Paris hiding in the bushes, Hoot hovers alongside me like a mosquito looking for a spot to bite. I wonder how much he knows about what happened last night.

"You should have listened to me, girly," he says.

"Get away from me, Hoot." I walk my bike in the opposite direction so he won't see Paris. After hearing what happened to Paris' father, I feel protective.

"You'd better tell me what you're up to." He narrows his beady eyes at me.

For several seconds we are in a standoff while he waits on me to spill my guts. It is so quiet I can hear Barbie ticking the time away.

"If you don't get out of my way I'm going to scream bloody murder and bring every policeman in Charleston County," I say to him. I push my front tire right up to his feet.

In the bushes, Paris edges his way closer in case I need help.

"Did you burn that cross in my yard last night?" I ask Hoot.

"I didn't do anything to no yard."

"I don't believe you for one second, Hoot Macklehaney."

Hoot grins.

"You best be getting out of my way."

He pauses, but then takes a step back. "Once I know what you're up to, I'm going to tell everybody," he says.

His pimples appear to stand at attention, and he glares at me before he walks away.

"Meet me at the corner of Meeting and Broad," Paris whispers from the bushes.

I agree and head in that direction. When I get there, I find Miss Josie sitting under a red umbrella surrounded by her sweetgrass baskets and two white buckets full of fresh flower bouquets. Colored women use umbrellas to keep the Charleston sun off their faces. White people only use them when it rains, which seems silly since we are the ones who burn to a crisp from getting too much sun. Paris stands next to her, Teddy's bicycle leaning against the curb. He must have taken a shortcut to beat me here.

Miss Josie smiles when she sees me and finishes weaving the feathery sweetgrass into her latest creation. Tourists, all white, stand and watch her as if she is part of a living museum.

"I've been making these since I was your age," Miss Josie says to me.

"They're beautiful," I tell her. "I don't know how to do anything like this."

"We all have a talent that's ours to grow, Miss Trudy. You'll find yours soon enough."

She winks at me and then takes ten dollars from a white woman who buys one of her largest baskets. She thanks the woman and folds the bill into a small leather pouch. I like thinking I have a talent that I will discover later. Something that will put money in a pouch.

"What's Paris' talent?" I ask after the tourist leaves.

She smiles again. "My grandson has the gift of persuasion. He's going to have a lot of influence one of these days." She looks at Paris like she believes this with all her heart. Paris smiles in response, and I step closer, proud to be his friend.

A couple of white people walk by getting an eyeful of me and Paris. Dark clouds move in on Miss Josie's sunny face. "I appreciate what you're doing, Miss Trudy, wanting to be friends with my grandson." She pauses like she is debating how much to say. "It worries me, though," she begins again. "You two better be careful. You can't push a river."

"Yes, ma'am," I say, wondering what a river has to do with anything.

Miss Josie hands me a daisy I stick behind my ear.

"Let's go to the Battery," I say to Paris.

The Battery is a fortified seawall and a public park. You can see Fort Sumter from there, where the Civil War started.

"But Miss Josie said we shouldn't be seen together," Paris says.

"We won't," I say. "I have an idea of how we can be together but not together."

Paris looks confused, but when I hop on my bike he follows a block behind. All this following business makes no sense to me. It seems like an insult to our new friendship.

Once we get to the waterfront, grand houses line the street. Some of them have widow's walks, little porches on the top of the houses where wives watched for their husband's ships to come into the harbor a long time ago. Nana Trueluck says sometimes these men were lost at sea and didn't come home and the women became widows, which explains where the name came from. Nana Trueluck has told me all sorts of stories like this one.

Because of the breeze from the harbor it is a few degrees cooler here but still hot. I leave my bike leaning against a tree, and Paris does the same, several trees over. I sit on one side of an old cannon and motion for Paris to sit on the opposite side. With the cannon between us, we can't see each other but we can talk. Battery Park has several cannons, tributes to the Civil War. The gray and black one that sits between me and Paris points toward Fort Sumter where the first shots of the War were fired in 1861. History is everywhere in this town.

A man with his suit coat draped over his arm smokes a cigarette nearby on a bench. He turns and stares like he is onto us, but he doesn't say anything. A minute later he stomps out his cigarette and walks away.

"Why do people feel like they have the right to stare?" I say. "I wanted to slap that look right off his face."

"Martin Luther King Junior doesn't believe in hitting people. He believes in non-violence and turning the other cheek."

I turn my cheek and look out over the harbor. Then I remember another story Nana Trueluck told me.

"Hey Paris, did you know that they used to hang pirates from these trees?"

"Oh my heavens!" Paris says, his southern accent pristine.

I lean forward to see his reaction and catch him looking up into the trees as if imagining the ghosts of pirates swinging in the coastal breeze.

"They were probably Hoot Macklehaney's ancestors," I say. "He reminds me of a pirate the way he's always lurking around, looking for ways to get us in trouble."

Paris doesn't answer. He is still looking up at the limbs of the trees as if spellbound.

"What is it, Paris? You look like you've seen a ghost."

"I've got a story to tell you, Trudy, but it's way scarier than pirates. Do you want to hear it?"

It is hard to imagine what would be scarier than pirates hanging in the trees, but I say yes.

He pauses for a long time, his voice almost a whisper when he finally speaks. "Have you ever heard of a lynching?" he asks.

I say no, and wonder if this story is going to be as sad as what happened to his father.

"I had a second cousin who it happened to," Paris says, his voice so soft my ears have to reach for the sound. "He lived in Mississippi."

Paris pauses again for a long time, and I feel sadness coming in like one of those storms that sometimes batter the harbor.

"What happened?" I ask finally, my patience battered, too.

"It's the same thing that happened to the pirates," he says. "Except my cousin didn't do anything wrong. They hung him because he was colored."

"That's a lie," I say before I can stop myself. But Paris isn't the type to lie. "I refuse to believe that people can be that mean," I say, more to myself than him.

"I swear on my cousin's grave," Paris says from the other side of the cannon.

"But how could somebody get away with that?" I ask.

"You'd be surprised what white people get away with, Trudy."

My face burns with the awareness that with my Scottish roots I am about as white as a person gets. Although, when I look at my own skin it isn't white at all, but a shade of light beige. And everybody knows that beige is boring.

"Sorry, Trudy, I know you're white, but you're different. Your family is different, too."

I scoot closer wishing we could be like regular friends, without a Civil War cannon sitting between us. Yet somehow that cannon there makes perfect sense.

"I'm so sorry that happened to your cousin, Paris. It makes me spitting mad." Then I remember his great-great-great-grandmother had to clean a whole mansion every day of her life, and I work up more spit.

"It makes me mad, too," Paris says. "But more than mad, it makes me determined. That's why I want to go to Hollywood and make movies. People look up to actors and listen to what they have to say. After I get famous, I'll march alongside Dr. King, and I'll tell the movie magazines how unfairly colored people are treated."

"I admire you, Paris. I do."

He thanks me. We sit in silence while a formation of six pelicans fly overhead toward the sea.

"Miss Josie says that if anybody took even five minutes to talk to colored people they'd see we were just like them, with the same wishes and dreams and feelings," he tells me.

"Your Miss Josie is very wise."

He agrees.

A colored nanny pushes a white baby in a fancy stroller. She gives Paris a look like she is thinking: *Why in the world are you sitting next to a Civil War cannon in downtown Charleston talking to yourself?*

Then she looks over at me.

She stops and puts her hand on her hip.

"Don't you have somewhere you need to be?" she says to him.

"No, ma'am," he says, his accent matching hers.

"Aren't you Miss Josie's grandson?"

He nods.

"Is this that girl you rescued?" she asks him. Her eyes point to me.

He nods again.

She gives me a long, slow look. For the first time I glimpse what it is like to be judged for the color of my skin. It never dawned on me that colored people might be prejudiced, too. All of a sudden I feel like I have fallen into the deep end of the swimming pool. I wish I were a stronger swimmer.

She walks away, tisking us like we don't have the sense God gave a lima bean.

"I forgot to tell you," Paris says. "My Uncle Freddie came by Miss Josie's this morning, and he's agreed to take me with him to Columbia on Saturday."

"Well, that's terrific," I say. "Nana Trueluck has agreed to take me and Vel, too. Now we need to come up with a good reason to go. If we tell people the truth, they'll try to talk us out of it."

We both go to pondering what a *good reason* might be.

"I'll say, if it isn't Trudy Trueluck." I look up from picking a knee scab to see Madison Chambers, a good friend of my Grandpa Trueluck.

He tips his hat to me to reveal a full head of white hair. He then looks over at Paris and bows, too. His eyes ask me if

I realize there is someone sitting on the other side of the cannon, so I introduce them. He insists that we call him Madison instead of Mr. Chambers.

During the centennial celebration of the Civil War, Mr. Chambers wrote letters to the editor of the Charleston newspaper about how white people should take colored folks' feelings into consideration. Daddy read them aloud at the breakfast table. If there is one person in the whole city of Charleston who might understand what it is we want to do, it would be Madison Chambers.

"Your daddy's doing a fine job as mayor," he says to me.

"Thank you," I say. "I'll tell him you said so."

"Please do," he says.

"How's your lovely grandmother today?" he asks with a smile.

I forget sometimes that Nana Trueluck and Mr. Chambers are friends.

"Did you hear about the cross burning?" I ask him.

"My heavens, no," he says.

I proceed to tell him the whole story.

"Is Ida okay?" he asks when I finish. The concern on his face tells me he may like Nana Trueluck more than I realized.

"Well, we were all pretty shaken up," I say.

He nods, showing more concern. "Something needs to be done," he says, glancing over at Paris.

Paris and I lean around the cannon and exchange a look where he gives me permission to tell Mr. Chambers.

"Well, sir," I begin, "you know that rebel flag that flies over the State House in Columbia?"

"Yes, I do," he says. "It's an abomination." His smiling mustache stops smiling. "Three years ago they put that flag up for the centennial celebration. Funny how they seem to have forgotten to take it down."

He arches his bushy eyebrows at Paris as if to offer an apology from the entire white race.

"That's okay, sir," Paris says. "I know you didn't put it there."

Like spies in old movies meeting to exchange information, we talk without looking at each other.

"You had a question about that flag?" he asks.

I pause, knowing how farfetched our idea might sound. "Paris and I were wondering how a person would go about getting it down," I say.

Mr. Chambers chuckles at first. Then he sees I am serious.

"You want to take that flag down?"

Paris and I nod.

"I've never heard of anyone ever trying," he says. Then he rubs his chin like he is wondering why he didn't think to do it himself. "I can tell you for a fact that petitions won't work," he continues. "You can't get the number of signatures you need." He goes to thinking again, petting his mustache into an even bigger smile.

"Couldn't somebody just go up to the top of the building and take it down?" I say.

He chuckles again. "I'd love it if somebody did that, but I'm not sure how they'd get away with it," he says. "As an attorney, I've been in that building many times. A guard stands right inside the door, and he makes it his business to know everybody's business. Plus, there is the old guard, too," he adds.

"An old guard?" I imagine someone even older than Mr. Chambers standing by the door with a cane.

"The old guard isn't an actual person, but an old way of thinking. I don't know how anyone would get past that old guard." He pauses and smiles at me. "You certainly ask good questions, Trudy Trueluck. You also have a most interesting imagination."

He pets his mustache once more and says his goodbyes.

"He seems nice," Paris says, still speaking from the other side of the cannon.

I agree but then pause, thinking about what Mr. Chambers said. "We need to figure out how to get past that old guard," I say.

"I didn't even know there was such a thing," he says.

"Me neither," I say. "But it kind of makes sense."

Just being Paris' friend has changed how I look at things. A big line divides our country that I never noticed before.

Sometimes I'd like to take an eraser to the pictures in my head, like that cross burning in our yard. Or the pictures on television of John F. Kennedy getting shot in Dallas. I wish I could forget all of that. I also wish I didn't know what a lynching was.

"People who burn crosses must be part of the old guard, too," I say. "Not to mention people who spit at other people and wave flags in their faces to make them afraid."

"At least now we know what we're up against," Paris says. "Martin Luther King Junior says that now's the time to do something about it. He has a dream that all of us will get free someday."

"Kind of like your dream of taking down that flag," I say.

Paris smiles, but there is also sadness in his eyes.

"My fourth grade teacher told our class once that when things get too bad, people will rebel in order to make things change," I say.

"It's way too hot for a rebellion," Paris says.

"Maybe not," I say. Then I smile with a breakthrough idea.

"What is it?" Paris asks.

"What if we say we're starting a school newspaper, and the first story we want to report on is the flag over the State House? We can interview people about whether or not they think it's a good idea."

"That will give you and Vel an excuse to be there, but what about me?" Paris asks.

"We can say our two schools are doing it together," I say.

"You think they'll believe us?"

"Why wouldn't they?" But I'm not so sure they'll believe us, either. "It's worth a try," I add.

Three seagulls land on the rail of the seawall and then fly over next to us like they may have some answers, but it will cost us bread crumbs. Bread crumbs we don't have. They squawk their dissatisfaction.

In the next instant a loud rumble of thunder shakes the ground underneath us, and the gulls scatter. I turn to see a dark gray sky behind us. Paris and I stand and exchange surprised looks. Neither of us expected a storm to come up so quickly. We get on our bikes and pedal as fast as we can down East Bay Street. At the crossroads he gets off Teddy's bike to give it back to me, but I tell him to keep it. He can bring it back to my house later. Then we turn to go in opposite directions to our houses. As the wind picks up I think about what Mr. Chambers said about the old guard and wonder if Nana Trueluck knows about them, too. If she does, maybe she can help us get past them. But for now this storm seems to have other ideas.

Chapter Fifteen

Ida

The thunderstorm passes and the air is dripping with humidity. Having lived in Charleston my entire life, I have seen quite a few storms batter the coastline, including tropical storms and hurricanes. When you live at sea level, things can get a little wild. Storms at high tide flood low lying streets. Barricades go up until the water recedes. Thankfully, this is simply one of the frequent afternoon thunderstorms that accompany summertime.

Trudy arrives home soaked and exhilarated. After she changes into dry clothes she joins me on the front porch. Water drips from the trees, making it sound like it is still raining.

"Were you with your new friend?" I ask.

Trudy looks to make sure nobody is around. "Yes," she whispers. "We went to the Battery. We ran into Mr. Chambers. He asked about you."

I surprise myself with a smile.

"Any new developments?" I ask, hoping the answer is no. The more I think about it, the more I am convinced going to Columbia is too risky. Not to mention the fireworks that will ensue if Abigail and Ted Junior find out the reason we are going.

"Paris' Uncle Freddie is willing to take him to Columbia," Trudy says. "Now we've got to come up with a story to convince Vel's parents and Mama and Daddy to let us go."

"Vel's parents are coming by after supper tonight for pie and pinochle," I say, relaying something Abigail said earlier.

"Perfect," Trudy says.

I find myself hoping that Ted Junior and Abigail nix the idea, or perhaps Oscar and Penelope Ogilvie—Vel's parents. Without Vel, Trudy and Paris may lose interest. Yet Trudy's commitment to the idea shows no sign of waning.

Later that evening, Ted Junior comes out of the attic, a sure sign that it is a special occasion. He has put on a shirt to go with his worn out Bermuda shorts. On the front porch, Abigail slices one of her peach pies usually reserved for Callie's Diner. Trudy pulls Vel aside, and I overhear her tell Vel to go along with whatever I say. What *I* say? Since when am I the one doing the persuading? I am not convinced it is a good idea myself.

The house across the street has all its lights out, and I am certain Widow Wilson is up to her usual spying. If not for the Trueluck family, I can't imagine what she'd do for entertainment. Of course, she would be welcome for pie, too, but I think she prefers her clandestine practices to real socializing.

A few minutes later a police car drives down our street really slowly like they did the night before. Ted Junior waves at the officer, who lifts his index finger in response.

"You would think the mayor of Charleston would deserve more than a finger," I say under my breath. At least it wasn't a different finger, but still.

"Don't worry about it, Mother," Ted Junior says. "Everything's fine." I wonder when my son took up lying. Nothing is fine, not in the current social environment. Plus, the smell of gasoline lingers in the front yard.

Greetings go around and Oscar and Penelope Ogilvie join us on the shady porch. Iced tea is served with plenty of ice that melts as quickly as our greetings in the Charleston heat. The evening progresses. Teddy does a few stunts that make us laugh as well as fear for his safety. Meanwhile, Trudy is silent, her leg shaking her jitters. With all that energy she could run to Columbia.

Surely she knows that getting parental permission is a long shot. Columbia is a hundred miles away, and we are without a purpose for going. Not one that I know of anyway. Ted Junior and Abigail typically err on the side of caution when it comes to parenting styles. And as someone who lives here as a result of their grace, I can hardly question that. But what about Trudy? Is my responsibility to encourage her passion or to keep her safe? My answer shifts like a weathervane on a wind current.

After pie, pinochle is suggested and I wonder how to bring up Columbia. Before I get a chance to pull together a story, Trudy stands.

"I have something important to ask you," she says to her parents.

She visibly swallows before jumping into her lost cause with both feet. I have to say I admire this burst of bravado to act on something she believes in. As for me, any fleeting boldness I possess was washed away by Abigail's tears earlier today. I have meddled enough.

Trudy begins to talk about a school newspaper project in a way that sounds believable and even admirable, including a part about interviewing people on their opinions about the flag. I have to admit, it is a good idea.

"Can Vel and I go with Nana Trueluck to Columbia on Saturday?" she asks.

"Trudy needs me to take notes," Vel says to her parents. She whips a pen and pad from her purse with the precision of someone who actually wants to go.

Vel is a follower. Being friends with Trudy almost requires it. But she is also someone who thinks about things. Someone who might do something with her life someday. Something more than getting married and raising children, though it is practically a sacrilege to even think this. In my day, to have only one child was looked down upon. Not that Ted Senior and I didn't try to have more.

"You have to be careful when you question people's views," Ted Junior says. "A lot of them see nothing wrong with that flag."

Vel's parents appear unmoved.

"Of course, I'll be there the whole time," I say, "to make sure they ask their questions in a way that doesn't challenge anyone."

The weathervane has shifted again, and I surprise myself with my intent on helping with Trudy's mission. She has never asked much of me as a grandmother. The least I can do is help her and her friends get to Columbia. I doubt they can get anywhere near that old flag anyway. To conjure up the courage to make the attempt is not without its merits, either.

"I've been meaning to go to Columbia to see my cousin for months now," I begin again. "We can perhaps even meet her at the State House so I can keep an eye on the children."

I do have a second cousin on my father's side who lives in Columbia—that part is true. However, my cousin is not someone whom I care to visit. Unfortunately, a stained sofa on the side of the road holds more luster than she does and is more inviting.

"I love how the girls have taken an interest in our state's history," I am quick to add. "Think of how this will widen their experience, as well as get them extra credit."

Oscar and Penelope look skeptical at first, but both girls offer persuasion, and they finally agree. Ted Junior and Abigail agree next, and Trudy and Vel exchange victory glances. It is decided. Next Saturday morning, I will drive the girls to the State House in Columbia where they will meet Paris and begin their secret mission.

Chapter Sixteen

Trudy

Friday night, Vel sleeps over and we set two Baby Ben alarm clocks to wake us up at four-thirty in the morning so we can be ready to go by five o'clock. Nana Trueluck says if we leave then we will arrive in Columbia by seven-thirty to meet Paris and his Uncle Freddie at the Farmer's market.

Vel is snoring when the first alarm goes off, and I have to shake her hard to wake her up. Vel can be a royal grouch in the mornings, and this morning is no exception. Her right leg flares out from under the sheet and nails me in the thigh. Not one to be nailed, I grab her foot and pull her halfway off the bed until she screams and gives me a look that reminds me of Hoot Macklehaney.

Eyes half closed, Vel's Toni curls spring to life much sooner than she does. She takes off her pink pajamas and puts on her other pink clothes for the day. Since Vel wears so much pink, I refuse to wear any, except for my Barbie watch.

By the time we get to the kitchen, Mama is up, too, making us eggs and toast. She puts coffee in Daddy's thermos for

Nana Trueluck. She also wraps up three apple turnovers she baked the day before.

As Vel and I eat breakfast, Mama tells us a litany of things we should be careful of. The list includes: strangers, crooks, dirty bathrooms, and rabid dogs. New to her list is rabid dogs, added after seeing *To Kill a Mockingbird* at the movie theater last year.

"Here's a nickel for the pay phones just in case you get lost." She hands a buffalo nickel to me and Vel.

Vel puts it in her training bra, but it falls straight through. Her face turns a color that matches her outfit. I put my nickel in my pocket. Vel tries her training bra again. I am not sure what she did differently, but this time it stays.

"If you get lost, find a pay telephone and call me collect," Mama says.

Mama is an expert at thinking up every possible thing that could go wrong in every situation. While Vel and I wait at the kitchen table, I imagine a stranger who is also a crook hiding from a rabid dog in a dirty bathroom.

Life is full of danger, I say to myself and then smile.

"I've changed my mind," Vel whispers. The outline of the buffalo nickel shows through her light pink shirt.

"It's too late to have second thoughts," I whisper back. "Nana Trueluck will be downstairs any minute."

Vel tugs at her curls as though trying to milk courage out of them.

"We may get there and not do a thing except turn around and come home," I whisper again.

She relaxes her grip on Nancy Drew.

At five o'clock exactly, Nana Trueluck comes downstairs looking like an aging canary. Instead of her usual wild skirt and high-top sneakers, she wears a yellow dress with a matching yellow hat and the low black heels she always wears to church. When she walks her legs swish from wearing hose.

Nana Trueluck takes a few sips of black coffee as if to fortify her commitment.

"Are you sure you want to do this, Ida?" Mama asks.

It is always strange to hear Nana Trueluck's first name. I forget she used to be Ida before she was Nana Trueluck.

"I've never been so sure of anything in my life," she says to Mama, looking over at me and Vel. Her smile isn't convincing.

Vel grips Nancy Drew again, as though needing her own fortification.

"I'm not sure why in the world you need to leave so early," Mama says.

"Traffic going into Columbia on a Saturday will probably be heavy," Nana Trueluck replies.

And taking down that flag may take a while, I want to add.

Meanwhile, Vel's hair looks like a mop that needs to be rung out. I wonder how long it will take me to get used to her perm.

When we leave the house it is still dark. The porch light reaches into the yard, the shadow of the cross burned into it, reminding me of our mission. When I latch the gate of our white picket fence behind us, it feels like from this moment on there is no turning back.

Nana Trueluck's 1940 Chrysler Plymouth has been moved from the garage by the house to the street. Daddy has the hood up in the dark and is checking the oil with a flashlight. Nana hasn't driven since she moved here, and I catch myself hoping she remembers how.

We pile into the front seat, Vel by the window, me in the middle, and the thermos and the food Mama packed in between me and Nana Trueluck. Over a year later the car still smells a little like Grandpa Trueluck's pipe tobacco.

Daddy closes the hood.

"I added air to your tires." He shines the flashlight into the car.

She thanks him and pats his hand.

"Stick to the main roads," he says, sounding protective.

"Ted Junior, I remember how to get to Columbia. Highway 176."

Nana Trueluck turns on the car, and the engine rumbles as though remembering how to do its job. She pulls away from the curb driving really slowly down Queen Street. So slowly it occurs to me that at this rate we won't reach Columbia until sometime tomorrow. Something sharp pokes into my thigh, and I realize it is Nancy Drew. Vel apologizes.

We are past Summerville before it even hints at daylight. But the minute the sun appears on the horizon we can tell the day will be a scorcher. Thankfully, Nana has sped up to five miles below the speed limit. We don't talk because the windows are wide open, and the wind flaps through the car like loose sails. We couldn't hear each other if we wanted to.

About thirty minutes in, Vel falls asleep, her head against the door of the Chrysler. Drool seeps from the corner of her mouth, and I time it with my Barbie watch, measuring how long the drool takes to reach her chin. Vel's snore blends in with the sound of the engine until it crescendos into a snort. Nana Trueluck and I exchange looks, and I cover my mouth to stifle the wild laughter that wants to escape.

The land between Charleston and Columbia is flat and dense with pine trees. Nana points to a deer on the side of the road and honks her horn to make it run back into the pines. When she honks, Vel startles awake and wipes away 11 minutes and 15 seconds worth of drool. A red crease crosses her cheek from leaning against the door. It looks like war paint.

"What are you looking at?" Vel yells over the flapping sails.

I smile and shrug while Nana Trueluck pretends she wasn't in on it.

We pull up at the farmer's market in Columbia right at eight o'clock. On the way we glimpse the enemy flag flying high above the State House. It waves in the slight breeze as if intent on spending the next hundred years there, maybe longer. My shoulders drop. All of a sudden it feels like we came all this way for nothing. Taking down that flag is an impossible task. We were crazy to even consider it. A sick feeling settles in the pit of my stomach when I think about Paris' dream dying so fast—except what I realize is that now it feels like my dream, too.

Nana parks the Chrysler nearby, and we find Paris and his Uncle Freddie next to a truck full of melons. It feels good not to be in the car anymore. I introduce Nana to Paris, and Paris introduces her to his Uncle Freddie. They talk for a while, and we find out that Freddie has a college degree and teaches at the colored elementary school. He only runs melons on Saturdays to help out his dad who owns a farm in Beaufort. Freddie gets busy with the melons, and Nana Trueluck greets a woman at a nearby vegetable stand.

"Why are you so quiet?" I ask Paris.

"It feels like a dream to be here," he says.

"Of course it feels like a stupid dream," Vel says. "That's how this whole stupid thing started."

We look at her. "Have I told you that Vel is always grouchy in the mornings, Paris?"

"I'm not grouchy," Vel says, sounding even grouchier.

"Are you ready to do this?" I say to Paris.

"I guess so," Paris says. "We're doing it for them as much as for me." He looks out over the farmer's market.

At that moment, I realize that Nana Trueluck and Vel and I are the only white people here. I wonder if all the colored farmers are also the descendants of slaves. Seeing that flag flying on top of a building that's supposed to represent everybody in the state must be like having a bunch of white folks scream right to your face that you don't belong here.

Paris is quiet, and I wonder if he is also thinking about how impossible this is.

"What if we get in big trouble, Trudy? What if my Uncle Freddie gets in trouble, too? And your Nana Trueluck? What if we all get arrested?"

For the first time since I have known him, Paris looks genuinely scared. In the seconds that follow, I catch his fear like a summer cold.

In the distance, the rebel flag waves in the wind like it is waving goodbye and telling us to have a nice trip back to Charleston. Its presence is a constant reminder of a war that nobody can seem to get over. A war that has defeated us again. Within minutes of arriving, we are about to raise our white flag of surrender.

Chapter Seventeen

Ida

The children stand around like lumps in search of a log. Their mood has shifted since we first arrived. Doubts are written on the brows of their young faces. Their eyes find me as though I hold the answers to their unspoken questions. Since I am the oldest by far, I guess that makes sense. But I don't have any answers, either.

Uncle Freddie puts a sign at the back of his truck that reads: WATERMELONS 25 CENTS. Paris agrees to be back at the farmer's market by one o'clock so Freddie can head home to Charleston. I like Freddie, and I like that he trusts me with his nephew.

With the hem of my dress I clean my glasses, a habit I often do when thinking hard about something. I am not sure why I dressed up, except that acting on our constitutional rights seemed as sacred an occasion as attending church. It is not every day one tries to overthrow bigotry.

As a lifelong follower, I wait for Trudy to step forward and lead her friends. Ever since we arrived, she has been unusually quiet. I remember how Ted Junior went quiet for weeks before he began his novel. And Ted Senior got quiet before he announced we were going to travel and see the world. Hopefully Trudy will snap out of it before it matters, but for now I have to lead the charge. We say goodbye to Freddie and walk to the corner.

"I suppose the first thing we need to do is get ourselves to the State House," I begin, putting an arm around Trudy. "Then once we get inside we can see what we're up against."

Their postures relax, and Trudy offers a brief smile.

She just needs to get her bearings, I say to myself. *Then she'll be fine.*

Meanwhile, Paris shoots me a smile as though thankful to have a grownup around, even if I am as white as a loaf of Sunbeam Bread.

I am reminded of how special he is. Like Trudy, he is intent on doing the right thing and has a sense of honor about him. He seems much older than he looks. Vel has possibilities, as well, but it is too soon to tell with her. She is a reluctant soldier in the cause, but at least she is here.

Grandmothers have a code of honor, too, and watch out for each other's grandchildren. Everyone in downtown Charleston knows Miss Josie. I imagine her sitting on the corner of King and Broad, straight and proud. Does she have any idea what her grandson is up to today?

Ted Senior was the one who made plans, not me. I wish he were here to help us figure out how to get that flag down. It may be that we get to the State House and turn around and go home. I can't imagine we will actually find a way to get to the top of the dome.

As the four of us walk up the street toward the State House, my hose swish the entire way. The closer we get, the more I sweat. I wish now that I'd worn my comfortable shoes and one of my cotton skirts and tops instead of this newfangled polyester dress that doesn't allow a person to sweat properly. So much for sacred.

Columbia is different than Charleston. For one thing it isn't nearly as pretty. For another thing, it is stifling hot but without the ocean breeze. At eight-fifteen in the morning, the sidewalk is already hot enough to cook two eggs over easy with a side of bacon.

The four of us walk, three children and a reluctant grandmother. I wish Trudy would stop being so quiet.

"My goodness, we're an unlikely band of rebels," I say, hoping to lighten the mood.

The mood doesn't lighten.

I find a folded up church bulletin from Easter in the pocket of my dress and fan myself in hopes of resurrection.

"Let's rest under these trees for a moment," I say, guiding the children to shade. They look as wilted as I feel, and the excitement has drained from their faces. As for Trudy, I can only hope that at some point her enthusiasm revives. I am not sure how long I can keep this up.

The troops are weary. We need a boost of morale, I tell myself, sounding like Ted Senior. He used to say this when Ted Junior was little and we were on one of our many long road trips to SEE ROCK CITY. Or SEE RUBY FALLS, as the billboards always read.

"Perhaps now's a good time to tell you the story about my great-grandmother," I say to them.

They remain unenthused, but I forge ahead anyway.

I wonder why I have told so few people this story. Perhaps it is too strong a reminder that I haven't taken a stand for anything in my life. But it appears that has changed. At least for now. At this moment, I am in downtown Columbia only blocks away from the State House where I will take a stand for Paris and Miss Josie and Freddie and all the colored people in this great state of ours. My throat tightens, and I haven't even said anything.

Who am I fooling? I say to myself.

Then Trudy looks at me like she is a thirsty plant waiting for rain. I clear my throat. The Easter bulletin goes limp, and I put it back in my dress pocket.

"My great-grandmother was an abolitionist," I begin. "Someone who was against slavery." I think of the trunk in the attic filled with her things and wish I had them to show.

Vel closes her book, and Paris waits as though hanging onto my every word. I wonder if this is what it is like to sing in front of a live audience, something I have never done but often dream of doing.

"She published articles in a Quaker newspaper in Pennsylvania under a man's name," I continue. "She wrote about what the conditions were here in the South for the slaves. It wasn't until years later that people found out that she was the one who had written the articles."

My audience appears unenthused. We leave the shade and continue walking. I won't tell the children the part about how my great-grandmother was disowned by her family and forced out of Charleston because she was seen as a traitor instead of a hero. Even today it is dangerous to voice your views, especially as a woman.

We stop at the entrance to the State House. A mountain of steps leads to the front doors. It is hard not to feel small. Our eyes lift. In the distance the rebel flag lies limp against the flagpole at the top of the dome. It looks harmless and almost beautiful. I attempt to swallow the lump in my throat. How can a piece of fabric hold so much meaning?

"Do you think Dr. King ever gets scared?" Paris asks.

I pause and forget my reluctance. "He wouldn't be human if he didn't," I say. "He puts his life in great danger every time he speaks out about what he believes."

Indeed, it is Dr. King and many like him who are the brave ones, as is Paris to attempt something so symbolic with these new friends. White friends, no less.

While we stare up at the flag, I put my arm around Paris. We stand for several seconds in silence, perhaps realizing the boldness needed to proceed.

"What do we do now?" Vel asks, putting a voice to everyone's question.

I resist saying I have no idea and imagine what my ancestor might remark in this situation.

"We must carry on in the name of freedom," I hear myself say. Perhaps I have some of my great-grandmother in me after all.

"What happens if we get caught?" Vel asks, always the practical one.

"Let's not talk about that because it's not going to happen," Trudy says.

"Trudy Trueluck, are you scared?" Vel asks. "I've never known you to be scared a day in your life."

Trudy denies the feeling, but there is no denying that she has acted strange ever since we got here. Almost petrified. I imagine we are all intimidated by the bigness of this place—not to mention the bigness of the task. Perhaps Trudy is having second thoughts, as well as third and fourth ones. Even Paris looks back toward the Farmer's market as if contemplating running back to his Uncle Freddie's truck.

For the second time today I wish Ted Senior were here to lead the charge. Actually, I would settle for Ted Junior. It occurs to me that maybe the smartest course is to retreat. But what message would that send to the children? Quit before you even try? Quit before you do something significant?

"You know, Nancy Drew would love this kind of adventure," I say to Vel, easily the hardest to convince.

"Nancy Drew would never break the law." Vel clutches her book to her chest like it is a bible that contains the gospel according to Nancy Drew.

"We're not breaking the law," I say. "We're exercising our rights as citizens."

They look at me as though I am Nana Pinocchio and my nose has grown six inches. It is true our rights probably don't extend to taking down a rebel flag, but we do have a right to protest in this country.

"We can go home if you want," I say to them. "Or we can stay here. But I can't do any of this alone."

For several seconds we sit in silence. Paris rests his head in his hands, and Vel has her nose in her book again. It is Trudy who has surprised me most. Where is that fire she had in her eyes earlier in the week?

Nearby, an old man rakes leaves on the State House grounds. Stooped over, he reminds me of the people of color who pass me on the streets of Charleston sometimes. They aren't proud like Paris' grandmother, Miss Josie, but broken down. Their own value hidden from themselves.

"He has to look at that flag every day," Paris says.

The four of us turn toward the man. I think of how strong Paris' ancestors must have been and the misery they have put up with at the hands of white people. But Paris' story doesn't have to be the same as the people who came before them. Neither does ours.

"We've come all this way," Trudy says. "We should at least try." Her voice grows stronger with each word.

Paris sits straighter, and Vel puts away her book. Low tide has ended, and a new tide is coming in. Growing waves of possibility wash ashore.

"We've at least got to try," Trudy says again. She glares at the flag as though looking into the eyes of a bully. The spark inside her has ignited again, and we can all feel it.

We stand. For the first time that day, we feel united.

"Come on, everyone," Trudy says. "Let's go make history."

Paris stands tall, and Vel sticks a hand down her shirt and pulls out a nickel to call home. Trudy makes Vel put the nickel back. This is the granddaughter I know and love.

As for me, I have waited my entire life to do something to make my great-grandmother proud. What is the point of having ancestors if you don't honor them? However, nothing this important is simple. The mammoth building looms ahead of us, the flag perched on the top like a cherry on a sundae.

Facing the building again, we take a step back.

"You can't bail now," Trudy says to us. "We're going to take down that rebel flag. You know why?" she asks, not giving us time to answer. "Because we are here to start a rebellion. We see something wrong, and we are willing to go against the old guard to make it right. We are the best kind of rebels. We are the new rebels."

Arm in arm—with the exception of Vel, who Trudy practically drags—we march up the sidewalk full of our cause to
the big front doors of the State House. Given the honor of
opening the heavy doors, I tug, but nothing happens. They are
locked. Trudy glances at her Barbie watch. It is only 8:30 A.M.
The building is not open yet. We give a collective sigh. Our
history making will have to wait.

Chapter Eighteen

Trudy

"Why don't we go get a soda?" Nana Trueluck says. "I saw a Woolworths on the next street over." Her momentary disappointment seems to evaporate. It never occurred to me that she might be thinking of her great-grandmother—my great-great-great-grandmother—while helping us. At least she is not thinking about Grandpa Trueluck and making herself sad.

We walk along the tree-lined streets to the Woolworths. Paris is wearing a red shirt, white socks, and dark blue shorts, an outfit that would make our founders proud. I wonder if he planned this. When we walk inside the store every single person at the soda fountain turns to look. Paris lowers his head and appears to shrink in size. In the next few seconds, I realize no one knows me here. I am not the mayor's daughter. Nor is Nana Trueluck the mayor's mother. In Columbia, no one knows the Truelucks, and at that moment I feel like a nobody.

Faking my bravery, I lead the way to four stools at the end of the counter. Paris sits between me and Nana Trueluck, with Vel at the end of the counter. People aim their hatred at us, like it is deer season and we are the deer. Nana Trueluck hands us menus to hide behind.

I wish I had a picket sign to hold up that says: I GET TO BE FRIENDS WITH ANYONE I WANT!

In the meantime, Vel reads Nancy Drew like the book is a life raft in the middle of a stormy sea. I probably couldn't pry it away from her if I had to.

The waitress pretends to be busy, wiping already clean counters and refilling coffee cups. I think she wants to make us wait. Nana Trueluck clears her throat several times to get her attention, but the woman just smiles and winks at the other customers like they are all in on the joke. A fake magnolia blossom is glued onto her name tag that reads Faye. According to Barbie, ten minutes and eight seconds pass before she comes over to us.

Faye's tiny dark eyes are lined with black eyeliner. Red circles of rouge dot her pale, wrinkled cheeks, and her lipstick matches her cheeks. Lipstick has bled onto her teeth and makes it look like she ate raw meat for breakfast. Faye looks about Nana Trueluck's age, but her hair is dyed blond, and she is so skinny her nylon hose droop around her ankles.

Finally, Faye grabs her order pad and saunters over to us. "What can I get y'all?" She looks at everybody except Paris.

Paris stares at his silverware, and I seriously question if this trip to Columbia was such a good idea. I don't like seeing him this way, so I kick his leg.

"Ouch!" He gives me a look that has some fire in it.

I nod my approval. I want him to get mad. Mad at me and mad at anybody who thinks he has no right to be here. But Paris probably knows much better than me how dangerous that can be. I remember what he told me about his second cousin and wonder if he has given up. But then I see his eyes twinkle and realize that he is acting. He is playing the part of the old man on the State House grounds, the one who doesn't look up.

"We'll all have sodas," Nana Trueluck says to the waitress. "All *four* of us."

Faye pops her gum, which smells like Juicy Fruit mixed with cigarettes, and then tosses her order pad behind the counter without writing our order down. The ice in our sodas has already melted by the time she finally brings them to us.

Nana Trueluck must be acting, too, because she doesn't get riled and even thanks Faye like she delivered our order in record time. I, however, am about to grab Faye's bleached blond hair and pull it out by the roots. The door jingles its bell, and Paris' eyes widen. The front door is blocked by a rotund man wearing a sheriff's badge. Fat bulges over the officer's belt and strains the buttons on his white shirt.

"They must eat grits by the truckload here in Columbia," I say.

Nana Trueluck shushes me. Something she rarely does.

Faye delivers a plate of breakfast to the man next to us. One half is piled high with scrambled eggs and bacon, the other is filled with grits, confirming my theory.

Grits taste like cardboard to me. But in the South they are as American as apple pie. Regardless, I'd eat them every day if it meant that Paris was treated with respect.

The sheriff walks over and stands right behind us. Paris' chin touches his chest like he is reciting the Lord's Prayer in case he dies in the next few seconds. Either that or he is going for the performance that will earn him the Academy Award.

"Is there a problem, Sheriff?" Nana Trueluck asks.

She swivels on the round stool with the red cushion and then stands. Compared to her, the sheriff looks massive, her head coming up to about his shoulder.

"Is your husband in the store?" he asks her.

"My dear husband died last year," she says.

"I figured that might be the case," he tells her. "Otherwise you wouldn't be sitting here in the Woolworths with a little colored boy." He says this like Nana should know better. I am surprised he doesn't pat her on the head.

Nana Trueluck narrows her eyes like she is about to offer a few well-chosen words.

"You kids about finished?" the sheriff says to me and Vel, ignoring Paris. "We have a lot of people waiting for seats."

I look back through the store toward the door. Nobody is waiting. In fact, there are several empty tables.

"Officer, we have just as much right to be here as everybody else," Nana Trueluck says, reaching for reason.

"The coloreds pick up their food and drink out back," he says. "They aren't welcome in the main dining room."

"This young man is with me," she says.

"I don't care if he's with Abraham Lincoln, he's not allowed in the dining room," the sheriff says.

Head lowered, Paris slides out of his chair to head for the door. I take his arm and tell him to wait, and Faye gasps as though I have touched a live electric wire. As a result, the sheriff rests his hand on his gun like we are four hardened criminals who stand in front of him instead of three kids and a grandmother.

"I'd like to speak to your superior," Nana Trueluck says.

The sheriff chuckles. "My 'superior' is on about the sixth hole of the country club by now, and I doubt he'd want to be disturbed."

"My son is the mayor of Charleston," she says.

"Is he?" the sheriff asks, like he couldn't care less. "Maybe you could call your son from the station and tell him about how you got arrested in Woolworths."

"But you seem to be forgetting about Greensboro," I say, remembering Walter Cronkite's report. A series of nonviolent sit-ins took place in Greensboro, North Carolina, in 1960. Those protests led to the Woolworth chain removing its policy of racial segregation in the South. I remember Nana Trueluck and I talked about what a big deal it was.

"This isn't North Carolina," he says to me. "This is Columbia. We do things different here."

"Let's go," Paris whispers, and I can tell he isn't acting this time.

The sheriff takes a step closer. His belly stretches the seams of his shirt and there are large half-moons of sweat under each arm. He smells like Vitalis hair grease. From his belt, he unhooks a pair of handcuffs like he might use them on Nana Trueluck.

I gasp.

"Come, children," she says, her teeth gritted.

Last year a photograph appeared in the Charleston newspaper of local students from the College of Charleston being arrested for having a sit-in at a local lunch counter on King Street. I imagine a similar snapshot of the four of us pulled out of the Woolworths in handcuffs.

Before we leave, Nana Trueluck opens her purse and slides four dimes on the counter to pay for our sodas. Then we edge past the smelly sheriff, Nana's firm jaw tilted upward, and a look on her face I have never seen before. The sheriff follows us to the front of the store. His shoes squeak as if screaming for mercy.

We step out of the Woolworths into the sunny, muggy day. Vel squints as though coming out of a cave. It feels ten degrees hotter than it was fifteen minutes ago. The sheriff follows us outside.

"Move it along," he says to Nana Trueluck, who clutches her yellow purse like she would like to hit him with it.

I take her arm and lead the way across the street. A block away, we stop and Nana Trueluck asks if we are okay. We say we are, though all of us seem shaken. When I look back the sheriff is still watching. We keep walking.

Once inside the State House grounds again we collapse onto the soft cool grass under the shade of an oak tree. I have never seen this side of Nana Trueluck. The side that will break the law if need be. Nearby, the old colored man still rakes leaves, but he is watching us from the corner of his eye as if he is a soldier and reinforcements have finally arrived at the scene of a long and difficult battle. Reinforcements wearing the uniforms of summer and that include three twelve year olds and a seventy-year-old grandmother.

Chapter Nineteen

Ida

"Who knew rebellions involved so much waiting?" I say, while Trudy checks her watch again.

As usual, Vel is reading, and Paris sits on the State House grounds as if deep in thought.

"I wouldn't blame you one bit if you're upset about what happened in the Woolworths," I say to him.

He shrugs like he doesn't want to talk about it right now. I try to imagine what it is like to be him and realize I can't.

"If I had known it would cause such a ruckus I never would have suggested we go inside that store," I say to him. "I'm sorry."

"It's not your fault," Paris says. "That old guard Mr. Chambers told us about really hates me." He looks at Trudy.

"I forgot you two talked to Madison," I say.

"We asked him for ideas of how to take down the flag," Trudy says. "He said an old guard protected it. Not an old man but old ideas."

"If I'm not mistaken, Madison was part of the Montgomery Bus Boycotts," I say. "He worked with a team of lawyers to challenge bus segregation laws."

"Do you think he met Dr. King?" Paris asks.

"I wouldn't doubt it," I say.

Paris nods as though this pleases him.

"If that sheriff had taken us to jail I would have been okay with that," Paris says. "Dr. King has been in jail many times."

"Well, I'm not okay with going to jail," Vel says, in case we hadn't figured that out by now.

"I have to admit that really scared me," Trudy says. "Do you think he would have arrested us?"

"I doubt it," I say, though at the time I thought it was a definite possibility. I don't mention how frightened I was in there, underneath all that anger. Or how powerless I felt. A woman. An old woman, at that. I think of Paris again. What must it be like to have almost an entire nation intent on keeping you in your place? I am not sure white women have it much better, but at least we can go into a Woolworths and order a Coca-Cola without being threatened with handcuffs.

I begin to hum "Sentimental Journey," one of my favorite Doris Day hits. Pressure builds in my chest, the sadness that revisits me from time to time now that Ted Senior is gone. Or perhaps it is the sadness of such a lovely boy as Paris who just wanted a drink, not being welcome in a store.

"You know, it's okay if y'all want to forget about it," Paris says. He lifts his head from his knees, the sadness in his eyes meeting mine.

"Well, that's the best idea I've heard all day," Vel says before anyone has time to answer.

Trudy rolls her eyes at Vel and then looks at Paris. "Is that really what you want to do?" she asks him.

He doesn't answer.

I think about the March on Washington last year, and Medgar Evers' murder in Mississippi, and the four girls killed while attending Sunday school at a church in Birmingham. All things that have happened in the last year. It suddenly occurs to me what a dangerous game we are playing. While a part of me wants to run back to the safety of my room, another part of me needs to do something.

Also, it is important for people to know that not all southerners are like those images on television. Some are, that's for sure. But some aren't. And the Trueluck family wants everybody to have a fair chance no matter what color they are.

"I wish I could teach that sheriff a thing or two," I say to break the tension. "Maybe put a box of Ex-Lax in his next plate of brownies."

The laughter that follows shifts our seriousness, and I realize how much I sounded like Trudy.

"That's the best idea I've heard all day," Paris says.

Even Vel is smiling and not reading her book.

Perhaps old people and children can not only be friends, but even change the world together. But first we need to get inside the building.

Two guards approach the side doors to the State House and knock to be let in. The door opens, closes, and locks again. According to Trudy, we have three minutes until they open. The dome soars several stories above us. Two flags hang limp at the top of the flagpole. The American flag is on top with its fifty stars. It was forty-nine for the longest time, and then Hawaii joined us four years ago. Below it is the Confederate battle flag put up in 1961 as a statement against desegregation. At least that's what Ted Senior believed.

"I wish I understood why that flag is so important to some people," Trudy says, as though reading my thoughts.

"I think it's about heritage more than anything," I say. "A lot of families lost loved ones in that war. But any symbol that hurts people is not going to help. Ted Junior used to say that it would be like flying a Nazi flag after World War II, not caring how it might hurt Jewish people."

Trudy moves from where she sits and puts her head on my shoulder. I am reminded again that she is only twelve. Everybody needs someone older to tell them things will be all right. But who do you turn to if you're the oldest person in the room?

"I still have no idea how we're going to get it down," Trudy says, "but I think it's important that we try." She looks at her watch and sits up as though an alarm clock has awakened her passion for justice. "It's not only Paris' dignity that's at stake. It's everybody's," she adds.

With that statement, I no longer see a little girl, but the woman Trudy will become. A lump of pride sits in my throat.

"So how do we get there?" Paris looks up at the dome.

"I guess we find the stairs and just keep heading up," Trudy says.

"Don't we need some kind of signal for if we get in trouble?" Paris asks.

"You mean besides screaming bloody murder?" Vel closes her book with a snap.

"No, he means like a hand gesture or something. Right, Paris?" Trudy asks.

"Yeah, something like that," Paris says.

The four of us pause. All I come up with are Doris Day songs, none of which seem to fit the occasion.

"How about we whistle?" Paris puckers his lips.

"That's a great idea," Trudy says.

I agree. "But what do we whistle?" I ask.

We pause for another few seconds, as if thumbing through a file folder in our brains labeled: *songs to whistle while in deep trouble*.

"How about 'Dixie'?" Vel says.

We turn to look at Vel, as if her brilliance has caught us by surprise.

"'Dixie' is the song people always sing in the South when they want to remember the good old days of cotton fields and plantations. The old guard probably loves it." She whistles the first two lines.

Paris tells her she is good at whistling, and Vel laughs.

For the next few minutes we all whistle "Dixie" at different times and out of key. We sound like a bunch of drunken songbirds and practice until our jaws are sore. Then the giggles start and cause us to lose all ability to pucker. The laughter chases my fear away.

At nine o'clock the front doors open and a man in a blue uniform pulls out a metal sign on a stand that lists the times of the tours.

"Maybe we could take a tour," I suggest. "Who knows, they may take us up to the top of the dome."

"I should stay here," Paris says. "I don't want y'all to get in trouble."

"Don't be ridiculous," Trudy says. She gives Paris a hand up from the ground. "We need you, Paris Moses. You've got to lead us to the Promised Land, like that Moses guy in the Bible."

"No relation," Paris reminds us.

We walk up dozens of steps to the front entrance, and I wish I were twenty years younger. A tall guard opens one of the big glass doors and tips his hat to us. I remember what Madison told the children. You would think the old guard would look meaner, but he actually looks a little bit like Ted Senior.

My companions push me gently from behind. Evidently, I am appointed spokesperson.

"Good morning, Officer."

I swallow the quiver in my voice. Trudy steps up and holds my hand, squeezing courage into my palm.

"My friends and I would like to take a tour," I say, my voice stronger.

The guard opens one eye wider than the other. It takes a moment to realize that he has a glass eye. One eye blinks and the other one doesn't. When the children notice it, Trudy shudders, and Vel backs toward the door like she and Nancy Drew may make a run for it. The blinking eye turns to look at Paris and hovers there for a while but he doesn't say anything. I wonder if perhaps the guard is color blind as well.

I can't decide which eye to look at but start to speak anyway.

"We're here from Charleston," I say. "My granddaughter and her friends work for their class newspaper."

The blinking eye doesn't look impressed. "What about the colored boy?" he says.

"A friend of the family," I say.

The guard answers a question from another tourist, and Trudy pulls me close to whisper in my ear. "He reminds me of that alligator who ate Miss Myrtle Page's unfortunate poodle."

I chuckle, and she makes a chomping noise that makes Paris jump.

The guard turns to us again, his one good eye looking skeptical.

"Our school newspaper is called the, um, *Gator Gazette*," Trudy says to him. "We're writing a story about our wonderful State House and the fabulous people who work here."

She smiles at the blinking eye as if to tame it.

"Can the children have your name for their story?" I smile and look at the others, who aim their pearly whites at the guard as well.

The blinking eye blinks and then blinks again.

"Les Lester," the guard replies.

"Excuse me?" I ask.

"That's my name," he says. "If they want to put it in their newspaper."

A smile now accompanies the blinking and unblinking eye. The four of us exchange a look of surprise. Vel pulls her notepad and pen from her pink purse. She makes a big production out of writing the man's name, asking him exactly how to spell it, like a real reporter might do and then repeating it back.

The guard's glass eye threatens to mesmerize me. I don't want to forget why we are here. Les Lester offers to give us a personal tour. We agree. As we walk into the rotunda he tells us facts about when the State House was built, about the governors who have worked here and about the paintings on the walls. Meanwhile, Vel writes everything down as if interviewing a curator for the Smithsonian, instead of a one-eyed, color blind guard.

For the next twenty minutes Les Lester shows us different rooms off the rotunda as well as the law library and the courtroom where cases are presented to the state Supreme Court. We sit in the balcony and overlook the court. Les Lester delivers information as fast as Vel can write it down, like how many windows and doors there are, as well as how many books are in the law library. He drones on. What we need to know is how to get up to the dome.

Trudy and I exchange impatient looks, and Paris stifles a yawn. When I look over Vel's shoulder I see that all this time instead of taking notes on Les Lester's tour, she has been writing her name over and over again in every way possible. *Velvet Ogilvie* is spelled out in cursive and block letters, as well as upside down and sideways, with little flowers drawn inside the O of Ogilvie.

"Too bad you don't have a camera." Les Lester straightens his Frankenstein hair. "I take a good photograph."

Trudy covers her mouth and swallows a giggle.

I smile at the non-blinking eye, then correct myself and smile at the blinking one. When I tire from watching his mismatched eyes, I notice the brown divot that sits on the top of his head, one of the worst toupees I have ever seen.

Just when I think I am destined to doze off, he finishes the tour and asks if we have any more questions. Trudy steps forward.

"Mr. Lester, how do those flags get up on the top of the dome?"

Paris and Vel and I freeze like the statues of dead statesmen who litter the place. Why did it never occur to me to simply ask for what we want, instead of waiting all this time for Les Lester to reveal it? In my defense, women my age were never taught to ask for what we want in life. But perhaps it is time for that to change. I take a step closer to Trudy, aware that I can learn from her, just as surely as she can learn from me.

Meanwhile Les Lester's bushy eyebrows meet in the middle of his forehead. Is he onto us? I pucker, ready to whistle. Once "Dixie" starts, we have agreed to meet back at the farmer's market in whatever way we can get there. Not that I actually run anywhere anymore.

Les Lester motions for us to follow.

The jig is up, I say to myself.

He takes us into a large room where men in suits talk and wait around for the next session to begin. A well-dressed young woman sits at a large information desk to the side. Her job must include friendliness because she is all smiles.

"Would you like a chair?" she asks me.

"No thank you, dear," I say.

My eyes dart like a bank robber casing a bank, learning where the exits are and where the guards stand in case we need to make a quick escape. The impossibility of the task never leaves me. How did I let Trudy talk me into this? Besides, I have no idea what I am doing. I haven't thought clearly since Ted Senior died. Or perhaps I have never thought clearly. Ted Senior always offered a dose of reality to my ideas. I counted on him for that. And maybe I also resented him for it. At least a little. If he were here now he'd tell us to forget this foolishness. But sometimes the fools in life are the truly sane ones. They can see things the rest of us can't.

Les Lester picks up the black rotary telephone and dials a number. The four of us wait for him, our eyes unblinking. Is he calling the old guard to come take us to that awful sheriff from earlier? I can only imagine that if Abigail and Ted Junior find out, the situation of me living in their home may be short-lived. Where will I end up then?

"Wally, I've got three kids and their grandmother down here that are asking about how we get the flags to the top of the dome."

Les Lester pauses and listens. "Yeah, that's what I was thinking, too." He chuckles. "Can you take them up there and show them in person?"

Our eyes blink in unison, and the four of us exchange disbelieving looks. Is it possible that a guy named Wally is going to take us right up to the flag?

Les Lester readjusts his turf and puts down the telephone. "We don't usually let anybody up in the dome. But I can tell y'all are special." His smile is so big I can almost see the non-blinking eye blink.

Minutes later, a short, apple-shaped man in a uniform similar to Les Lester's walks down the side stairs and over to us. Sweat leaks down his face from under his blue hat, as if there is a sponge full of water on his head getting squeezed. I feel ten degrees hotter simply looking at him.

"This is Wally," Les Lester says.

I realize he doesn't know any of our names and that this is probably a good thing. Wally smiles at us, and I am relieved to see that both his eyes blink at the same time. Ted Senior had a facial tic after he came home from World War II, but thankfully it only lasted for a few months. What must Les Lester's wife do to keep herself from going crazy when one eye blinks and the other doesn't? Then there is the divot. Does she wash it at night for him? Ted Senior had a full head of hair with only a slight bit of thinning from wearing his hat. A sigh slips from between my lips. I wonder if I will ever stop missing him.

Wally glances at Paris and then looks at me.

"Friend of the family," I say.

Thankfully, Wally lets it go. Anyone who watches the news knows Lyndon Johnson's Civil Rights Bill may go into effect any day. It prohibits segregation in public places. Perhaps the guards are being cautious right now.

"I hope you don't mind stairs," Wally says to us.

"Always good exercise," I say. But actually I am not that fond of stairs. Or physical exertion of any kind—especially in this heat.

"Do you live around here?" Wally asks me.

"Charleston," I say.

"Beautiful place," he says. "Do you have an interest in flags?" Wally is as friendly as he is rounded.

The four of us shrug in unison, just like we blinked. It is as if the tension has all our thoughts and feelings wired together. Trudy is quiet again. I hope she snaps out of it soon.

Wally leads the way. We walk past the elevator, and then he opens a door that leads into a gray stairwell. We pause to stare up into the stairwell that contains dozens of narrow steps. Feeling dizzy, I grab the door-jamb.

"Perhaps I should wait here," I say. "I've never been good with heights."

"But we need you to go with us," Trudy says.

The dizziness returns, and I touch her arm. "I'm sorry, sweetheart, but a body can do only what a body can do." But the truth is, my mind isn't cooperating, either. I am thinking of all the ways this could go wrong. I am a coward at heart, it seems, without an ounce of my great-grandmother's bravery. Trudy is our only chance.

"You can't desert us now," Trudy says to me. "We need you to come up with a plan." She pulls me and Vel and Paris back out to the elevators where Wally can't hear.

Paris looks as uncomfortable with me leaving as Trudy does. And Vel has her nose so far into her book the picture of Nancy Drew on the front looks like she is wearing a Toni perm.

"I know you think you need me," I say, "but you can do it. I promise you can. It just never occurred to me that our mission would require this many steps." I hold my head feeling dizzy again.

I can't imagine that Wally will let the children get anywhere near those flags anyway. At best, he might take them up a couple of flights where the flag will still look like a postage stamp. Meanwhile, I can catch my breath and put this rebellion to rest. I was silly to think I could do this. Confidence is not my strong suit.

"I'm sorry, but this is as far as I can go," I say. "I'll wait for you in the lobby." I press the down arrow to call the elevator. A wave of cowardice seems to have come on with the dizziness.

Wally steps into the hallway, and I tell him that my heart palpitations are acting up and that I will wait downstairs. He asks if I need him to call someone and I say "no." Then I thank him for looking after the children.

"I'll be waiting downstairs," I say to them, thinking *cowering* is a better word than *waiting*. Who was I to think I could do something so audacious? I am not a rebel. I am a grandmother. A dizzy, anxious grandmother. A grandmother who has never made a bold move in her life, with the exception of a few clothing choices.

And with that thought I step into the elevator.

Chapter Twenty

Trudy

The elevator door closes. My shoulders drop. Do all adults fall short of what kids need them to be?

"What do we do now?" Paris whispers. "How are we going to get that flag down by ourselves?" The look on his face mirrors how I feel.

Meanwhile Vel stares at the elevator like she wishes she had gone with Nana Trueluck.

"We've got to try," I whisper back to Paris. "Then we can go home knowing we did the best we could." But *the best we could* doesn't feel nearly good enough.

Wally, the guard, waits for us in front of the main stairway. Is he part of the old guard we have been warned about? He turns to ask our names.

I pause and swallow hard. Has our luck run out? The last thing we need is for Les Lester or Wally Whatever to know our real names and be able to trace us back to Charleston. Paris and Vel shoot panicked looks in my direction.

"I'm, uh, Ida," I say. I am not sure why I chose Nana Trueluck's name, except I wish she were here.

All eyes turn to Vel, who for a wide-eyed moment appears speechless.

"I'm Nancy," she says finally. "Nancy An-drew." She flashes a huge smile, and then tucks her pencil behind her ear and shakes Wally's hand like Nancy Drew might do.

"Pleased to meet you, Nancy," he says. "And you?" Wally asks Paris.

"Martin King," Paris answers in his best southern accent.

To my surprise, Paris' color hasn't seemed to bother Les Lester or Wally Whatever. Maybe they don't want to answer to Nana Trueluck.

We walk up dozens of steps, and I am glad Nana Trueluck is in the lobby. The higher we go in the State House building the hotter it gets, like the world is backward and we are ascending into hell instead of heaven. Sweat pours down my back and into my sneakers at world record pace.

Vel, who I have never seen sweat, is covered in it, as is Paris. We are all starting to smell like the marsh on a hot day. Vel and I look like goopy globs of white paste. Her Toni perm is the only thing that hasn't wilted. In contrast, the sweat on Paris' skin practically glistens.

Wally's face is red, and his whole shirt is covered in sweat. He takes a wet handkerchief from his wet shirt pocket to mop his wet, bald forehead. With each step, my guilt grows. He is making all this effort for three kids, with an absent grandmother as an accomplice, who want to take down a flag.

We stop at a metal door. From his pocket Wally takes out a set of keys that are big enough to choke a gator. They jingle their importance. He pulls a key from about halfway and unlocks it. Inside the door is another set of steps. Vel and I exchange eye rolls, and then she throws in a glare to voice her displeasure.

The stairway of the building is narrow now, and we have to walk in single file. It is musty and reminds me of our attic at home. Add to that the body odor of three almost-teens and one grown man on what may be the hottest day of the year.

We come to a final door. Wally uses three different keys to open the three different locks. When he finally opens the door, it creaks like in a horror movie. I imagine ghosts of Confederate soldiers rushing out to protect their flag. Except it is a hundred years later, and they don't realize what their flag now represents.

The three of us look up the narrow ladder that ascends to the dome. Wally explains that this is as far as we get to go. Evidently only authorized personnel get to use the ladder and only when absolutely necessary. I can't imagine Wally fitting on that ladder and climbing the steep steps anyway.

Paris and Vel and I lean into the stairwell. At the top of the ladder, at least twenty feet away, is the glass dome with the flag flying on top. For some reason I thought we could walk right up to it and take it down. No such luck. Butterflies bump into each other in my stomach.

We exchange looks and then gaze into the dome again. The American flag flies at the top, and below it is the Confederate flag. There is no way we can get to it, much less take it down—especially if we have to somehow overpower Wally to get there. That would be like three kids bringing down a walrus. The truth is, we are probably as close to the flag as we will ever get.

Paris sighs, and it stops me cold. Who runs a marathon and quits the race twenty feet from the finish line? Paris and Vel look at me to see what to do, but I am empty of answers. It was crazy of us to think that we could do this in the first place. We are just kids, after all. Although I can't imagine Nana Trueluck would know what to do, either.

My leftover hope drips to the floor with my sweat. It doesn't seem fair to come all this distance to simply turn and walk away. I guess rebellions are harder than people realize or there would be more of them. We've come to the end of our adventure, and we all know it.

In the meantime, Wally jiggles his keys as he talks on and on about the history of the dome. None of which reveals how to get up there.

"Mr. Wally?" I interrupt.

"Yes, Ida?" he says.

I look around for Nana Trueluck and then remember that *Ida* is me.

"Mr. Wally, I think there's a hole in the bottom of that flag." I point to the top of the stairs.

He turns and strains his eyes toward the dome.

"What a shame," I say. "And such a beautiful flag, too."

"What a shame," Paris echoes.

"I bet you get fired since you didn't notice it was damaged." Vel can be counted on to point out ways people can get in trouble.

To my surprise, it appears to work. Wally's forehead now has deep creases for his sweat to cross over. He looks at his hips and then at the ladder as though taking a measurement.

"You know, I've actually never had to climb up to the dome," he says with a nervous laugh.

A look passes from Paris to Vel to me.

"I can do it for you, Mr. Wally." I swallow. What am I saying? I am not so fond of heights myself.

"That's awfully nice of you, Ida," he says. "But I could get in big trouble if I let you go up there. It's dangerous."

"It would be easy for her," Paris says. "Have you heard of the Flying Wallenda trapeze act? Ida's been climbing tall things her entire life."

Paris sounds so convincing, he almost has me persuaded, too.

"Is this true, Ida?" Wally asks.

My nod isn't convincing, but he doesn't seem to care.

"Then I guess that would be okay," he says, "but you have to promise you won't tell my boss."

I wonder if the old guard answers to a guard that's even older.

We do a pinkie swear for Wally's benefit. Then I say my final goodbyes to Vel and Paris.

"Remember your heritage," Paris says.

I wonder if he means the made-up Wallendas or my great-great-great-grandmother.

Vel holds Nancy Drew close to her heart as though prayer is required.

I remember Nana Trueluck's words: *You can do this.* At the same time, I realize she would never go along with this plan. It is too risky. If something happens to me, my parents will never forgive her. I pause long enough to wonder why I am doing this. Then I remember the guys in the pickup truck on the Marsh road, the Macklehaneys and the cross burning in our yard, and the stupid sheriff in the Woolworths. Then I think of Nana Trueluck waiting downstairs, and my great-great-great-grandmother and her abolitionism. I am simply the latest person in our family to take up the cause.

My knees shake, trying to convince me to give up this foolishness. They are right. This is foolish, and not only foolish, but dangerous. Then I remember the Sunbeam Bread truck swerving in my direction. My life might already be over if not for Paris Moses, who hopes to become Paris France someday so everyone will remember his name. Maybe I was saved so I could do this one thing for Paris.

Pretending I am one of the Flying Wallendas, I begin to climb the ladder. But didn't one of the Wallendas recently fall to their death during their high wire act? I saw it on the news while watching Walter Cronkite. I cross my fingers for good luck and quickly realize that you can't climb a ladder with crossed fingers.

As I ascend, I count the rungs, keeping my eyes focused on my hands and refusing to look down. At thirteen, I stop counting and think my luck has finally run out. I touch the top of the ladder and take a deep breath. Then I climb seven more rungs and unlatch a small window. A blast of fresh hot air hits me in the face. It reminds me of the heat in our attic at home, and I wish Daddy were here. I pause and close my eyes and wonder what to do next. I hear Daddy tell me to be part of the solution, not the problem. Isn't taking down this flag part of the solution? Then I hear Nana Trueluck tell me I can do it and that she believes in me. And after that a voice from somewhere deep in the past tells me she is proud of me. In the one hundred degree heat, I get chills. It must be my great-great-great-grandmother. Perhaps I am imagining it, but it feels absolutely real. My ancestors are like the rungs of this ladder, all of them supporting me on this journey.

When I open my eyes, the rooftops of downtown Columbia stretch before me. I have a bird's-eye view of the entire city. If I weren't so terrified, this would be truly cool.

Wally yells instructions up the ladder to pull the cables that attach the flag to the pole. I do as I am told. The flag doesn't move at first, and I wonder if I am even strong enough to do it. Then the cable finally gives, and I pull the flag toward me. It smells like stale laundry off a clothesline. It is bigger than I am and much heavier than I anticipate. I release several hooks and then stagger on the step with the weight of the flag. Gasps come from below.

"I'm coming up!" Paris yells.

Wally stops him. If one dead kid doesn't get him fired, two most definitely will. I steady myself and then drop the flag into Wally's waiting arms. Then I slowly begin my descent and breathe again.

Vel and Paris applaud when I reach the landing. I take a slow bow as Wally searches the flag for holes.

"Well, Ida, this flag looks fine to me," Wally says finally. Sweat pools on top of his bushy eyebrows. He takes out a white handkerchief to mop up his moist forehead again, as if our adventure has worn him out.

"I guess it was the sun's reflection," I say, trying to sound innocent.

Wally frowns, the flag in his arms. "I'll get somebody else to put it back," he says, sounding irritated. "You wait here and hold this. Don't let it touch the floor." He drops the flag into our arms. Then he walks away.

Paris, Vel, and I exchange long looks. Disbelieving looks. Holding the flag, we glance at the door, as if we are all thinking the same thing. Can we make a run for it?

But my feet feel nailed to the floor.

"What should we do?" I say, just above a whisper.

"It seems kind of obvious, doesn't it?" Vel says, her voice as loud as we normally talk.

Paris flashes a smile like a cartoon character who has a lightbulb materialize over his head.

"Since I got us into this, I'll take it from here," he says.

We carefully drape the flag over Paris' shoulders like a huge Superman cape.

"Wish me luck," he says.

We wish him luck.

"This is for Dr. King," he says.

"This is for all of us," I say.

Then Paris begins to run. Within seconds, he is down the narrow hallway and out of sight. Vel and I follow, running, too. Two floors down, Wally rests on the steps. Paris runs past him. When he realizes what is going on, he yells for Paris to stop. Then when Vel and I pass, he looks at us like we are co-conspirators, which is exactly what we are. Wally follows us faster than I thought possible for a sweat-soaked, apple-shaped man. A man whose deodorant wore off hours ago.

We follow Paris into the main corridor. Fortunately Wally tires fast and falls behind. In the distance, Paris flies down the marble steps, two at a time. The Confederate flag flows behind him like he is a caped crusader charged with saving the world from ignorance. In sporadic gasps, he whistles "Dixie." Vel and I join in. We sound like canaries finally free from their cages.

As Paris sails by, people in the State House stop and stare. Nobody seems to know what to do. Many of the tourists think it is some kind of staged performance and clap and smile as

Paris flies by. Others stand with their mouths gaping like they never expected in their lifetimes to see a skinny colored kid run though the State House with a Confederate flag flying behind him. It occurs to me that this scene has probably never played out in the whole history of the world. I sprint after Paris feeling proud to be an American. Proud to be a daughter of the South, and proud to be Paris' friend.

He sails down another flight of steps onto the main floor. A hundred more steps and Paris will be out the door. He is like a football player who catches the opening kickoff and sprints the entire length of the field to claim a winning touchdown. Three guards play defense and are at Paris' heels. But Paris outruns them. Vel and I aren't far behind. We slow to go around a corner. I smile at Vel, whose Toni-permed hair runs faster than all of us.

In the distance Nana Trueluck waits. A look of stunned surprise is followed by a huge smile. She crosses the rotunda to protect her team member. I have never seen her move so fast.

The four of us never talked about what to do with the flag once we got it. I guess we never thought it would actually happen. Paris is only steps away from the front entrance. Once he gets outside, no one will be able to catch him. Tears come to my eyes and blur the scene. History is taking place right in front of us. I make a wish that Paris' great-great-great-grandmother is watching from heaven and holding hands with my great-great-great-grandmother the abolitionist. Both of them have waited over a century for this moment. A moment where their descendants pick up the banner of freedom.

Les Lester waits at the front doors, a defensive guard about to sack the other team's quarterback. When Paris realizes what is happening, he jags right and runs around the rotunda like a track star sprinting a victory lap before leaving the stadium. He is a blur of red, white, and blue. But how will he leave? There is no way he can get away. Vel and I stop, and Wally clamps a moist arm around each of us. Guards are everywhere and tourists watch from the sidelines. Everyone waits to see what will happen next.

Nana Trueluck waves her arm from the center of the rotunda like a wide receiver ready to receive a Hail Mary pass in the last seconds of the game. Her yellow hat and dress make her hard to miss. Paris runs toward her as the guards close in. Then Nana Trueluck takes the handoff at the same time Les Lester jumps to make the tackle.

When Les Lester hits the ground, his hair flies in one direction and his glass eye in another. Everyone gasps. Paris' sneakers shriek as he dodges the twirling glass eye. He trips and lands with a thud at Les Lester's feet. Inches away, the blue glass eye stares up at us.

The crowd gasps again as Les Lester scoops up his eye and returns it to its socket. Then he returns his Frankenstein hair to his shiny bald head. Paris stands, his arms up in victory. The crowd applauds as if the curtain has come down at the end of a hit play on Broadway, and Paris has given the performance of a lifetime. But the game isn't over yet. My seventy-year-old grandmother circles the rotunda wearing the rebel flag like a southern shawl, singing as loud as she can her favorite Doris Day song:

> *Que sera, sera,*
> *Whatever will be will be.*
> *The future's not ours to see.*
> *Que sera, sera.*

Chapter Twenty-One

Ida

Trouble closes in from every angle. I am surrounded by guards while several tourists take pictures. The flag is removed from my shoulders, and I am escorted to an office. Trudy and Vel are detained, too, and Les Lester has Paris by the arm.

Minutes before I took the flag from Paris, I had tears in my eyes. I felt useless, and I hated myself for being old and letting down the children. Then Paris ran through the rotunda with the flag soaring behind him, and it brought more tears to my eyes. Different tears. Happy tears. What a beautiful moment that was.

Trudy and her friends actually did the impossible. Then, it seemed, I was to play a part in it after all. An action was called for. An action taken for all grandmothers of every color in the name of justice and honor. We all hope for a moment when we meet our potential. This was clearly mine.

After having regrets for most of my life that I didn't pursue a singing career, I sang as though my life depended on it, as though everyone's life depended on it, my heart wide open. If only Ted Senior had been a witness to all this. He would have been so proud of me. Tears come to my eyes again. This time they are bittersweet.

But it seems now a price must be paid for that moment. Les Lester orders Wally to resume business as before. The flag is draped over his desk. It looks so innocent lying there. A lifeless piece of faded fabric instilled with meaning. Meanwhile, the four of us are left alone in the room with the blinking and the non-blinking eye staring straight at us—thankfully from its socket and not the floor. It is then that I notice a piece of lint stuck on the outside of the glass eye, picked up from the rotunda floor. I take off my glasses and wipe my eyes so that maybe Les Lester will take the hint and remove the fuzz stuck to his left eyeball. No luck. I cringe. Things like this make my teeth itch.

"What did you think would happen?" Les Lester says. "Did you think you would get away with it?"

"It was all my idea," I say, wiping my eye again. "You should let the children go. They didn't do a thing."

"No, it was my idea," Trudy says.

"No, I put them up to it." Paris' voice wobbles in and out of a southern accent. His eyes are dark and serious, as if Les Lester is the latest Sunbeam Bread truck to endanger Trudy.

Les Lester lets out something that sounds like a growl.

Am I really being detained? Until now, I have gone my entire adult life without even a speeding ticket.

"Let the children go," I say again. "You can take me to jail if you want." I can't resist wiping my eye again, and then I wink. His good eye looks offended or perhaps intrigued. It is hard to see past the floor lint.

As the adult in the mix, I am clearly the one responsible. I imagine Abigail packing my bags as soon as she and Ted Junior get the call to come and bail me out of jail.

"Nancy, tell them it was my idea," Trudy says to Vel.

Why did she call her Nancy? I wonder.

"I think you're confused, *Ida*," Vel says. "It was Martin's idea."

Martin must be Paris. Evidently, names have been changed to protect the innocent. Then who am I?

Trudy grits her teeth and glares at Vel, who shrugs her betrayal of Paris. In the meantime, Les Lester looks pleased thinking the whole thing was Paris' idea. Perhaps putting him away is preferable to putting away two girls and a grandmother.

"Martin didn't do anything wrong," Trudy says. "I was the one who took down the flag. I took it down myself while Wally watched."

The blinking eye narrows.

"Do you honestly think these children are the ones who thought this up?" I say.

Les Lester looks at Paris. "I doubt anyone would have done anything without the boy's input."

"For goodness sakes, he's twelve years old," I say.

"Enough of this," he says. He asks my name.

"She's Doris," Trudy says, before I have time to answer. "Doris Day-vis."

My partners in crime smile. Fake names are one thing, but how do we get out of this office?

Les Lester leaves the room to talk to Wally and the other guards. They take turns looking through the glass at us until he comes back.

"You can all leave except for Martin," he says.

"No way." Trudy stands next to her chair, one fist clinched.

"Let me handle it," I say to her and look back at Les Lester.

"You have no right to detain this young man," I say.

"Actually, we do," Wally says. "Anyone who defiles the contents of the State House faces Federal prosecution."

The alarm in Paris' eyes causes me to stand, too.

"But what about me? I carried that flag, too."

Both men ignore me.

"I'd like to telephone my son in Charleston," I say. "He'll tell you what a misunderstanding this is."

"You can do that, Doris, once you leave the State House grounds."

For a moment I wonder who he is talking to. This is hard enough without having to keep all the names straight.

"But I refuse to leave without, uh, Martin," I say.

Another guard enters the room to escort the girls and me out. He towers over us.

"We can't just leave him here," Trudy says to me as we leave the room.

Paris sits straight in the chair as if he has no regrets. But I am worried about leaving him behind. Does the state of South Carolina prosecute children for running with a flag? Surely not.

Once we get outside it must be a hundred degrees. I miss the breeze from the coast, even if it is a hot breeze. Les Lester steps forward again.

"Look, I understand you want to help the boy, but it won't do any good." He sounds halfway sympathetic, and I am relieved to see the lint on his eyeball is finally gone.

"I want to telephone my son," I say again. "Aren't I allowed one telephone call?"

"You aren't being arrested," Les Lester says.

"What about Martin?" Trudy asks.

"The authorities are just going to ask him some questions," he says.

"The authorities?" I ask.

Trudy and I exchange a look, and I am reminded of the night the cross was burned in the front yard. Vel is silent, her knuckles white from clutching her book. Les Lester tells us to go on home.

"Let's go," I say to Vel and Trudy.

"But we can't leave Paris," Trudy whispers to me.

"We won't," I say. "We'll get help. We'll figure this out."

She doesn't look like she believes me—and who can blame her after my earlier disappearing act?

Vel pulls Trudy out the door, but then Trudy runs back into the building. A guard grabs her arm and escorts her back outside.

"Stop it," I say to the guard. "That's my granddaughter you're manhandling."

He doesn't let go.

"We have rights," I say. "You're violating our rights."

The guard releases Trudy's arm with a scoff.

"Who do you people think you are?" he asks.

"Patriots," I say.

Trudy comes to my side. Vel looks frightened as well. We are in a dilemma even Nancy Drew can't solve.

I tell the guards that we will be back, but I feel shaken, too. We leave the building and walk down the steps and re-group under one of the giant oaks on the grounds.

"Why didn't you take up for Paris?" Trudy asks Vel.

"Because he's the reason we did it," she says.

"No, he's not," Trudy says to her.

"Are you telling me that if Paris hadn't saved your life, we would have come to Columbia to take down that stupid flag?" she asks.

"That doesn't mean you abandon your friend," Trudy says.

Vel lowers her eyes as though she might have a point.

"We need to stay calm," I say, exuding calmness, though that's not what I feel at all. I clean my glasses hoping it will clear my thoughts.

Vel holds up a nickel.

"I don't want to call my parents yet," Trudy says.

"What are you waiting for?" Vel asks. "It can't get much worse than this."

They both look at me.

I don't want to telephone Ted Junior, either. Nor do I want to give Abigail fuel for the fire.

There's got to be a way to outsmart these nitwits, I say to myself.

We sit on a wooden bench underneath a giant magnolia tree. Metal stars are hammered into the outside of the building to mark where General Sherman's cannons tried to destroy the place over a hundred years ago. This was one of the bits of information from Les Lester's tour. At the top of the dome the American flag flies by itself. I point to it, and Trudy smiles.

"You wanted to take down that flag, and you did it. At least you can be proud of that," I say.

As if the old guard planned it, the tiny window opens at the top of the dome, and the Confederate flag is reattached.

"So much for a rebellion," Trudy says, her voice soft with our defeat.

"I hope that Wally guy gets stuck up there," Vel says.

Trudy looks at Vel as though she is not yet ready to forgive her for selling out Paris.

"What do you think they'll do to Paris?" Trudy asks me.

"I honestly don't know," I say.

"Well, I hope he doesn't tell them his real name," Vel says. "Wait. Can you get in trouble for using a fake name?"

"Surely not," I say, still thinking.

"Maybe I should go get Paris' Uncle Freddie," Trudy says. "I got Paris into this mess and want to get him out."

"Not yet," I say. "We don't want to get Freddie in trouble, too. We've got to come up with a plan to save Paris ourselves."

"We?" Vel asks. "You can count me out, Nana Trueluck. I don't want to end up in jail. My parents will kill me."

Trudy aims her disappointment in my direction.

"Okay, kiddo, it looks like it's up to us," I say to her. I always thought she would be the one to do great things, but maybe it is not too late for me to have a chance at it. We need a rescue plan, but I am empty of thoughts. The urgent look on Trudy's face doesn't help.

Seconds later, a black sedan pulls up in front of the State House. Three men wearing dark sunglasses get out of the car with the letters FBI on their shirts.

"Uh, oh," Trudy says.

"H-e-double-hockey-sticks," Vel says, her words soft.

A hot flash confirms the trouble we are in. I fan myself. All this for running through the building with a flag draped behind you? What about me? I had my hands on that flag, too. When I think of Paris in a room surrounded by white men pushing their authority around, I get mad. Boiling mad.

Charleston mad. And the whole problem of how to rescue him gets much more serious.

Chapter Twenty-Two

Trudy

"We must have really riled up the old guard if they called in the FBI," I say to Nana Trueluck.

She looks worried.

I envision Paris serving time in a federal prison and feel like I might be sick.

A nearby church bell rings twelve times. We are running out of time. We are supposed to be back at the farmer's market by one o'clock.

"Tell me what to do," I say to Nana Trueluck, who has cleaned her glasses so many times they sparkle.

Meanwhile, Vel is useless. With every turn of the page, she gives me a look that says, *I told you so.*

"We need to distract the FBI," Nana Trueluck says.

"How?" I say.

"That's the big question," she says.

"Maybe I should go back in and explain everything to them," I say. "Tell them the whole story."

Vel looks at me like I have just announced I am going back into a cage of hungry alligators dressed in a white poodle suit.

"Do you have a better idea?" I ask her.

She sighs and turns back to her book. If the Russians released the atomic bomb, she would grab a book and read while she waited to be obliterated.

"Wait," Nana Trueluck says, "maybe we could trick them into letting Paris go."

"How will you do that?" I ask, surprised by my grandmother's willingness to take on the FBI.

She bites her bottom lip.

"Maybe we should telephone your father," she says. "Maybe he can pull some strings."

"That could take forever," I say. "I can't just sit here and do nothing. What if they take Paris somewhere, and we never see him again?"

"We won't let that happen." Nana Trueluck stands again.

"Trudy, would you be willing to go back inside and look around? Maybe see where they're keeping him? See if there's a back door, a way to get him out? If you can do that, I'll come up with some kind of distraction."

"Well, I'm not moving from this spot until you get back. *If* you come back," Vel says to me.

"Velvet Ogilvie, you are a coward," I say. She nods like she couldn't agree more.

I am not feeling so brave myself, but I owe Paris a life-saving moment.

"Trudy, be careful," Nana Trueluck says.

I say I will. Then I approach the building again. This time I circle around to one of the side doors. Two men stride up the walkway dressed in suits and ties. I duck behind the bushes to wait until they pass. One of them is complaining about his boss, a state senator. Then the complaining guy holds the door as the two of them go inside. I guess this must be an employee's entrance since nobody else seems to be using it. Just inside the door is another guard who is reading a newspaper. He must not know what has been going on upstairs.

"I need to give my dad something he forgot at home," I say to the guard, pointing at one of the men up ahead. To my surprise, he waves me on. I duck behind a pillar and then take the stairs to the rotunda.

People mill around, which makes it easier for me to go unnoticed. I find Les Lester's office again, and the door is still closed. The glass door has blinds that are left open just enough to see three FBI agents standing over Paris, who looks tiny compared to the large white men. I should never have left him in that room, but it is not like I had a choice.

A family of redheads stands at the front entrance. Behind them, I see Nana Trueluck's yellow hat sticking above the crowd, ready to rescue me if I need help. A new guard is there and doesn't seem to know who Nana Trueluck is. He lets her inside, and she goes to a far wall and stands. I wonder what she has in mind as a distraction. In the next instant, she takes a deep breath and begins to sing another Doris Day hit. A crowd gathers. I never realized how nice her voice is. Even the guard turns to watch, his back to me now.

With the guard preoccupied, I sneak down the hallway to look for another way into Les Lester's office. Just past the bathrooms I find another hallway that circles back around to the front. Like a cat burglar searching for jewels, I enter the empty office next to the one where Paris is held. Nana Trueluck hits the chorus, her voice echoing in the marble building. Chills crawl up my arms.

Through the open door I see the FBI men questioning Paris. He stares straight ahead, his legs jiggling as though warmed up and ready to run if given a chance. I wonder if he is acting or if he is as courageous as he seems. Only a few feet away, I am close enough to hear the agents talking. They ask Paris all sorts of questions. They want to know who put him up to this and what other people were involved. They use words like *conspiracy*, and they ask Paris again what his real name is. Paris keeps silent, which is probably the smartest thing he could do.

If only I could distract those FBI guys and Les Lester, then Paris could make a run for it. I glance at my watch. 12:30 P.M. Paris' Uncle Freddie expects us back at the farmer's market in thirty minutes and it is a ten-minute walk. We need to get Paris back to Charleston. Otherwise, I will have to tell sweet Miss Josie that I left her grandson in Columbia, all alone, in a roomful of FBI men.

In the background Nana Trueluck's singing continues. She is doing her best to buy me time. I hide behind a desk that has a framed photograph of three dorky-looking kids with big ears that look just like Les Lester. Minus the glass eye and hair rug, of course. Huge filing cabinets line a whole wall. A large table, like Daddy has at City Hall, sits in the center of the room. At the far end is another door that leads to where they are keeping Paris.

People clap after Nana Trueluck finishes her song. Evidently Les Lester hasn't figured out who is singing and walks down the hallway in my direction. I scoot under the desk and hold my breath. He enters the dark office and pulls two paper cups out of a cylinder by the water cooler. He aims his eye that blinks at the spigot.

The water cooler gulps loudly as he fills the two cups. I hope my stomach doesn't growl, because he is so close he could hear it. Then he carries the water back into the next office. When the door opens, Paris turns his head and sees me before looking away.

Nana starts singing songs from "Annie, Get Your Gun," one of her favorite Broadway musicals, and I wonder if this is the best choice given the situation. Her voice gets stronger with every song, like she has been waiting her entire life to give this one concert.

We have twenty-two minutes to get Paris out of here and back to the farmer's market. I massage my temples like Daddy does when he is hoping for inspiration. Then I see it: the perfect solution. A fire alarm is mounted on the wall. I crawl across the cold tile floor toward a sign that reads: PULL ONLY IN CASE OF EMERGENCY.

If this isn't an emergency, I tell myself, *I don't know what is.*

With all my strength, I pull the fire alarm. For a few seconds nothing happens, but then the alarm shrieks to life. It is so loud I have to cover my ears. I run and duck behind the desk again. Les Lester and the FBI men look around and then at each other. Nana Trueluck's singing has stopped. A flurry of people run for the exits.

Les Lester tells Paris to stay put. Then he and the other three men leave the office and close the door. How could they just leave Paris in there? What if this actually was a fire? Then I realize how grateful I am for their stupidity. It is the perfect moment to get Paris out of here.

When I enter the office Paris smiles the widest smile I have ever seen. We leave the room and go into the rotunda. Guards and FBI agents usher tourists out the front door telling them not to panic. Nana Trueluck swims through the crowd and joins us. Amid the chaos, Paris grabs my hand, and I lead him through the rotunda toward the side door, where there are fewer people. Nana Trueluck follows. The alarm continues to hammer out its warning. The family of redheads I saw earlier almost knocks us down as we make our way to the door.

We find Vel at the far end of the State House grounds. For once, she is about as animated as her Toni perm. She gives each of us a hug, even Paris.

"Don't look so surprised," Vel says to me.

My smile at Vel turns into a giggle. I pet her head like I have decided I love poodle perms.

"Stop it," she says, but I can tell she isn't angry.

"Trudy saved my life," Paris tells her.

"Well, you saved mine first," I say.

In that instant, it is like I have a crystal ball, and I know that Paris and I will be good friends for the rest of our lives.

"I couldn't have done it if not for Nana Trueluck's singing," I say. "She distracted everyone and drew a crowd."

Nana takes a bow, and we all applaud. "Ted Senior always told me I missed my calling as a lounge singer," she says.

For the first time, she doesn't look as sad as she usually does when she talks about Grandpa Trueluck, and I wonder if this adventure has been good for her. I glance at my watch, and Nana nods like she is thinking the same thing.

"Let's get out of here," I say.

We hide behind an oak tree and wait for the best time to flee. Two fire trucks pull up in front of the State House as the fire alarm continues to blast. More people billow out the front doors like thick smoke, followed by the three FBI agents and Les Lester. We scrunch closer to the oak to avoid being seen.

"We need to get back to Woolworths as fast as we can," I say. "Then we'll see if anyone has followed us before we go to the farmer's market."

"I can't run in these heels," Nana Trueluck says. "I'm not sure I can keep up."

"Maybe we could split up and then meet there," Vel says. This sounds just like something Nancy Drew might do.

"Are you sure you remember how to get back?" I ask.

"I remember," Paris says.

We agree that Nana will join the crowd going in one direction, and we three kids will go in the other. We need to get Paris back to Charleston before the FBI finds him.

The chaos grows. Firemen run into the building with their hatchets and hoses drawn. Nana Trueluck's yellow canary hat bobs among the crowd going in the direction of the farmer's market. Meanwhile, Paris and Vel and I sprint toward Woolworths as if the flames from the imaginary fire nip at our heels. We dash one block, then two, and then have a short wait at the traffic light before we dart across the street.

After we reach the store, we bolt through the front doors and stand panting at the front windows. Large fans overhead do a poor job of cooling us. Other people are standing at the windows, too, looking toward the State House, including Faye, the waitress who treated us so badly. Her look tells Paris he doesn't belong here.

"Where's the old lady?" she asks us.

"She already went home," I say.

Faye pops her gum and scoffs. "That old lady had an attitude." She turns to look at what is going on outside.

Two more fire trucks go by and another police car with sirens and lights flashing. But no one seems to have followed us.

"Do you think it's against the law to pull a fire alarm?" I whisper to Vel.

"Probably," Vel whispers back.

What if Paris and I are both fugitives now? My knees shake, and my worry grows into full-fledged fear. What if I never get to finish grade school because of a jail sentence? My parents will be so disappointed.

"We need to get out of here." Paris motions toward the people next to us. They look familiar. Then they seem to recognize us, too.

"Hey, isn't that the kid who ran with the flag?" The father of the redheaded family points at Paris. "He ran through the State House with the Confederate flag draped around his shoulders."

Angry faces turn toward us. The fat cop from before squeaks his way to the front of the store. I check my watch again. We have seven minutes to get to the farmer's market and then get out of town.

We run down an aisle full of beach balls, sand buckets, and metal picnic coolers, as if the South Carolina coastline extends all the way to Columbia. The fat cop follows. On our way out the back exit, Paris turns over a basket of beach balls and they bounce in every direction. When the fat cop stumbles and falls, it reminds me of one of my brother's stunts. Either that, or a Laurel and Hardy movie.

After busting through to the back door of the Woolworths into the alley, we pause to look around. The backs of stores look totally different from the fronts, and it is hard to decide which way to go. We run past four trashcans with smelly, sunbaked garbage inside. We hold our noses and keep running.

As we maneuver our way through the alleys, I am reminded of the coastal waterways around Charleston. Some are like a maze with dead ends that circle back to where you started or lead you deeper into the marsh. We need to find the right way, the alley that will lead us back to the farmer's market. I look behind us. The fat cop isn't following, but he is probably calling all his cop friends.

We take one wrong turn, then another. We pause long enough to look at each other. Panic fills Vel's eyes. If she had known this would happen, she would never have agreed to come.

"This way," Paris says, choosing a direction we haven't tried yet.

We run down the alleyway until we arrive at the back side of the farmer's market. We made it! We exchange smiles. Winded, the three of us lean against Uncle Freddie's truck and take in big gulps of freedom. Nana Trueluck arrives soon after, fanning herself with her canary hat, a smile on her face, too. She hugs us like she hasn't seen us in ten years, much less ten minutes. Luckily the chaos from the State House hasn't made it this far.

Freddie looks at us and closes up the back of his truck empty of melons. "Did you all have a race or something?" Freddie asks Paris.

"Something like that," he says.

Paris opens the door to the truck and retrieves a mason jar full of Miss Josie's lemonade and passes it around. We each take huge sips. The drink is as warm as the day but refreshing all the same. Then he opens a brown paper bag filled with Miss Josie's cookies. While we eat and drink, Uncle Freddie says goodbye to some nearby farmers, and we take turns watching the street to make sure no one is coming after us.

"We did it," Paris says. "We took down that flag."

"If I hadn't seen it for myself I would have never believed it," Nana Trueluck says. "You children did the impossible. I'm very proud of you."

But our adventure isn't over yet. Those FBI agents are probably still looking for Paris.

Moments later, we say our goodbyes to Paris and his Uncle Freddie. Then Vel and I get back in Nana Trueluck's Chrysler. On our way out of town a police car flies past us in the direction of the State House. Vel and I duck below the seat.

"I wonder what all this commotion is about," Nana Trueluck says with a grin.

"Shouldn't we pull over or hide or something?" Vel pulls herself up into the seat.

"Well, if they catch us, they catch us," Nana Trueluck says. "Besides, I'm not sure what we've done wrong. We displaced a flag for a few minutes. Sang a few Doris Day hits and a few songs from *Annie, Get Your Gun*."

"I pulled a fire alarm," I say.

"Yes, well, there is that, too," she says.

While I keep an eye on the side mirror to make sure no police cars are following us, Vel and I hold hands. For once, Vel isn't reading. Has life become more interesting than a book?

An hour out of town my worry fades, and my relief turns to laughter. Uncontrollable laughter. Vel joins in, and then Nana Trueluck gets the giggles, too.

"Can you believe that poor man's glass eye popped out of his head?" she asks.

We laugh more.

"I'll never forget Paris running through the rotunda," I say, "and that Confederate flag soaring behind him. Then just when it looked like it was curtains, Nana Trueluck takes the flag at the last moment and runs out the door singing 'Que Sera, Sera.'"

Vel and I collapse into giggles, and Nana Trueluck has to pull off the road because she is giggling, too. The three of us laugh until tears roll down our cheeks. It is the first time I have seen Nana Trueluck truly happy since Grandpa Trueluck died.

I decide that no matter what happens next, even if I get in trouble for tripping that fire alarm, it has all been worth it. At least that flag came down for a few minutes. Paris got to act out his dream, and Nana Trueluck got to laugh again.

Chapter Twenty-Three

Ida

Spanish moss in the pine trees signals our approach to the coast. The air turns salty as we near the ocean. The laughter from earlier energized me for the rest of the drive. The girls are quiet now. Both are dozing. It has been a long day and a surprising day. The children's courage has made an impression on me. Especially Paris'. He may be the bravest young man I have ever known. I want to tell Miss Josie what a wonderful grandson she has, but no one must find out what happened today. No one. But that doesn't mean our adventure was without merit.

All of us changed today. For once I wasn't just watching history on television, but I was a participant. And honestly, after all those images on the six o'clock news of the horrible things going on in Alabama and Mississippi, I wanted Paris to know that southern white people aren't all like that. Some of us are compassionate folks.

It is three o'clock in the afternoon—almost twelve hours since I woke up this morning. Because of all that happened, it feels like it has been even longer. I park in front of Ted Junior's house—my home—at least for now, given Abigail doesn't find out what happened today.

"Is it possible the house has shrunk since we left it this morning?" Trudy asks with a yawn.

"Compared to the State House, it does look small," I say.

"I'm sure glad they don't know our real names," Vel says, matching Trudy's yawn. "Do you think they'll come looking for us anyway?"

"I doubt it," I say, even though I have plenty of doubts.

Vel walks toward her house with Nancy Drew stuck in the waistband of her shorts, her pink purse thrown over one shoulder.

"You don't think she'll tell her parents what happened, do you?" I ask Trudy.

"Not in a million years," Trudy says.

"That's good," I say. "As the grownup in charge, I'd have some explaining to do."

For several seconds we sit in the car without moving. It has been a bigger adventure than either of us anticipated.

"Paris would still be with the FBI if left up to Vel," Trudy says.

"It's also true that we couldn't have done it without her," I say. "She was great at keeping Les Lester occupied by taking all those notes."

Trudy laughs.

Our peaceful, boring street is totally opposite of the pandemonium at the State House a few hours earlier. I roll up the car windows, get out of the car, and wave at Widow Wilson behind the curtains. As we walk up the sidewalk, I put an arm around Trudy's shoulder.

"Good job today," I say.

"You, too," she says. "Do you think Paris is safe?"

"I'd be surprised if they came looking for him here," I say. "Surely the FBI has bigger fish to fry."

We walk into the house, and Trudy lets the screen door slam at her heels, something we both know irritates Abigail. We pause in the entryway to listen to the sound of the typewriter clicking away in the attic. We exchange smiles. Then Teddy barrels around the corner, Band-Aids flapping in the breeze. He stops inches from my feet, looks up, and smiles a goofy smile.

"Hi Nana," he says.

"Hello, Teddy. What have you been up to today?"

"Nothin'," he says.

"Us, too," I say, giving Trudy a wink.

"I can't believe I'm even glad to see my dorky brother," Trudy says, giving him a hug.

Teddy screams and then pretends to throw up in a potted plant in the hallway. Grandsons have a special quality all their own.

"Nana and Trudy are home, and they're acting weird!" he yells to anyone listening.

The smell of an apple pie baking makes me practically giddy. I am so glad to be home. Even if it isn't exactly my home, it feels comforting, like a cotton nightgown just off the clothesline. Abigail comes into the hallway and asks about our trip to Columbia.

"It was good," I say. "But I think I'll go upstairs to take a nap before dinner."

"A nap?" she says. "Since when do you take naps?"

"Since today," I say with a smile.

In addition to fatigue from the trip, my throat is tender from my impromptu concert. Time alone in my room will do me good.

"You two can tell us about your trip at dinner," Abigail says, studying me.

Trudy and I exchange a look that confirms our lips are sealed forever about what actually happened in Columbia. If our true exploits are found out, Trudy will be grounded until the space program puts a man on the moon—the moon being where I may have to live next. But even if we told them every detail, I don't think Ted Junior and Abigail would believe us anyway.

Chapter Twenty-Four

Trudy

The next day, Paris and Vel and I meet at Hampton Park underneath a maze of azalea bushes. We are getting good at hiding our friendship. Meanwhile, for the last 24 hours, I have been waiting for the FBI to show up at my door.

The bushes shake, and a voice startles us from behind.

"I've been looking all over for you," Hoot says, crawling into the bushes after us.

We make room for him. He has a rolled up newspaper in his hand, and I think how strange it is that Hoot Macklehaney might actually read a newspaper.

"I knew you were up to something," he says, "and it looks like I've finally got proof. He unrolls the newspaper and drops it in my lap.

On the front page of the Sunday edition of *The Charleston Post* the headline reads: CONSPIRACY AT THE STATE HOUSE. Next to the headline is a photograph of Les Lester and Wally, whose last name turns out to be Wiggins. Underneath the photograph is the story:

Authorities are searching for an elderly woman and three juvenile suspects—two females and a Negro male—responsible for defiling the Confederate flag on Saturday. They believe the elderly female, who also gave an impromptu music concert in the building, may have been the master planner of the uprising. Anyone knowing the identities of these suspects must come forward immediately. A $500 reward will be given for any information leading to their apprehension.

For a few seconds I forget to breathe and Vel spells DAM under her breath. I don't take the time to correct her spelling. Paris looks like he is wondering whether to fight Hoot or run away. I wonder the same thing. I never expected for Hoot to put two and two together and actually get four, as in the four of us going to the State House.

"We weren't anywhere near Columbia yesterday," I tell Hoot, crossing my fingers behind my back.

"Liar," Hoot says. "You two and your grandmother were gone all day yesterday." He points at Vel who holds Nancy Drew like a brick she might pelt him with. "You must have ridden with somebody else," he says to Paris.

All this time I have watched out for the FBI when I should have been watching out for Hoot Macklehaney.

"How dare you watch my house," I say, but it comes out half-hearted. His spying is the least of my worries. Shutting him up is my big concern now.

"What do you want?" I ask him.

Hoot looks like a cat whose claws are sunk into three juicy mice. He aims his pimples heavenward. "I want money for starters," he says. "The newspaper is offering five hundred dollars as a reward. That's a lot of money."

Vel, Paris, and I look at each other. You would think Daddy makes a lot of money as mayor, but the job actually doesn't pay that much. Vel's dad probably makes more at the bank. At least they can afford to have Rosemary.

"We don't have five hundred dollars," I say. "If you haven't noticed, we're just kids. Besides, that's blackmail."

"Exactly," he says, looking pleased with himself.

He motions for us to put any money we have in his hand. Paris pulls out a couple of quarters from his shorts pocket, and Vel digs seventeen cents out of the bottom of her pink purse. I have a dollar bill in my back pocket that I got for babysitting Teddy three nights ago, but I am not about to hand that over to Hoot Macklehaney. At any rate, this isn't adding up to anything close to five hundred dollars.

"Where's your money?" Hoot asks me.

"I'm broke," I say, pulling my empty front pockets inside out.

Hoot taps his head like he is trying to knock some sense into it.

"If you don't have money, then I want you to be my girlfriend."

I don't know whether to laugh, cry or barf. Instead, I toss the dollar bill from my back pocket at Hoot.

"There's your stupid money," I say.

He tosses the bill back at me.

"That's not enough. I want you to be my girlfriend," Hoot repeats.

"Vel can be your girlfriend. She is much more girly than I am," I say.

Vel shoots me a look like I have thrown her into an alligator infested swamp.

"I don't like Vel," Hoot says. "I like you. You're funny." He flashes his yellow corn kernel teeth at me, and Vel gives me a wicked smile, like this is what I get for suggesting he choose her.

"You must be blind as a bat if you didn't see that one coming, Trudy," Vel says. "Hoot's been sweet on you for years."

His face turns red like Vel has just spilled the one secret he wants to keep.

"Are bats blind?" Paris asks, as if this—like freckles—is news to him.

Despite my rising panic, I tell myself to stay calm. The last thing I want to be is somebody's girlfriend, especially if that somebody is Hoot—middle name Moron—Macklehaney. Not to mention that I resent being called a blind bat by my best friend.

Hoot waves the newspaper as if to remind me of his threat.

"I would consider being your girlfriend, Hoot, but my parents won't allow me to have a boyfriend yet." My words sound sweet, like he is a Thanksgiving turkey, and I am buttering him up.

"We can just pretend for one day," Hoot says, his voice cracking in earnest. "If you could just come by the Esso station, then maybe my oldest brother, Hank, will quit kidding me. He says no girl will ever like me because I'm ugly as sin."

"His brother has a point," Vel says to me.

I shush Vel, and for a split second I actually feel sorry for Hoot Macklehaney. This is something I never thought possible until the freezing over of hell and the flying of pigs.

"If I pretend to be your girlfriend for one day, will you keep our secret?" I ask.

"I swear," he says, as though the winner of the better deal.

"Trudy Trueluck, don't you dare agree to this," Vel says. "Once you do, he'll just want something else."

I wonder how Vel got so versed in blackmail.

"How do we know you'll keep your promise?" I ask Hoot.

He puts his hand over a mustard stain on his shirt. "Cross my heart, hope to die."

I ask Hoot to give us a minute so we can talk things over, and he climbs out of the bushes.

"Do you really want to do this?" Paris asks me.

"Not in a million years," I say, "but do I have a choice?"

Not only do I not want Paris and Vel and me to get in trouble, but I have Nana Trueluck to think about, too. The newspaper said she was the ringleader. I can't imagine Nana Trueluck the ringleader of anything, except maybe Doris Day songs, and I surely can't imagine her in jail.

"You don't have to be Hoot's girlfriend," Paris says. "If the news comes out, it comes out. I'm not ashamed of anything we did."

"But if my parents find out, I'll be in huge trouble," Vel says.

"I agree that we've got to keep Hoot quiet somehow," I say.

"Let's knock him out and put him on an Amtrak train to Alaska." Vel's eyes glimmer.

"Don't you think someone would miss him?" I ask.

"Probably not," Paris says.

We pause to come up with a more viable plan. I peek out of the azaleas. Hoot waits under a magnolia tree reading the comics.

"How much harm could it be to act like his girlfriend for one day?" I ask.

"What if he wants to kiss you?" Vel grimaces as though this is the most disgusting thought imaginable.

The oatmeal I ate that morning rises with the thought, and I glance over at Hoot again, who is now picking his nose and flinging his findings like they are darts. Does he think no one sees him? Does he *think* at all?

"It would definitely be the longest day of my life," I say. "But it's only one day."

Hoot Macklehaney needs to keep his mouth shut. If he doesn't, Nana Trueluck could be arrested for being a ringleader, and Paris could get in big trouble for running with that flag. Plus, who knows what happens to girls who pull fire alarms when there isn't even a fire. I could be in more trouble than anybody. After yesterday I was actually looking forward to being bored for the rest of the summer. But no such luck. Our adventure is still going strong.

Chapter Twenty-Five

Ida

I take my coffee to the front porch along with the Sunday newspaper. I haven't slept in on a Sunday for years. But after the trip to Columbia yesterday, I needed my rest. Ted Junior and Abigail left a note in the kitchen that after church they are taking Teddy to the beach and that Trudy is meeting with some friends at Hampton Park. It is strange to have the house to myself. But not at all a bad strange.

Positioning myself on the porch swing, I rest my coffee cup on the small table nearby and give myself a slight swing. Two of the cats Trudy rescued rub against my bare ankles. In a way, I think Trudy rescued me, too. Not that she was the one to give me a home, but she has certainly made me feel welcome, as well as relevant. It is nice to be needed and involved in projects that don't only involve bake sales or knitting.

The lyrics of "Que Sera, Sera" go through my mind again. I can't believe that at my age I managed to surprise myself. Who knew I could sing in public at the top of my lungs and carry a flag out the door in protest? Certainly not me. If Ted

Senior were still alive, I doubt he would have believed it, either.

Most of my life I have never put up a fuss about anything. Even about things I knew were morally wrong. It is easy to go through life without rocking any boats. But last night when I couldn't sleep, I realized the events of yesterday were something I felt gratified by. Keep in mind, the list of things I have felt proud of in my life isn't a long list. I was a good wife and mother; I suppose that counts for something. And I took care of my parents at the end. But other than that, I have a hard time thinking of things.

But now, as I anticipate my final breaths on this earth, I imagine I will look back on yesterday as a time when I took part in something grand. I take a sip of coffee and remember Paris running through the rotunda with that flag flying behind him. Such a statement. It is moments like these that define a life.

No harm done, I say to myself. The children got a lesson in civic responsibility, and I got a lesson in . . . What? How to be bold?

Enough of this, I think, unrolling the newspaper. *Time for life to get back to normal.*

When I see the headlines, I release a half-gasp, half-shriek. A grainy photograph is at the top of the fold. With my back to the camera you can't tell it is me, but there I am with the flag over my shoulders going out the door.

My coffee cup falls onto the porch, the cup breaking into a dozen pieces. My proud moment did not involve being a fugitive from the law or having my photograph plastered on the front page of the Charleston newspaper.

Two cats come to lap up the cream in my coffee. A figure approaches from down the street. Vel's father waves at the front gate, newspaper in hand. I wish now I had put my hair up. I look practically unkempt. A criminal in the making. Or perhaps I am already made.

Does he know it is me on the front page? Is he going to accuse me of endangering his daughter? He would have a right to be angry. While at no time was Vel in real danger, she was on the scene, and she did witness the scary parts of Paris being held by the FBI. My argument would be that it was good for her to widen her horizons, like it was good for me. But does someone at twelve years of age need her horizons widened? I suppose you could think of it as a history lesson that got a little out of hand. I flash back to the sheriff at the Woolworths reaching for his handcuffs.

"Did you see any of this happening while you were at the State House yesterday?" he asks, walking up to the porch.

I hesitate and wonder how much to say. "There was a flurry of activity when the fire alarm went off," I say, "but we were already on the grounds by then." I exhale, pleased with my selective truth-telling.

"What were those nut cases trying to accomplish?" he asks with a roll of his eyes that reminds me of Vel.

"I wouldn't call them *nut cases*," I say. "They believed in a cause and thought something needed to be done about it."

"Like I said, nut cases." He laughs a short laugh.

My hackles rise, but I caution myself not to react. It would be hard for anyone to understand if they weren't there. This was more than about a flag. This was about the principles this country was founded on. Liberty. Freedom for all. But this is too much to discuss on a Sunday morning with a banker who thinks anyone is crazy if they question the powers that be.

"It was a lovely trip, regardless," I say. "I'm so glad Vel went with us." I think again of her asking Les Lester all those questions and then seeing her name written in a thousand different ways. "Would you like a cup of coffee? I was just about to go inside to get another cup."

He thanks me and says something about needing to get back to his wife.

Alone again, it occurs to me that at least Vel's father didn't recognize me from the photo, but that doesn't mean someone else won't. I look back at the headline and carefully read the article. A $500 reward is offered for information on where to find the "ringleader." Five hundred dollars is enough for some people to turn in their own mother.

"Me, a ringleader?" I laugh a short laugh and turn serious again. Ted Junior would have a conniption. Not to mention, Abigail.

I wonder briefly if the children could help me confiscate all the newspapers in Charleston. The thing about newspapers is that the story is alive for a day, at most, before the next story grabs our attention. If I am lucky, maybe everybody will go to the beach today and not get around to reading the paper.

However, I know that Ted Junior always reads it from front to back. It is part of his job to know what is going on in the city. Abigail will be reading, too, while her pies bake. The newspaper always sits on the kitchen table until put in the trash the following morning.

Should I start packing my bags?

Trudy runs down the sidewalk calling my name. She holds another copy of the newspaper, her eyes wild with *What are we going to do?* When she reaches the porch, Ted Junior, Abigail and Teddy pull the car up in front of the house.

"Uh oh," I say. Like yesterday, trouble surrounds us on all fronts. It is time to confess and show Ted Junior and Abigail the article. Trudy joins me on the porch, and we clasp hands to await our fate.

Chapter Twenty-Six

Trudy

Things at my house aren't good. Daddy even yelled at Nana Trueluck in the kitchen. Then he went up to the attic to think, and he hasn't typed a word on his novel. He didn't even put on his lucky shorts. If I had known she would get in this much trouble, I never would have asked her to take us to Columbia. But now we have even bigger problems. If anybody recognizes her in the photograph and turns her in, she could be blamed for everything.

Later that night, Vel and Paris and I got to the cemetery again for an emergency meeting, along with Nana Trueluck. I can barely stand to see how guilty she looks. But the mood lightens when Paris attempts to give me a few acting lessons in order to pull off being Hoot's girlfriend. He stands on the grave of the unknown girl and shows me how to flutter my eye lashes and flip my hair with one hand. Every now and again, Vel looks up from her book to laugh. The truth is, Paris is much better at being a girl than I am.

Something rustles in the far corner of the cemetery, and the four of us duck behind a large gravestone. Even Nana Trueluck's eyes are wide.

"Why do we meet out here anyway?" Vel whispers. "It's creepy."

"Because it's private," I whisper back.

"It doesn't seem all that private if we're always ducking behind tombstones," she says.

"Do you want to go home?" I ask her.

Nana Trueluck shushes us. Seconds later, a raccoon waddles out of the shadows. We all exhale.

"Are you ready, Trudy?" Paris asks.

"Ready for what?" I say, wanting to forget why we're here.

"Ready to play the role of a lifetime?"

"Being Hoot's girlfriend for one day is the role of a lifetime?" Vel smirks.

Paris ignores her. "Don't worry, you'll bring the house down," he says to me.

"One day, one performance," I repeat, matching his seriousness. "Then the whole thing will be over, and our secret will be safe." I flip my hair and give a quick flutter of my eyelashes. Everyone laughs except Nana Trueluck who looks worried again.

"Unless someone recognizes me from the newspaper," she says.

"It's good you dressed the way you did that day," I say. "If you'd been wearing your high-tops and one of your wild skirts you would have been much more recognizable."

"That's true," Nana Trueluck says. "Sometimes it's good to try to blend in."

I wonder what I should wear when I pretend to be Hoot's girlfriend and then shudder with the thought.

As Vel, Nana Trueluck, and I walk home, silence stretches between us. Vel follows a few steps behind and lingers whenever we walk under a lamppost so she can read. It is quiet this time of night, especially on a Sunday.

"You are brave to do this," Nana Trueluck says to me, breaking the silence.

"It feels more stupid than brave," I say.

"You wanted a summer adventure, and here it is," she says. But she doesn't sound convinced that this is a good thing.

Today was the first time I ever heard Daddy raise his voice to her. I hope this doesn't mean she won't live with us anymore. Before Nana Trueluck came to Queen Street, life wasn't exciting at all. Now it is almost too exciting. We are hiding from the FBI, dealing with blackmail threats, and having emergency meetings.

We settle into a rhythm as we walk, and I take Nana Trueluck's hand. She squeezes it like she always does to tell me she loves me. We walk Vel to her house and say our good-byes. When we get to our house we go into the living room where Mama, Daddy, and Teddy sit on the couch ready to watch *Bonanza*. We join them as the opening music plays and the Cartwrights ride across the screen on horses. Any hard feelings left over after our confession are pushed aside for the latest drama taking place at the Ponderosa.

Later that night it takes me forever to fall asleep. When I do, my dreams are full of old white guards hitting me over the head with rebel flags, me shielding myself with Miss Josie's red umbrella. I wake up tired the next morning. Too tired to be anyone's *real* girlfriend, much less a *fake* one.

When I go into the kitchen Nana Trueluck sits at the table alone reading the newspaper.

"Anything about Columbia?" I ask.

"Lots of things, but nothing about you-know-what." She folds it to the crossword and puts it to the side to save for later.

"You look nice," she says, looking over at me.

I wear a sleeveless dress and sandals, the only thing I could think of that might be considered "girlfriend" clothes.

"Nana Trueluck, why did I ever agree to do this? My palms are already sweaty."

"Maybe you could pretend that you're Doris Day and he's Rock Hudson."

I make a face that causes her to laugh.

"Yes, well, maybe that's stretching it a bit," she says.

After I finish breakfast, she wishes me luck. I leave the house to meet Hoot at the corner of Meeting and Mary Streets as we arranged the day before. Then we will walk to the Esso station together where I will pretend to be Hoot's girlfriend in front of his brother Hank.

The things a granddaughter will do to keep her grandmother out of jail, I say to myself.

When I reach the corner, I almost don't recognize Hoot. Instead of his usual ratty shorts and tattered T-shirt, he wears slacks and a short sleeve shirt with a brown tie hanging around his neck that looks like a burnt piece of bacon. He is clean, and his hair is combed. If I didn't know better, I'd think he was going to a wedding. Except from where I stand, it is more like a funeral.

Forcing a cheerful look onto my face, I pretend I am Doris Day like Nana Trueluck suggested. But Hoot Macklehaney is the farthest thing from Rock Hudson that I can imagine.

"Hello, Miss Trudy," Hoot says, all polite.

The theme song to *The Twilight Zone* plays in my head. It seems I have entered an alternative universe where Hoot Macklehaney is nice.

"Shall we go?" Hoot offers me his arm. He must have Clearasil on his face because his pimples look tamer than usual.

I refuse his arm, but walk a little closer to him so he won't get mad. I think of Captain Hook forcing Peter Pan to walk the plank, except there aren't any pirates or lost boys or planks, only the sidewalk and the gas station up ahead. In contrast to my feelings of doom, Hoot whistles like it is the happiest day of his life.

We approach the Esso station, and he stops at the gas pumps. "Can I hold your hand for this part?" he asks.

I grimace.

"You agreed," he says, his happiness disappearing. "If you don't do this, I'll tell my relatives what you did, and your little colored friend will regret the day he ever saved your life."

"Okay, okay," I say.

I shake off my disgust and imagine myself as Doris Day again. I even hum a few bars of "Que Sera, Sera." Thankfully, that reminds me of why I am doing this in the first place. Nana Trueluck should never have to go to jail for something that was mine and Paris' idea. Besides, as Nana Trueluck has told me many times, she does not look good in stripes—jailhouse or otherwise.

Hoot holds out his hand. At first I stare at it, but then I take a deep breath and slip my palm in his. At the same time, I hope he hasn't picked his nose lately or gotten zit juice on his fingers.

Hoot's palms are sweaty, and my hand slides around a little before it suctions to his. Paris would be proud. I could definitely win an Academy Award for this performance. We walk the last few steps to the Esso station. Meanwhile, I pray I don't see anyone from school because I could never explain how I got myself into this mess.

Both bay doors are open to the garage. Hoot leads me to a white Ford Fairlane suspended in the air. Hoot's brother is underneath looking up at the engine and doesn't see us walk up. Hoot's sweaty hand begins to shake. His brother finishes tightening a bolt and then turns to look at us, grease on his face.

"Hank, I want you to meet my new girlfriend, Trudy Trueluck." Hoot says this with a slight stutter.

Hank's name is stitched onto his blue shirt. He takes an oily rag and wipes his hands, but they still look as dirty as ever. "Are you playing some kind of joke on me?" Hank says to Hoot.

"No, I'm not," Hoot replies.

He doesn't stutter this time. But Hoot's hand gets even sweatier, and I have to hold on tightly to keep my hand from slipping off.

"How long have you two been going out?" his brother asks, his eyes narrow.

"Since we saw you last," I answer. I unlock my hand from Hoot's and take his arm and lean in a little like I have seen high school girls do with the boys they are dating. Hoot smiles at me, and his eyes send me a message about how grateful he is. Unfortunately, Hoot's arm is sweaty, too. I will have to take at least six baths after I get home just to get his slimy sweat off me.

"I don't believe you," Hank says. "No girl would go out with a reject like you." Hank laughs.

"What right do you have calling somebody names?" I ask. "If anyone is a reject it's you."

I stand straighter with the same feeling I had at the State House when I saw that Confederate flag flying. Nobody has the right to put anybody else down. Even if the person getting put down is Hoot Macklehaney.

Hank mutters something under his breath. Then he pauses as though remembering where he has seen me before. "Hey, aren't you the girl who took up for that nigger?"

The hatefulness of his words causes me to hesitate. "I take up for anyone I please, colored or white."

Hank throws a wrench that clangs close to my feet. I jump out of the way.

"Oops," he says, like it was an accident, but then he smiles.

"You'd best be getting your little girlfriend out of here or she might get hurt," Hank says to Hoot.

"Let's go," Hoot says. He pulls me outside next to a stack of used tires. The rubber is heating up in the sun and smells sour.

I let go of his sweaty hand and wipe the excess moisture on my dress.

"Trudy, you shouldn't have said those things to Hank," he says.

"Why not?" I ask. The last thing I need is a lecture from Hoot.

"You should know by now that Hank's got friends."

"So do I." I think of Paris and Vel and Nana Trueluck.

"Not like these," Hoot says.

We walk back to where we met up, and my anger makes me step so fast Hoot has to hurry to keep up. At the corner I stop, determined to forget this day forever.

"Thanks for being my girlfriend," Hoot says. "I appreciate all those nice things you said."

My determination melts in the summer sun. "I don't think it did any good, Hoot. Your brother is a total dingbat."

"I come from a long line of dingbats," he says.

I take a long look at Hoot Macklehaney and appreciate his honesty. Then it occurs to me that he might not always be this disgusting, that it is something he might outgrow, just like his pimples.

"So you'll keep your promise?" I ask. "You won't tell any-one about Columbia?"

"I promise." Hoot extends his hand for me to shake.

This time it feels a little less slimy.

"Watch out for Hank," he says. "You made him mad back there."

"He made me mad, too," I say.

"Just watch out." Hoot spits a hocker on the sidewalk, and I see the family resemblance.

It occurs to me that our families have a lot to do with who we become. If not for my great-great-great-grandmother, I might never have become Paris' friend and gone to Columbia to take down that flag. And if not for Nana Trueluck giving me and Vel a ride, I never would have gone there in the first place. My grandmother has surprised me in the last few days. But I have had enough surprises. I am ready for a normal summer again. Then I remember Hoot's warning and realize it may be too late.

Chapter Twenty-Seven

Ida

While Abigail delivers pies with my grandson, and Ted Junior is busy being mayor, I sit in the kitchen to work a crossword with Trudy. Thankfully, no one has recognized my posterior on the front page and things have died down. Even Ted Junior and Abigail seem to have forgiven me for my part in the Columbia fiasco.

"What's a seven letter word for *clandestine?*" Trudy asks, pencil poised.

Before I can answer someone knocks on the front door with such force, Trudy and I jump. We are still jumpy from our adventure last week.

We go into the living room, and I peek through the sheer curtains. For a moment, I feel like Widow Wilson and hope no one starts to call me Widow Trueluck. Widowhood is not a club anyone wants to join.

On the front porch stand two men who could be Laurel and Hardy lookalikes. One is tall and thin, the other short and round with a mustache. The tall one knocks again.

"They don't look like FBI," Trudy says. "Or policemen."

"I thought that adventure was behind us," I say. "You don't think this is about Columbia, do you?"

We exchange an intrepid look.

"Should we pretend we're not at home?" Trudy asks.

"Might as well see what they want," I say.

Trudy follows me to the door. The good thing about being a grandmother is that I look like one. By that I mean I look harmless. Being seventy is like traveling incognito everywhere you go. I am convinced a team of grandmothers could rob banks just by pretending to knit in the lobby beforehand. No one the wiser. A thought that first occurred to me when I realized Ted Senior hadn't provided enough money for me to live on after he'd passed.

"Can I help you?" I ask through the screen.

"I'm a reporter from the *Post*," the tall man says. "I'm here to ask about your role in taking down the Confederate flag in Columbia last weekend."

Trudy and I exchange a look. Someone has told our secret.

A flash bulb goes off as the shorter man, a photographer, snaps a picture that must capture the surprise on our faces. He is more casual looking than the tall guy, but still wears a tie with his short-sleeved white shirt. His arms have muscles, probably from carrying his bulky camera bag all over the place. The bag hangs down past his hip, and I notice that we stand eye to eye. I wonder if he ever cuts the heads off the people in his photographs like I do.

"I'm afraid I have no idea what you're talking about," I say. I have never been good at lying and give a nervous smile.

"We believe you know *exactly* what we're talking about," says the tall one.

Trudy and I exchange another look.

"May I offer you gentlemen some iced tea?" I ask.

As usual, it is a hot day and they accept with eagerness. I tell them to have a seat on the porch while Trudy and I go inside to get the tea.

Trudy paces the floor and wrings her hands while I pour two glasses of iced tea. Sometimes she acts more like a grandmother than I do.

"What are you thinking, Nana? Are you actually going to talk to them?"

"What choice do we have?" I say. "If we don't tell them our version, then they'll make up their own."

"I thought you didn't trust reporters except for Walter Cronkite."

Trudy knows I have a crush on Walter. It is a running joke of ours. Walter is the only newscaster I trust. Him and Edward R. Murrow.

"I think we should just be honest," I say. "Honesty is the best policy, right?" I wonder if this is true.

"But what if they put Paris in jail?" Trudy asks.

"He's just a boy. They won't put him in jail." I bite my bottom lip. After seeing on the news the happenings in the

Deep South, I wonder if there is anyone left with a lick of sense in regard to treating our colored citizens with decency.

"Should I answer their questions, too?" she asks.

"That's up to you," I say.

I imagine my mug shot up in the downtown post office next to the photos of hardened criminals of the *Most Wanted*. At least a white-haired grandmother will add a little diversity.

"That stupid Hoot Macklehaney must have told," Trudy says. "Who else could it be?"

"It's always the person you least suspect," I say. "Think of all those Alfred Hitchcock movies we've watched."

I slide two peach turnovers onto plates, thinking it wouldn't hurt to try to influence them favorably. Meanwhile, Trudy telephones Vel and Paris and tells them that the newspaper is asking questions and to get over here quick. We go back to the front porch with turnovers and tea.

By the time we come back outside, Vel is already on her way up the street, poofing her hair. After the men eat their turnovers, the tall reporter, Charlie, gets out his pad and a pencil.

"So when did this idea of taking down the Confederate flag at the State House first occur to you?" he asks me.

"It was my idea," Trudy says. Then she tells him the entire story about Paris saving her life and about the dream he had. As she finishes, Paris gets off a bus at the corner and walks in our direction. Vel and Trudy meet him at the street.

"So the mayor's daughter and the boy became friends after he saved her life?" the reporter asks me. "Did the mayor not mind his daughter having a Negro friend?"

"The *mayor* didn't even know about it," I say. "The children hid their friendship for fear of what others might think."

"But you knew?"

I hesitate. This feels like a setup.

Another flashbulb goes off as Paris approaches the porch. The reporter turns to the children, asking more questions, including their full names. Then the photographer asks the three of them to stand arm in arm next to where the cross burned in our yard.

"That should sell a few newspapers," the reporter says to his photographer.

I straighten my spine and my anger crackles. Yet at the same time it appears I have been struck mute.

"Mrs. Trueluck, aren't you a descendent of one of Charleston's famous abolitionists?"

"Well, I don't see how—"

"Are you saying that you had nothing to do with taking down that flag?" the reporter asks.

"This is the young man you should talk to." I stand and put a hand on Paris' shoulder. "He'd be happy to tell you his side of the story, including how the FBI tried to hold him against his will for questioning."

"How did the mayor react to you taking the children to Columbia?" the reporter asks, giving Paris only a glance.

"Leave my grandmother alone," Trudy says to him.

The photographer snaps another photo, this time of Trudy pointing her finger at the reporter, a scowl on her face.

"I think it's time for you to leave," I say to them.

"Does the mayor think that white children and Negro children should be allowed to be friends? What does your son think about the Civil Rights Act that was just voted into law today?" The reporter fans himself with his note pad.

"This interview is over," I say.

I usher the children into the house and close the door and lock it.

"I may never watch a Laurel and Hardy comedy again," I say. "Not after putting up with those two."

We go into the kitchen, where my crossword lay unfinished.

"What just happened?" Trudy asks.

The four of us sit at the kitchen table.

"It seems they wanted the story to be more about your father, not about what happened in Columbia," I say.

What I don't tell them is how much trouble I imagine I am in again. Especially with Ted Junior and Abigail. The photographs alone could be damaging to Ted Junior's bid for a second term. The reporter mentioned the passing of that Civil Rights Act I have read about lately. It was John F. Kennedy who put it into motion, but now President Johnson has taken it up. I don't trust Johnson. Not that he has personally done anything to hurt me. But he is not Jack Kennedy. And he has kept that war going on in Vietnam much longer than it has needed to be.

I think of those fateful events in Dallas seven months ago. The whole family stayed glued to the television for four days watching the aftermath. It was one of the saddest times in our nation's history as far as I am concerned. Ted Senior had died in May of last year and what grieving I hadn't finished up for him, I lumped in with President Kennedy's death.

I give the children Jell-O salad from the refrigerator, Abigail's staple dessert when there isn't a pie around. They sit at the kitchen table, and I hand them bowls and spoons. Children are always hungry, and it gives me time to think while they are eating.

"I'm sorry if I got you in trouble," Paris says to me, as if my upset might be about him.

"No, no, this isn't about you, Paris. I was just remembering my dearly departed husband."

Paris nods, as though remembering someone he lost, too.

"That stupid Hoot Macklehaney must have told, even after I pretended to be his girlfriend." Trudy gets up from the kitchen table with a huff and puts her bowl in the sink.

"Hoot didn't do it," Paris says. "I was the one who told."

Trudy's jaw unhinges, her disbelief tangible. "It was you?" she asks.

"I called the newspaper this morning and told them everything," Paris says.

"Why'd you do that?" Trudy asks, her voice raised.

"I bet it was for the reward." Vel scoffs, as though she knew not to trust him all this time.

But I already know that Paris wouldn't do something like that for the reward. He has something that few people have today, even old people my age with plenty of time to develop it. It is called integrity. Perhaps that has something to do with Miss Josie being his grandmother. Perhaps not. Sometimes children are just born with something special and you don't know where it came from.

"I didn't do it for the reward," Paris says. "It was for other reasons."

Trudy gives him a look like those *other reasons* better be good.

"As long as what we did was a secret, it was like we were ashamed of it," he begins. "The funny thing is, I'm not the least bit ashamed. I'm proud that we acted on what we believed. I'm sorry I didn't ask y'all first," he continues, "but I didn't want you to talk me out of it. I wanted to tell the truth. Even if it meant I got in trouble."

I wonder how a boy of twelve could be so eloquent as well as brave.

"I wish you'd asked us first, Paris," Trudy says. "But I understand what you're saying about it being a secret. I just didn't want you to get in trouble." She pauses as though his honesty has challenged her. "Truth is, I didn't want to get in trouble, either."

"I don't mind getting in trouble about this," Paris says. "Even if I have to go to jail like Dr. King, I'm proud of what we did."

"Now that we've all decided to be proud," I say, "we've got some extra thinking to do. There's no telling what will come out in that newspaper article and we need to prepare."

"Prepare for what?" Trudy asks.

"The unexpected," I say.

Trudy doesn't look too pleased with the prospect of preparations or the unexpected. It is then that I decide to call in reinforcements: my old friend Madison Chambers.

Chapter Twenty-Eight

Trudy

Two days later, on our nation's Independence Day, I am the last to go downstairs for breakfast. Since nothing appeared in the newspaper yesterday, Nana Trueluck and I are hopeful that the reporter tossed the story and that we have heard the last of our trip to Columbia.

When I enter the kitchen, my entire family is sitting at the table, the newspaper spread across most of the table. Mama is tisking, Daddy is holding his head like he has a whopper of a headache, and Nana Trueluck has her head bowed. Gracing the front page is the photograph of me and Paris and Vel standing next to where the cross burned in our front yard. A photograph of Daddy is there, too, with the headline:

Mayor Trueluck Signs His Own Civil Rights Bill

The first few paragraphs are about how Daddy allows his kids to play with Negro children at their home and how his mother, Ida Trueluck, took these same children to Columbia to defile the Confederate Centennial flag flying over the State

House. The last line of the editorial states: *Is this the kind of mayor we want for the city of Charleston?*

Nana Trueluck has not lifted her head from her personal prayer meeting, or maybe she is just too mortified to look up.

"Are we in trouble?" I ask.

"We?" Mama laughs a short laugh.

Though I am certain she is pointing the finger at Nana Trueluck, she doesn't look at her.

"This is all my fault," I say.

"No it isn't," Nana Trueluck says, finally looking up. Her eyes are rimmed in red. I want to help, but I don't know how.

"That reporter tricked us," I say.

Daddy taps the kitchen table with his index finger. "They are a tricky bunch," he says, glancing at Mama.

I haven't asked my father if he likes being mayor, but from the looks of things, he wishes he at least had the chance to a second term.

Teddy kicks the chair leg with his sneaker, and Mama makes him stop. Teddy forgoes his stunts and smiles at me as though enjoying me getting in trouble for a change. He asks to be excused and goes into the backyard. With all that has been going on, he has been practically invisible this summer, which is fine by me.

"I should have known better," Nana Trueluck says.

"But there must be something we can do," I say.

"I doubt it," Daddy says. "The good news is it will die down eventually."

The kitchen is quiet. Contriteness is called for, and I lower my eyes. But like Paris, I don't feel sorry at all. I am glad we went to Columbia and took down that flag, even if it was for only a few minutes. And I am glad we told the newspaper the truth, even though they didn't print it. We were modern-day rebels who believed in our cause and got in trouble for it.

"There is some good news," Nana Trueluck says. "Yesterday, Madison Chambers met with the FBI in Columbia and because of the young ages of the juveniles involved and the advanced age of the grandmother—"

She pauses to roll her eyes, which I am pretty sure she learned from me.

"Well, somehow, Madison talked them into not filing charges."

My relief comes out in a short squeal. "Nobody is going to get arrested?" I ask.

"Well, that is good news," Daddy says.

Mama agrees, but she still won't look at Nana Trueluck.

After dinner Daddy doesn't go up to the attic like he usually does, but sits with us in the living room. We wait for *The Andy Griffith Show* to begin. Nana Trueluck loves Aunt Bea and Barney Fife makes her laugh. She knits, and even Teddy acts like a normal kid and isn't tripping over the rug. I try to relax, but feel uneasy. If we are not in trouble, then why do I feel like something bad is about to happen?

Seconds later, right in the middle of a Kraft macaroni and cheese commercial, something crashes through the picture window. Mama screams, and Teddy jumps behind the couch as if someone has just thrown a hand grenade. We all drop to the floor, including Nana Trueluck, who brandishes her knitting needles like weapons.

A rock the size of a softball sits in the center of the living room. Shards of glass cover our living room rug.

"Stay down!" Daddy says. He runs out onto the porch just as a car speeds away.

Tires screech at the end of the road in front of Vel's house, and we hear glass shatter in the distance. Mama pulls Teddy and me close to her like a mother hen gathering her chicks. Nana Trueluck's eyes are wide. We are all shaking. The car turns around and speeds back past our house. The hair prickles on the back of my neck. Is Daddy in danger? Through the hole in our picture window I watch a blue Ford Torino drive by with two white men inside. They whoop and holler like they are at a Carolina football game.

Daddy runs back into the house repeating the numbers and letters on the license plate. He finds a pen and paper in the kitchen to write them down. Then he returns to the living room to make sure we are okay. Somehow a rock thrown through the window feels much scarier than a burning cross in the yard. It is like these men threw their meanness right into our living room instead of leaving it outside on the lawn.

"I need to check on Vel," I say. I walk toward the door, glass crunching underneath my sandals.

"You're not going anywhere without me," Daddy says, joining me at the door.

Before we leave, he picks up the rock. A string is wrapped around it attaching the first page of the newspaper where the story ran. Words are written in black magic marker on the newsprint. When he reads it his face turns red, and he makes a fist. He shows the note to Mama and Nana Trueluck.

"Don't do anything crazy," Nana Trueluck says.

"What does it say?" I ask.

Daddy hesitates as though deciding if I am old enough to see it. Then he hands the note to me. It contains the most hateful words I have ever read. So hateful I figure I will still remember them when I am a hundred years old. Jagged, hand-written letters goad us from the newspaper page:

GOD HATES NIGGER LOVERS

"Why would anybody say something so mean?" I ask. My hands continue to shake from the scare, though the shaking is lighter now.

"Pure ignorance," Nana Trueluck says. "They're scared of what they don't understand."

"But I don't see how someone being scared could make them throw a rock through a window," I say.

"Beats me, too, sweetheart," Daddy says. He starts to say more, but Mama stops him.

I have been told I am wise beyond my years and also that I am too young to know certain stuff. I wish my parents would make up their mind.

Daddy and I walk down the street to Vel's house where all the lights are on, inside and out. Vel's dad and older brother stand outside with baseball bats like they are waiting on the car to come back. Vel is on the porch in her pink pajamas, holding a note that looks exactly like ours. The look on her face says again, *I told you so*. To Vel, making friends with Paris was never a good idea.

Chapter Twenty-Nine

Ida

While Vel and Trudy huddle together on the porch swing. I sit unmoving in the nearby rocking chair. A cross burnt in our yard was unnerving enough. Now they have thrown a rock through our window with a hateful message attached.

"What is this world coming to?" I say to no one in particular and think about how the national news has become more and more alarming since the Kennedy assassination.

Abigail stands in the doorway with an arm around Teddy. "I wonder the same," she says to me, an apology in her glance.

The porch light casts shadows into the yard, and the darkness takes on a sinister look. Trudy and Vel look so young sitting on the swing, and I question why I went along with their Columbia plan. Ted Senior used to say I can be naive, but I would call it wishful thinking. I like to pretend the world is a nicer place than it actually is.

Trudy stands, an urgency evident in her look.

"I need to call Paris and warn him," she says. "What if they're headed over to his house?"

Of course she would think of Paris. He is her friend. Trudy goes into the kitchen to use the telephone, and I follow her there. "Would you like me to make the call?" I say. "I could talk to Miss Josie."

Trudy looks relieved at my suggestion and goes back outside to sit with Vel.

I dial the number she gave me, and Miss Josie answers. She sounds like I do when I am fighting mad.

I introduce myself as Trudy's grandmother. "Did you get a rock thrown through your window, too?" I ask her.

"I don't, for the life of me, know what gets into some people," she says.

I hear Paris in the background ask, "Are Trudy and Vel okay?"

I relay that they are, and that they are concerned for him, too.

"They got our house and Vel's, too," I tell Miss Josie. She sounds like someone I would like. Someone who could be a friend.

"I'm afraid this is because of what my grandson told the newspaper," Miss Josie says. "But I have to respect his choice to do that."

"I respect his choice, too," I say.

A police car pulls up in front of our house, red and blue lights flashing, a repeat of the week before. The policeman gets out and walks over to Ted Junior.

"The police are here," I tell Miss Josie. "I guess I'd better go. Have they come to your house, yet?"

Miss Josie pauses. "Mrs. Trueluck, the police don't come when colored people call about something like this, so we don't even bother calling."

I pause. It never occurred to me that people like Miss Josie wouldn't get the same protection as white citizens. Perhaps naïve is exactly what I am. Next time Ted Junior and I have time to talk, I am going to mention this to him. In the meantime, I apologize for the ignorance of those people and get off the telephone.

At the street, I listen in on Ted Junior talking to the police officer. The officer sounds sympathetic, but just like the one who came when the cross got burnt in our yard, he doesn't write a report.

"If you want to catch these people, why aren't you writing anything down?" I ask the officer.

He aims an angry look at me, and Ted Junior puts an arm around my shoulder, which I take as my signal to keep quiet, that he'll handle it.

I think of Miss Josie again and the daily injustice she has to live with. Ted Senior used to say that you can never understand a person until you walk a day in their shoes. I try to imagine what it would be like to have dark skin and live in a place where a majority of light-skinned people think they are better than you every minute of every day. At that moment, I feel the need to apologize to more than Miss Josie.

The only thing that keeps me from weeping is knowing that my family is different. They aren't perfect, that's for sure, but we believe in basic freedoms. We believe that everybody should be treated with fairness and dignity. When I think of the dignity Miss Josie and her family don't get, it makes me spitting mad, as Trudy would say.

Within minutes the reporter and his photographer show up again and flashbulbs begin to go off. Abigail takes the children into the house. Trudy protests, of course. She doesn't like being treated like a child, but I agree with Abigail that they have witnessed enough.

The reporter stays on the other side of our fence, but yells questions at me like: *Do you know who did this? Was it the same people who burned the cross in your yard?* I think about how his article in the newspaper skewed everything I said. I charge up to the fence. Only a few white pickets separate me and the reporter.

"I want to tell you how unfair your interview was," I say, looking up at his tall frame. His five o'clock shadow is pronounced, as is his accomplice's, who aims the camera in my direction. I lift a hand to block his view and give him a look that says he may be singing the girl parts in his church choir soon. He backs away, his camera now to his side.

"I was just doing my job," the reporter says to me.

"Bull malarkey," I say. "Manipulating the truth isn't your job. Your job is to report the news—truthfully—not twist what someone says to make the most sensational story. And now here the two of you are back like vultures circling. You should be ashamed of yourselves," I add, looking them both in the eye. "Would your mothers and grandmothers be proud of you right now?"

I hear myself speak the words and can't believe I actually said them. In the past I might have thought these things, but I never would have spoken them. Is it possible that after seven decades I am finally growing a backbone?

The reporter shows no remorse and walks over to ask Ted Junior the same questions.

The photographer, however, apologizes. He tells me that the reporter is trying to keep his job, and that the editor at the newspaper is the one who wants more controversial stories. I thank him for telling me.

In the background, Widow Wilson is in full view in her window. I give her a wave that she doesn't return. Since we are both widows, and of a similar age, you would think we could be friends. Of course, she may believe I am the reason for all this trouble, since it seemed to start after I moved in.

Finally, the policemen, reporter, and the photographer leave, and Ted Junior and I walk back toward the house.

"They think it was the Klan again," he says to me on the porch.

"Makes sense," I say. "Their whole reason for being is to keep everybody off balance and afraid."

"Well, they're doing a good job of it," he says.

Ted Junior looks tired. I imagine these last few days have been hard for him.

"You okay?" I ask him.

"I've been better," he says. "How about you?"

"I've been better, too." Truth is, I thought I was awake before, but it seems I have just been sleepwalking, with no idea what my neighbors on the other side of the city have been dealing with. My face grows warmer just thinking about it.

Ted Junior and I go inside. On the television, the end credits run and the theme music plays for *The Andy Griffith Show*. Has it only been thirty minutes? What would Aunt Bea have done if a rock had been thrown through her front window?

When Trudy looks over at me, her face reveals the same spark she had at the State House. Looks like this roller coaster ride isn't over yet. Not that I ever liked roller coasters. But once you are strapped in, it is not like you can get off. For now, I guess I'd better hold onto this ride with both hands.

Chapter Thirty

Trudy

We spend the morning sitting in the cemetery talking about what we should do next. Paris and I sit on the grave marker of the unknown girl, while Vel sits against a tombstone that serves as a back rest as she reads.

We stay hidden so our friendship won't be noticed and we won't get rocks thrown through our window again. In the daytime, the cemetery isn't the least bit scary. Turns out the scariest things happen outside a cemetery, perpetrated by people who are living not dead.

Paris sighs. "We're fighting a losing battle," he says.

I can't say I blame him for his frustration. I haven't a clue what to do next, either, and tell him so.

While Paris sits nearby, I lie across the large, flat crypt and stare up into the limbs of a live oak tree that was probably a seedling during the Revolutionary War. Its arms stretch and cover the whole back corner of the cemetery. Even through wars, beautiful things grow.

The ancient grave marker is cool and leaves its texture imprinted to the back of my legs. With the help of the wind, a ray of sunlight breaks through the leaves. I hold up a hand to block the sun.

"Do you think Martin Luther King Junior ever wants to give up?" Paris asks finally.

"I bet he does," I say. "I don't think he'd quit, though."

Paris stands. "Maybe that's the answer. Maybe we need to ask ourselves what Dr. King would do in this situation."

"Uh, oh," Vel says. She looks at Paris before turning a page.

Then I have the craziest idea I have ever had. So crazy I wonder if I should even voice it.

"What is it?" Paris asks.

"It's even bigger than taking down that flag," I say to warn him. "And we're going to need Hoot Macklehaney's help."

"Why in heaven's name would we need *his* help?" Vel asks. "You going to pretend to be his girlfriend again?"

I pretend to gag, which makes her laugh.

"We need Hoot to help us get the names of the people in the local Ku Klux Klan," I say.

"What?" Paris raises his voice before lowering it again. "The Klan is dangerous, Trudy," he whispers.

"I overheard Daddy tell Nana Trueluck that the Klan was responsible for the rock through our window," I say. "And the burning cross."

"I'm not sure this is a good idea, Trudy," he whispers again.

"What's the worst that could happen?" I ask.

"I end up like my cousin in Mississippi," he says.

We both get somber.

"By the way, since when did you become fearless?" he asks.

"I learned it from you," I answer, which is true. Paris is brave every day of his life just by walking down the street.

"What did you learn from me?" Vel asks, with a huff.

I put a hand on my hip, poof my hair, and roll my eyes. A perfect imitation of Vel. Paris laughs. For about two seconds she acts angry, but then she laughs, too.

In the distance someone comes out of the side door that leads to the church office. I shush everybody. We wait until the sound of footsteps fade and the creaking gate opens and closes. I wonder what Nana Trueluck will think of my latest plan. She seemed as shaken up about last night as I was.

Before bed, when we talked in her room, she said that something had to be done. But this plan could prove more dangerous than taking down that flag, and I question if I should even mention it to her.

"Think about it, Paris," I begin again. "Every club has a list of its members, right?"

"I guess so," he says, like he has never even thought about it.

"And this is a secret club, so the list is even more important. None of the members want anyone to know who they are," I continue. "This is how we catch them by surprise. We get that list of names and then release them somehow.

They'll be like ants that scatter when you put cornmeal on their mounds."

"But these aren't ants, Trudy," he says. "These are more like hornets. Hornets don't scatter, they attack."

For several seconds we are quiet. Whether we are dealing with hornets or ants, I am convinced we can pull it off.

Vel snaps her book closed and puts Nancy Drew back in her purse. "Are you seriously trying to get a membership list of the KKK?"

I nod.

"Trudy Trueluck, you are out of your mind."

Like Mama, Vel only uses my full name when she wants to keep me in line.

"You can't do this, Trudy. This is dangerous. Dan-ger-ous," she repeats.

"But somebody's got to do something," I say to her.

"If smart grownups haven't been able to do something, what makes you think that you can?" She stands and puts a hand on her hip and poofs her hair, but leaves out the eye-rolling.

I pause to think up a good answer. "Because nobody even notices when kids are around, Vel. It worked at the State House didn't it? We got all the way out the door with that flag."

"Maybe we should ask your Nana Trueluck what she thinks," Paris says.

"She got in trouble with Mama and Daddy for helping us last time," I say. "We need to keep her out of this one or she might not get to live with us anymore."

"You can keep me out of this one, too." Vel secures her pink purse to her shoulder as though ready to leave.

Paris and I exchange a look.

"She'll come around," I say to Paris. "She always does."

Vel rolls her eyes.

We sneak out of the church cemetery. Paris walks in the direction of Miss Josie's flower and basket stand, Vel toward home, and me toward the Esso filling station where Hoot is known to hang out. I can at least ask him if a list exists.

As I walk to the filling station, I imagine myself marching with Dr. Martin Luther King Junior in Birmingham, like in the images on television last year. I think of my family, and how brave my father is to be mayor even though half of Charleston hates him. I think of Nana Trueluck, who carried that rebel flag out of the State House, and I think of my great-great-grandmother who was a witness to slavery and tried to do something about it. The thing I try *not* to think about is how nervous I am to ask Hoot Macklehaney for a favor.

When I approach the gas station, Hoot is sitting on the curb throwing rocks into the storm drain. He winks at me like he knew I couldn't stay away, and I have to remind myself not to vomit.

"We need to talk," I say. Hoot stands and follows me to the corner.

"Do you know about last night?" I ask.

He picks at a pimple until it bleeds, and I take this as a "yes." Then Hoot looks back at the Esso station, a dead give-away that he probably knows who did it, even if he wasn't part of it.

"If you ever want me to have anything to do with you ever again, here's how you're going to make it up to us, Hoot." I pause for dramatic effect like Paris taught me. "You need to get us a list of names of people in the Ku Klux Klan." I don't tell him who "us" is, but I imagine he can figure it out.

Hoot laughs, like I have just told a funny joke. "That's like asking me to swim Charleston Harbor with barbells in my pockets," he says. "Those names are top secret," he adds in a whisper.

"I promise we'll never tell where we got them," I say. "We'll even do a pinkie swear." I hold out my little finger like I am ready to swear right here.

"But you don't understand, Trudy. They'll kill me."

"Oh come on, Hoot. You know they wouldn't really hurt you. You're one of them. Besides, they won't find out."

The one thing I have going for me is Hoot's crush, which appears to be waning.

"You know it's the right thing to do," I tell him. "People shouldn't get away with throwing rocks through people's windows or burning crosses in their yards."

Hoot mumbles a swear word and picks another pimple. Instead of gagging, I call on my feminine wiles, which is what

Daddy says Mama uses when she wants him to do something like mow the yard.

"Will you do it or not?" I flutter my eyelashes and flip my hair. My awkward attempt appears to work. He motions for me to come with him, and we go over to a shady spot at the side of the gas station where we can't be overheard.

"It may be the stupidest thing I've ever done, but I'll try," he says.

The color drains from Hoot's face, and he looks as though he is about to go in front of a firing squad full of guys wearing white hoods.

"My uncle has a list of names. But he keeps it locked up in his gun cabinet."

"Where's his gun cabinet?" I ask.

"In his house. With two bulldogs inside that don't let anybody get close," he says. "Even if I got in, I don't know if I could get out of there alive. Besides, the key to his house is hooked on his belt, and there's no way I can get that away from him."

"Let me worry about the key," I say. "As for the bulldogs, I bet Paris can think of something to do with them."

"As soon as I have the key, we'll come by, and you can take us to your uncle's house, okay?"

Hoot agrees, but he doesn't look at me.

"Where does your uncle work, anyway?" I ask.

"He's a deputy with the sheriff's department," Hoot says.

No wonder the police didn't write down their reports. They were probably told not to.

Meanwhile, I contemplate my plan. We have to go into the sheriff's office and somehow get a key from Hoot's uncle's belt. Then we have to sneak into his house, past two guard dogs, and take a list of names. I have to admit it sounds impossible. But it could be worse. There could be alligators involved.

Chapter Thirty-One

Ida

Trudy is quiet again, a sure sign that she is up to something. We pass in the hallway.

"Would you like to go out for an ice cream?" I ask.

Our eyes meet and she looks away, as though not wanting me to see what is hidden there.

"I told Vel I'd come over," she says.

"Vel can come, too," I say.

She hesitates. "Maybe you could take Teddy," she says. "He's due some grandmother time, anyway."

Trudy and I have barely spoken since the article came out in the newspaper. At first I didn't worry about it, but this latest silence feels even more serious than our trip to the State House. At least Abigail and I are talking again, and Ted Junior is back to working on his novel. But somehow it seems our summer drama is still going on.

This morning when the children weren't around Ted Junior told Abigail and me about receiving hate mail, letters that threaten to hurt him and us. But he says the people who write letters are not the people to worry about. It is the ones who never say a word.

In case Trudy wants to talk, I leave my bedroom door open. At twelve, she is not like other girls. She is almost too ardent. Was I ever that passionate? With age comes caution. Although it seems I was born cautious. Compared to my granddaughter, I feel dull. Perhaps that's how it should be. It is her turn to shine, not mine. My turn was over a long time ago. Or maybe it wasn't. Maybe this world has room for grandmothers and granddaughters to shine at the same time.

After Trudy leaves, I go into the kitchen to find Abigail and tell her of my plan to take Teddy for an ice cream.

"Don't spoil his supper," she says without looking up from the newspaper.

Supper is four hours away. I couldn't spoil it if I tried. But I don't tell her that. Instead, I agree. I certainly don't want to fight with Abigail in the kitchen over something so trivial.

The outbreaks that are going on all over the South over the signing of the Civil Rights Act have distracted me. The newspaper is full of stories of unrest, and the evening news adds images to go with the same stories. Tomorrow is the Fourth of July. A day we celebrate our independence. But not everybody is entirely free.

At the ice cream shop, Teddy and I run into Madison Chambers inside the entrance. He holds two scoops of strawberry ice cream stacked in a cone. A dash of pink graces his white mustache. When he greets me, he kisses the back of my hand, his mustache leaving behind a postage stamp of sticky strawberry.

"Lovely to see you again," he says.

I return the greeting. "Thank you so much for clearing all that up in Columbia," I say. "I owe you at least a hundred ice cream cones for that."

"I look forward to you paying me back." He lifts his eyebrows with a strawberry smile.

While we are in line, Teddy hangs from the counter like a baby chimpanzee until his scoop of vanilla is handed to him. To the extent that Trudy is headstrong, Teddy has energy. Sometimes just watching him makes me tired. But I suppose it's a child's job to have boundless energy. And as a grandmother, my job is to keep him from hurting himself. A task that is sometimes easier acknowledged than accomplished.

After I get my scoop of chocolate we go over to a table and sit with Madison. Within seconds, Teddy finishes his cone and begs to go outside to the nearby playground. I tell him to stay close. Then I tell Madison that my grandson is never to be left alone given his propensity for accidents. I also can't afford to make Abigail angry again so soon after the Columbia incident. Not to mention the newspaper article. He agrees to help keep an eye out.

Outside, we sit on a bench in the shade, our ice creams melting faster than we can eat them. With his napkin, he wipes a drip of chocolate from my arm. I take note of how strange it is to spend time with a man again. In a way, it makes me miss Ted Senior even more. In another way, it reminds me that I am the one who is still alive.

Madison and I are the same age, yet he seems older. After he and Ted Senior graduated from Duke, we often invited Madison over for dinner to our one-bedroom apartment near the courthouse. Even in those early days, I was comfortable with him.

"Has that granddaughter of yours been staying out of trouble?" he asks. "She's got gumption, that one."

"I think she's up to something she isn't telling me about," I say.

"Well, everyone has secrets." He offers a smile that could be perceived as wicked.

I wonder what his secrets are.

Then I wonder about my own. I suppose it is a secret that I have always had a tiny crush on Madison Chambers. Or at the very least, a bit of admiration.

From our proximity on the bench, I smell his subtle aftershave. Not the same that Ted Senior wore, thank goodness, that would almost be too painful, but a scent that is all his own.

"I met Trudy's friend, Paris, the other day," he says. "They were sitting on either side of a cannon at White Point Gardens. He impressed me."

"I like him, too," I say. "Do you think children give us glimpses of who they'll later become?"

"Yes," he says, "just like we give them glimpses of who we were as children." He smiles and with a dash of playfulness, pops the remainder of his strawberry cone in his mouth.

We sit in silence now, and I wait for it to feel awkward, but it doesn't. It is an easy silence. Not empty at all, but full of potential. We watch the children play, and even Teddy is blending in, playing normally. This is the same playground I brought Ted Junior to when he was a boy, perhaps hundreds of times. Yet it is as though I am seeing it for the first time.

"Have you noticed there are no children like Paris at this playground?" I say to Madison. "Where do you suppose those children play?"

I look around, shamefully aware of how I never noticed the absence of an entire race of children. I am like a goldfish oblivious to its fish bowl.

"There is so much work to do," Madison says. "We mustn't lose hope, though, Ida." He squeezes my hand.

Am I betraying Ted Senior by feeling so comfortable with Madison?

Teddy is now on the tall slide.

So much for playing normally, I say to myself.

As soon as his feet hit the ground, he goes into a roll. I hold my breath until he stands with his arms up in the air. Some of the tumbles he takes frighten me. We will need to go home soon. Abigail likes him to have quiet time in the afternoon—something that Dr. Spock character recommended. I wish Abigail would quit reading childrearing books and just get to know her children. Of course—even with this new backbone I appear to be growing—I won't be telling that to Abigail anytime soon.

Madison and I watch the children play. White children. I try to imagine a world where there are children of every color and every nationality playing on the same playground. With all the unrest around the country, it seems impossible. Like Madison said, we have a lot of work to do.

Yet I can't help thinking the young people will save us. People like Trudy and Paris and maybe even Vel, if she stops reading long enough. The thought nags at me again that Trudy is up to something. Something she doesn't want to tell me about. Something that may be more dangerous than one of Teddy's stunts. On the way home I decide to ask her about it and not give up until she answers.

Chapter Thirty-Two

Trudy

Paris, Vel, and I hide behind the bushes across the street from the Charleston sheriff's department. It is a summer of hiding in bushes. The building is small, beige, and rectangular, all on one floor. The police cars are parked to the side, and it is easy to see when anyone comes and goes.

We spot Hoot's uncle driving up in a patrol car. He looks like an older version of Hoot and Hank, except wearing a uniform.

"Those Macklehaneys all look alike," Paris says.

"They all look like morons," Vel says. She repositions a pink barrette in her poodle perm that matches her pink fingernail polish.

In order for Vel to help us, I had to promise to go to the library with her later and help her carry home some books. This means she can check out twelve, which is the maximum allowed. A small price to pay if it helps us get those names.

Hoot's uncle gets out of his patrol car, and we duck deeper into the bushes. He lights a cigar and talks to another deputy.

A set of keys sparkle on his belt in the summer sun. They remind me of Wally's keys at the State House. Somehow we managed to outsmart Wally, so maybe we can outsmart Hoot's uncle, too. It helps that this isn't our first run-in with the "old guard" as Madison Chambers called them. Although it may be our last.

While Paris and I wait in the bushes, Vel begins to execute our plan. As usual, Vel is dressed in pink from barrette to sneakers. She resembles a giant azalea blossom wearing a blond wig. With my nod, Vel poofs her Toni perm and walks up to Hoot's uncle. Fanning herself, she tells him she is not feeling well. Then she pretends to faint on the grass next to the sidewalk. Earlier this morning, Paris showed her how to do a pratfall without hurting herself.

With Vel on the ground, Hoot's uncle says a cuss word, like the last thing he needs today is a fainting kid. He leans over Vel to ask if she is okay. I run to her side, pretending to be out for a stroll. With him distracted, I am to unhook his keys. What I didn't anticipate is when he bends over, his keys totally disappear underneath a roll of flab. There is no way I am putting an arm in there to dig them out.

I whisper to Vel that it is not going to work, and she pops up like she is the Jack in a Jack-in-a-Box and fans herself with her hand.

"I feel better now," she tells Hoot's uncle. "I just got a little hot. But that cool breeze really helps."

The officer and I exchange a quick look. Charleston hasn't had a cool breeze in months. If anything, the breeze feels like car exhaust without the gasoline fumes.

"Thank you for your help," I say to him, my smile as fake as Vel's fainting attack. We walk away and drop into the bushes again.

"Well, that was a disaster," I whisper to Vel and Paris. "What do we do now?"

We look at each other, empty of ideas.

Just when we are about to give up and go home, Hoot walks around the corner. When he passes us in the bushes, he winks. Has he been watching the entire time?

"If that moron rats on us, it's your fault, Trudy Trueluck." Vel's whisper feels like a shout.

Nobody moves. We wait to see what Hoot's got up his sleeve along with his skinny arm. If he does rat on us, we will have the entire Ku Klux Klan burning crosses and aiming rocks at us.

When Hoot arrives, his uncle slaps his shoulder in a greeting that nearly knocks Hoot over.

"I'm glad nobody greets *me* that way," Paris whispers. "I'd be in the hospital afterward."

Our eyes stay focused on Hoot.

"Hank says you need your brakes looked at," Hoot says, loud enough for us to hear. "He sent me over to get your keys so we can pick up your car later."

Hoot's uncle takes a step back, probably because Hoot is talking so loudly.

"Hank heard your brakes squealing as you drove by the filling station this morning," Hoot continues. "You know you can't be too careful with brakes. Especially if you're chasing criminals all day."

Even from a distance, Hoot's smile reveals his corn kernel teeth.

It occurs to me that his uncle will never fall for something this lame. Then, to my amazement, he removes a key from his chain and tosses it to Hoot.

"We don't need the car key, we need the house key," I whisper.

"Why don't you give me your house key, too," Hoot says, like he heard me. "When we go to drop the car off I'll go let your dogs out in the backyard for a little while."

Hoot's uncle hesitates. Is he on to him? We hold our breath. But then the big man shrugs and tosses Hoot the house key, too. We exhale one long breath while Hoot walks away. After his uncle goes back inside, Vel and I take off after Hoot, who waits at the corner for us.

"I thought we should have a backup plan in case yours didn't work," Hoot says to me.

I resist telling him it was a brilliant idea since I don't want him to get any more ideas about holding my hand.

"I told my brother this morning that Uncle Ray's brakes were squealing," Hoot says, "and just like I thought he would, Hank told me to go get Uncle Ray's keys."

He looks proud of himself, and I give him a smile for payback, like carrying Vel's library books.

"Well, let's go over there and get that list," I say.

"But I thought you said there were bulldogs," Vel says. "How will we get past the dogs?"

We look back at Paris, who is still in the bushes. He motions for us to follow him.

A few minutes later we arrive at Paris' house and go inside. He asks Miss Josie if he can pack up several of her leftover barbequed ribs, and she agrees, wrapping them in a big piece of aluminum foil. She doesn't seem the least bit suspicious. In the meantime, Hoot acts totally weird, like he has never been in a colored person's house before. His shoulders are practically even with his ears, and he keeps looking around, like he can't believe how normal the house looks.

Before we leave, Miss Josie offers each of us one of her homemade oatmeal raisin cookies. Hoot says no at first, but then he changes his mind when he sees how much we enjoy them. By the time we leave, Hoot's shoulders have relaxed, and he thanks Miss Josie for the cookies. He even calls her "ma'am."

"Maybe Dr. King should take oatmeal raisin cookies on his Civil Rights marches," I say to Paris. "They sure won Hoot over."

Paris laughs.

We walk west for several blocks and stop short of a rickety house near The Citadel, the military college of South Carolina. We hide in another set of bushes and watch Hoot's uncle's house like we are on a stakeout. A lawn ornament stands at the end of the driveway. It is a little colored man dressed up like a horse jockey. I think of how much trouble colored people would get into if they had little statues of white people in their yards.

While Hoot tries the key, Vel and I stand on the porch, and Paris waits behind the small garage a few feet away. My neck hurts from all the looking around to make sure nobody sees us. The door opens easily. As soon as we inch ourselves inside, the growling starts. It sounds like two saber-tooth tigers are trapped in the bedroom determined to get out. They sniff the crack under the door with so much force I am reminded of Hoover vacuum cleaners.

Vel's eyes are as wide as the silver dollar-sized pancakes my mom makes sometimes. Vel has never liked dogs, even friendly ones, and these don't sound the least bit friendly.

"I just can't do this, Trudy." Vel sounds like she might cry any second, even though she isn't the type to cry.

Instead of being angry, I tell her to go home and wait for us. In a rush of pink, Vel dashes for the door.

With Vel gone, Paris and Hoot and I stand in the living room with our backs to the wall. A huge Confederate flag covers an entire wall in the living room. Over the television are two swords crisscrossed with "C.S.A." carved into the blades. Next to that, in a glass case under the picture window, are Confederate pistols and rifles next to a whole collection of Confederate caps.

"This is like a museum," I whisper.

"A Confederate museum," Paris whispers back. He shudders, and I put a hand on his shoulder.

To the right of the television is a large photograph of Fort Sumter, the birthplace of the Civil War. A place nearly every school kid in South Carolina visits on field trips.

Meanwhile, the dogs get wilder by the second. Paris approaches the bedroom door and opens the paper bag containing the ribs. He waves one of them in front of the crack at the bottom of the door. The dogs stop growling and clawing and take deep sniffs of the ribs.

"Are you ready?" Paris says.

Hoot stands by Paris and reaches up to the top of the door-jamb. He finds another key that's for the bedroom door. He slowly turns the key in the lock until we hear a loud click. Hearing the click, the dogs lurch at the door. Hoot holds it closed with two hands, a desperate look on his face.

My heart beats so loudly I can hear it in my ears.

"Open it on the count of three," I say, thinking we can't give up now.

The sniffing continues, like the dogs are going to sniff the floorboards right off the foundation.

I begin the countdown and debate whether to continue. What if it doesn't work? What if the dogs go for our throats instead of the ribs? I should have told Nana Trueluck my plan so she could have talked me out of it. But it is too late to turn back now.

Paris stands behind Hoot, ready to throw the meat.

I yell "Three!" Courage and cowardice surge in equal amounts.

Hoot opens the door, and the dogs run out at the same time that Paris throws the meat across the living room floor toward the front door. When the dogs lunge for Miss Josie's barbeque ribs, we rush into the bedroom and slam the door behind us.

Safely inside, the three of us lean against the wall. Deep claw marks are etched in the back of the door and puddles of drool are everywhere. After my heartbeat returns to normal, I realize the bedroom is a museum, too. The walls are covered with old photographs of Confederate generals who watch our every move. Thick curtains cover the only window making the room dark and musty. It looks more like a burial chamber than a bedroom.

For several seconds we are silent.

"This place is full of ghosts," Paris says.

"Tell me about it," I say. I tell Hoot to hurry up. I am ready to get out of here.

He tries to open the gun cabinet, but it is locked. "I don't know where he keeps the key to this," Hoot says. He feels around for a key on top of the chest and comes up with a handful of dust.

"You mean we needed a key for the gun cabinet, too?" I ask.

"I bet it's somewhere in this room," Paris says. "Some-where close."

I turn on the overhead light, and the three of us look around the small room. We look in drawers and under the bed. The dogs have finished the ribs and now sniff at the bottom of the door like they would like to chomp on our ribs next. As they growl and claw, the door dances on its hinges. Then they begin to bark.

"That racket is enough to wake General Robert E. Lee from the dead," Hoot says. To the side of the gun cabinet is a framed black and white photograph of a white-haired man with a beard, the general himself. A brass plate at the bottom gives his name.

"We've got to hurry," Paris says, "With all this noise, the neighbors may call the police."

The search for the key continues, except faster. I wish Nana Trueluck were here. I wish I'd confided in her and told her my plan. A plan that at this point appears doomed. We search on top of things, inside drawers, under the bed. All we find is a great big nothing. By now we have to yell at each other to hear over the dogs' barking. We sit on the bed that is lumpy enough to have dead bodies under the mattress.

"What's his most prized possession in this room?" Paris asks Hoot. "Sometimes people hide things there."

Hoot looks at the photograph over his uncle's bed. The engraved nameplate underneath says that it is a photograph of Nathan Bedford Forest. A black funeral ribbon is attached to the top right corner of the frame.

"He must really like that guy," I say.

"Who is he?" Paris asks.

"Bedford Forest started the Klan," Hoot says.

Paris shudders again.

Hoot stands on the bed and runs his fingers along the top of the frame, sneezing from the dust. He then takes the frame off the wall and turns it over. He smiles. The key to the gun cabinet is in an envelope taped to the back of the frame.

Hoot tosses the key to me, and I catch it easily. I test it in the keyhole, and it opens. Inside the gun cabinet are several rifles and shotguns. I have never seen so many weapons in one place, and I refuse to touch them. Some look new and some look very old. The old ones have C.S.A carved onto the barrels. I have no idea what the initials stand for, but it is not like I have time to look it up in a dictionary. At the bottom are two long drawers. I open the top drawer. It is full of boxes of different bullets. The second drawer is full of knives.

"Your uncle could fight the entire Civil War from his bedroom," I say.

"That's the whole point," Hoot replies.

"There's nothing here," Paris says, rummaging through the knife drawer.

"There must be a list of members somewhere," I say.

"What if he's not the one who has the list," Paris says.

He could be right. We are almost ready to give up again when Hoot finds a secret drawer behind the knives. He pulls out four sheets of yellowing paper with names and addresses written on them.

"Pay dirt," Hoot says.

In the next second we hear sirens.

Chapter Thirty-Three

Ida

The hairs stand on the back of my neck as though a hurricane is coming ashore. I remember Hurricane Gracie that swept in at the end of September 1959. Ted Senior and I lost the roof on our house, and our windows blew in. I have never gone through anything scarier. Except maybe this: Trudy is in trouble. I can feel it.

When we get home, Teddy goes into his room for his quiet time, albeit reluctantly. I look all over for Trudy, but she isn't here. I will have to wait until she comes home to make sure she is okay. To distract myself, I go into the kitchen to report to Abigail. She is baking early today and has a bigger order of apple pies than usual because of tomorrow being July Fourth. She asks about our time at the ice cream parlor and the playground, but I don't mention that Teddy and I saw Madison there or that he kissed and held my hand. I wish sometimes that Abigail and I could share these intimacies. We are, after all, two grown women living in the same household. So far, all my attempts to connect in that way have failed.

"Can I help you cut apples?" I ask.

"I've got it handled," she says, as if I am criticizing her preparedness.

"I'm sure you've got it handled. I just wanted to be useful."

She glances at me as if to discern if I am telling the truth. Then she offers me a knife and cutting board.

"What is Trudy up to these days?" Abigail asks. "She's barely been home."

"Whatever it is, she hasn't shared it with me," I say, which seems to please her.

Until recently, it never occurred to me that Abigail might be jealous of my relationship with Trudy. Yet more and more it makes sense.

Then I remember something that Ted Junior told me before they got married. That Abigail and her mother were at constant odds. Even from a distance, I would call their relationship strained. Though Abigail's family lives in Georgia, she rarely goes there. And the few times I have interacted with the "other" grandparents—at christenings and a couple of Thanksgivings—I remember thinking that Abigail was definitely the warmest member of her family. When around Abigail's mother, I feel the need to put on a sweater. Her personality is chilly, at best. In fact, I made a comment to Ted Senior about how her mother reminded me of an iceberg, and with Abigail as an only child, she was doomed like the *Titanic*. Not the nicest thing to say, for sure, but unfortunately it felt true.

"You know, I was an only child, too," I say. I do this sometimes. Say something out loud when I am actually having a conversation with myself.

"You've told me that before," Abigail says, not inviting further comment.

She flours her rolling pin and rolls out the dough for six pies. I wish she would let me help her. I also wish she would show the tiniest bit of interest in me. That is all anyone wants. At least she is interested in what Trudy might be up to. Knowing Trudy, we have reason to be concerned. Is she hitchhiking to Mississippi to march with Martin Luther King Junior?

"I'm sure you have no need to worry about Trudy," I say. The lie sticks in my throat, and I cough to dislodge it.

"Are we talking about the same child?" Abigail says, with a short laugh.

Before I have time to answer, Ted Junior walks into the kitchen.

"Why are you home so early?" Abigail asks.

"I needed a break," he says.

He enters the kitchen, his suit coat tossed over one shoulder. Sweat pools in puddles under the arms of his white shirt. He takes off his navy-blue tie with a red stripe running through it and tosses it onto the kitchen table.

"We've been told to cancel vacations for policemen," he says. "The governor has received word from the White House that all southern states should be on high alert for demonstrations on the Fourth."

Abigail washes the flour from her hands and turns to face him. She asks if it is because of the Civil Rights Act.

He nods.

"Why did Johnson have to force that on us now?" she asks.

"We're in the midst of another Civil War," Ted Junior says. "We need this. Otherwise things will never get better."

He gives me a quick hug and then gets himself a cola from the refrigerator and drinks it in several gulps. "Where's Trudy and Teddy?" he asks.

"Teddy's having quiet time, and your daughter is god-knows-where," Abigail says.

Ever since the Columbia trip, Trudy has become Ted Junior's daughter. She wants nothing to do with the independent part of Trudy, whereas I would take credit for it in an instant.

"Do you know what she's up to?" he asks me.

"I don't," I say, which is the truth.

"I'm not sure I can deal with much more this summer." He stands in front of the oscillating fan.

Every now and again I catch a glimpse of him as a boy. He was like Vel in terms of how much he read. He always had a book with him, yet he loved the outdoors, too. One summer he read *Don Quixote* and climbed live oaks like windmills. Another summer he created a nation of Lilliputians in the backyard with twigs, glue, and acorns.

"Will you talk to her?" he asks me. "Make sure she's not taking down another flag or something?"

"I will," I say, wishing I had thought of a way to talk to her this morning.

He kisses Abigail on the cheek. "I need to put on a clean shirt and get back," he says to her. Even if I don't entirely see the connection, the love in his eyes is real. I think of Madison and how his strawberry mustache tickled my hand.

I am too old for this, I tell myself. Then the hairs on my neck prickle again. I need to find Trudy and talk to her before it is too late.

Chapter Thirty-Four

Trudy

The dogs howl with the sirens and claw the floorboards like they are digging to China to reach us.

"Let's get out of here!" I yell.

We slam the drawers and lock the gun cabinet. Then Hoot hands me the papers, and I put them in the elastic of my shorts. The pages are cool and crinkly. After Hoot hands me the key, I jump on the bed to return it to the back of the frame. Once I am off, Paris straightens the bedspread so it will look like nobody's been there.

For our escape, Hoot unlocks the window and pushes it wide open. I put one leg out and am about to leap before I realize that I am at least six feet from the ground. But if I don't jump, I have got some major explaining to do to the police, as well as my parents.

"You can do it, Trudy." Paris' words push me from behind. "Keep your knees bent and roll when you fall."

Has Paris been talking to Teddy? The sirens get louder and our options are running out. I follow his instructions and jump. Then I stumble into a roll with an *oomph*. For several seconds I stay on the ground to make sure I am okay and all my limbs still work. Then I get up and wipe the dirt from my shorts before securing the papers again. Energy tingles through me and in that instant I understand my brother a little better.

Paris jumps next and rolls just like he told me to. He stands with his hands on his hips like he is part of the Flying Wallendas, too. If I had time, I'd applaud.

Hoot has one leg out of the window preparing to jump when I yell for him to stop. "Hoot, we need to put the dogs back into the bedroom," I say. "We have to make it look like we haven't been here."

With obvious reluctance, he turns and goes back inside.

Paris drags a rusty metal lawn chair over to the window, and we stand on it so we can see inside the room. Hoot stands by the door, wiping sweat from his forehead, his hand on the doorknob.

"We'll distract them as soon as you let them in," I call to Hoot.

The sirens sound like they are three or four blocks away.

Paris yells at him to hurry.

Hoot looks up at the ceiling as though to say a final prayer. Then he opens the door and runs toward the window. The dogs charge after him and go right for Hoot's ankles. He screams.

To distract the dogs, Paris and I begin to pound on the window and howl as loud as we can. One of the dogs stops and looks at us, her head turned sideways. When Hoot reaches the window, he dives straight through, head first. Paris and I have to duck out of the way so he doesn't crash into us.

I slam the window shut. The wild barking is suddenly muffled. Dog slobber covers the glass. The sirens stop mid-scream in front of the house.

Paris leads the way through a thick hedge that pokes at us. Then we run down the alley behind the houses. Hoot limps as he runs. When we are finally far enough away, we stop to look at Hoot's ankles. Both are covered with bite marks and blood, enough to make me wish I had my dad's first-aid kit.

Hoot sticks a finger in a hole of his ratty undershirt and tears off a piece to make a bandage. He insists he is okay.

"You got them?" he asks me.

I lift my shirt enough to reveal the folded papers. Papers with all the names and addresses of the rock-throwers and cross-burners in Charleston and Dorchester Counties.

"Now what do we do?" I ask.

The three of us exchange looks. We haven't thought this far ahead. Like the rebel flag incident, we never actually thought we would pull it off. But we have.

"I'll talk to Nana Trueluck and ask her what we should do," I say.

"Well, I'm done," Hoot says. "You asked me to get the names, and I got you the names."

"Sorry about your ankles," Paris says to Hoot.

Hoot shrugs it off. "It's not that bad," he says. He seems more concerned about other things. "Do you two swear on a stack of Bibles that you will never tell a soul where you got that list?"

"I swear," Paris says.

"I swear, too," I say.

"You better be telling the truth," he says, "or I'll end up like one of those barbeque ribs."

We do a quick pinkie swear, and Hoot limps off down the alley.

Paris and I turn in the direction of my house and do our usual routine of pretending we don't know each other, him following twenty yards behind and on the other side of the road to throw people off. We are getting good at walking this way—together but apart.

When we arrive at my house, I pass Nana Trueluck's car in the side driveway and go through the gate into the backyard. A few minutes later Paris does the same. No one can see us in our backyard. But I tell Paris to hide in my treehouse anyway, while I go into the house to get Nana Trueluck. He hesitates at the tree.

"I know it looks rickety," I say, "but it's perfectly safe."

The papers tucked in my pants start to get wet from my sweat. I need to put them someplace cool and safe.

"What about Vel?" Paris says. "She's in on this, too, even though she didn't stay for the bulldog part."

He has a point. I tell him to wait in the treehouse, and I walk through the backyards to get to Vel's house. When I go in the back door, Rosemary is ironing in the kitchen.

"Hello, Miss Trudy," she says, smoothing a sheet with her hand.

"Hello right back, Miss Rosemary," I say.

I have never called her "Miss" before, and the look she gives me confirms her surprise. As far as I know, Miss Josie is the only colored person I know who white people and colored alike call "Miss." Rosemary is darker than Miss Josie and Paris, and I wonder if white people come in shades, too. In the winter I am very light, but in the summer I turn a light pink. I never tan like some of the girls in my school do. But even if I did, I don't much see the point of baking in the sun.

"Vel around?" I ask.

"She's up in her room reading." Steam rises from one of Vel's pink shirts that Rosemary is pressing into the ironing board. "That girl is going to turn into a book someday, she reads so much."

It makes me smile to picture Vel as a pink book with blonde curly hair. I take the steps to Vel's room two at a time and lean against the door-jamb.

"We did it," I say.

She looks up from her book, and I show her the yellowing notebook paper under my shirt, damp with sweat.

She jumps up from her bed, and I hand her the sheets.

"Holy moly!" she says. "And you didn't get eaten by those dogs?"

"Miss Josie's barbecued ribs worked," I say, not telling her how close we came to being kibble.

"What do we do now?" she asks.

I like that she is saying "we."

"Paris is hiding in my treehouse. Can you go wait with him while I talk to Nana Trueluck and ask her what we should do with them? He can tell you all about what happened at that house."

Vel slides on her flip-flops and the two of us walk to my house.

With Vel and Paris in the treehouse, I stand on the small side porch that leads to the kitchen. I take a deep breath and wonder how to explain to Nana Trueluck what we have just done. But we need her to tell us what to do next. Otherwise, we may have risked our lives for nothing.

Chapter Thirty-Five

Ida

Abigail and I spoon sliced apples into pie crusts. It is a rare moment when she lets me help her, and I am happy to let her be the expert at this task, even though I have baked my share of apple pies.

"Where have you been?" Abigail asks when Trudy enters the kitchen.

I have to resist showing my relief at seeing her standing there and beam a smile at her instead.

"I was with Vel," Trudy says after a beat of silence. When she looks away, I take this as a signal that there is more to the story.

"What were you doing?" Abigail turns to face her daughter.

With her third degree, Abigail can sound like the Gestapo sometimes.

"We took a walk along the marsh road," Trudy says.

She is not the type to fib unless other people might get in trouble, too. I wonder where Vel and Paris are. The look she gives me tells me she needs to talk. What I don't know is how to finesse my way out of Abigail's kitchen and risk losing her temporary good graces.

"You want a cheese sandwich?" Abigail asks Trudy.

"No, ma'am," Trudy says.

Now I know something's up. Trudy rarely turns down food—especially food that contains cheese.

"Abigail, can you excuse me a moment? I need to get something out of my car."

I leave the house with a nod to Trudy to join me. Seconds later we stand under the magnolia tree in the side yard, out of view of the kitchen window.

"You look like the cat who swallowed the canary," I say to her, but actually she looks more worried than chagrined.

Trudy's words rush forward like the force of holding them back was almost too much. "You know that rebellion we started a few days ago?"

"Yes, of course," I say. "It's a miracle we didn't get in more trouble over that one."

She waits another beat. "You know how we thought it was over, and then the newspaper article came out, and we got a rock thrown through the window?"

I nod.

"Well, it's not exactly over."

"Trudy, what have you done?" I hide my alarm.

Abigail and Ted Junior made me promise to not let Trudy do anything the least bit dangerous or there would be far-reaching consequences. I am not sure exactly how to stop her from doing things she doesn't tell me about. I am not a mind reader. Although in these last few weeks of living here, I have a sense of what makes Trudy tick. And one thing is injustice.

She motions for me to follow her to the treehouse. Paris and Vel appear in the door, guilty looks on their faces.

Ted Senior built this treehouse for Trudy when she was five. It consists of pine boards hammered together that make up four primitive walls, with two windows sawed out, as well as a door. A sturdy homemade ladder has eight steps leading to the door. Despite the storms that hit the coast from time to time, this treehouse has withstood them all.

For a moment, I wonder where I will live next and glance at the treehouse.

Trudy climbs up the ladder in record time and invites me up.

"Can't we talk down here?" I say. As a girl, I'd have climbed up those steps in a flash. But at this moment, I feel old.

"You can do it," Trudy says, sounding like Ted Senior.

I hesitate.

Come on, old girl, I tell myself.

I remind myself that I have been in this treehouse before. Ted Senior invited me up after he put on the finishing touches. We kissed there. One of those unexpected kisses that makes you feel young again.

As I ascend, the handmade steps creak. I hate heights, even the height of a stepladder, and I already wonder how I will get down. I sit with an *oomph* on the wooden floor. Paris and Vel sit opposite each other under the windows, and Trudy sits in the corner by the door where Ted Senior carved his initials. My eyes mist, and I tell myself I don't have time to grieve right now.

"You need to tell me what you've done," I say to the three of them.

Trudy tells me the details of getting a list of names of people who might not appreciate exposure.

"Lord, in heaven." I turn the volume down on my voice as soon as it raises. "Taking down a flag in a public place is one thing," I whisper to Trudy. "Breaking into someone's house? That's—"

I am not often at a loss for words.

"What were you thinking?" I ask.

"But they burned a cross in our yard and threw a rock through our window," Trudy says. "How is that any different?"

I have to admit I see her point. "We have to let the police handle these things. That's their job," I say, sounding my age.

"But there are policemen on the list," Trudy says, her eyes wide.

Words escape me again. I can't say in seventy years of life a situation of this level of morality has ever come up. And it is probably time it did.

"We want to expose these people," Trudy says.

Paris and Vel remain silent, and I can't say that I blame them. It occurs to me that Vel looks different, and I realize she doesn't have a book with her.

"Are you sure no one saw you?" I ask.

The three accomplices exchange uneasy looks.

"I don't think so," Trudy says.

"Where are these documents?" I ask.

Trudy hands me several yellowed pages from under her blouse. A list of over a hundred names line the pages. A few of the surnames are ones I recognize. All members of the local Klu Klux Klan. This is like realizing that your beloved home is infested with termites. Who do you call if you know some of the exterminators are in on the infestation? Not to mention what might happen if anyone finds out Trudy has these. It could be more trouble than we ever imagined.

"We need to talk to Madison Chambers," I say to them. "He'll know what to do." At least I hope he will.

They agree to my idea.

We file down the ladder one at a time, which doesn't seem nearly as harrowing as being in possession of this list.

"Get in the car. I'll get my keys," I say to them.

In the kitchen Abigail cleans mixing bowls.

"What are you and Trudy up to now?"

"We need to run an errand," I say.

"You aren't going to Columbia again are you?" Abigail laughs another short laugh, but her eyes are serious.

"Of course not," I say.

How could I possibly tell her that her daughter has done something potentially even more dangerous?

"We'll be back in about an hour," I say, sounding practically chipper instead of panicked.

I go out the back door and find Trudy and Vel in the front seat and Paris lying down in the back. Not only does he walk a block or two behind the girls, now he is hiding in the back seat. I tell him to sit up and change places with Trudy and Vel. The children do as they are told without complaint, and now Paris sits beside me in the front seat. It may be 1964 in Charleston, but every decision helps to move things along. Who knows, maybe Trudy's list will help, too.

I drive over to Tradd Street, where Madison lives, and park in front of his house. The four of us walk up to the door. It has been years since I have been here. Ted Senior usually invited Madison to our house so he could get a home-cooked meal. I ring the buzzer and wait. My young friends stand on the front porch with me. Paris stands in the bushes, and I motion for him to join us. He has been hanging out in shrubs long enough.

The door opens, and Madison Chambers radiates a smile that makes my knees a bit wobbly.

"If it isn't Charleston's newest and youngest civil rights leaders," he says.

"You have no idea," I say with a sigh.

Madison kisses my hand again, and my companions exchange looks. Then he shakes Trudy's hand, followed by Vel's and Paris'. He commends the children on their strong hand-shakes and then invites us into his garden behind his house. The four of us sit on white, wooden benches with green and gold cushions. A vine of tiny white flowers weaves its way around the bench creating an aroma that is indeed celestial. The shade envelopes us. I am a great lover of shade. I could spend the rest of my life in this very spot. If this were purely a social visit, spending time in this lovely garden would be heavenly.

"To what do I owe this honor?" Madison asks. Even in casual around-the-house clothes he looks like a gentleman.

Everyone turns to look at me, as though I am appointed ringleader again, a position I do not relish, although I am getting used to it.

"It seems that Trudy and Paris have come across some interesting documents," I say to him. I leave out the part about how they got them.

Madison pulls a pair of reading glasses from his shirt pocket, and Trudy hands him the list. For several seconds his eyes narrow before widening again.

"Is this what I think it is?" he asks, looking over his glasses at us.

"Yes, sir," Trudy replies. "It's the names of every member of the local KKK."

Madison pets his mustache. His seriousness permits a brief smile.

"How did you come by these?" he asks.

Trudy tells him the whole story of having to be Hoot's girlfriend and getting his uncle's key and so on.

Madison appears impressed by the children's audacity, but also more than a little concerned.

"When Trudy told me what they'd done, I thought we'd best talk to you," I say. "I imagine this list might be of some use if it got into the right hands. Maybe it could even change things a little if certain people were exposed?"

"Interesting," Madison says. He looks over his glasses again. "What do you think you want to do with these?" he says to Trudy.

"We want to stop all those rocks getting thrown through windows and crosses burnt in yards," Trudy says.

"And lynchings," Paris adds.

Madison and I exchange a look. It no longer seems to matter that the names were taken illegally. Doesn't the public deserve to see a list of criminals in our midst no matter how the names were obtained?

Ted Senior liked to say that sometimes things aren't black or white. For sure this is a gray area.

Madison looks at the papers again and then back at me. "You know how dangerous this is, don't you?"

"That's why we came to you," I say. "The last thing I want is for anybody to get hurt."

The look on Trudy's face suggests that she never considered the consequences of her actions might involve physical violence. Who at age twelve does? That is left for people like me who have lived in the world long enough to know that people have been hurt for a lot less than this. Miss Josie can undoubtedly verify this as well.

"Are we the only five people in Charleston who know about this?" Madison asks.

"Hoot Macklehaney knows," Trudy says. "But he'll never tell. If he did, he would be in worse trouble than any of us."

Madison gets quiet for a long time, his white eyebrows knitted in a conversation of their own. Finally he looks over at me, and I am struck again by the kindness in his face.

"I have an idea, but I'm not sure it will work," he says.

"One idea is better than no ideas," I say and wonder when I became so awkward with words. It reminds me of when I first met Ted Senior. I literally ran into him on the street like a scene in a movie. I said something flimsy then, too. Something like *Come here often?* My face warms in the hot day. I turn away from the past and lend my full attention to Madison.

"I have a friend at the newspaper who would be very excited to see this list," he says. "Maybe he'll even publish it. But nobody must ever know who or where it came from. Understand?"

We agree.

"I'll say the list came from an anonymous, yet reliable, source," he begins again. "Of course I must remind you that this doesn't mean my friend will publish it. You must try to be satisfied with whatever result."

The four of us agree again.

"I'll telephone my friend at the newspaper and set up a time to meet with him this evening," he concludes.

We stand, and I shake Madison's hand to thank him for helping us. He holds on longer than I expect. We file out of the garden and say goodbye to him, leaving through a side gate. We get back in my car, which has become a pressure cooker in the heat, even with all the windows down.

When we get back to the house we sit at the picnic table far enough away from the kitchen so that Abigail won't over-hear. My companions are twelve, going on twenty, with hints of wisdom already evident. Perhaps with their help, the unrest in this country will calm down and freedom will prevail.

Chapter Thirty-Six

Three Years Later
1967
Trudy

History didn't take much notice of our trip to Columbia three summers ago. Nothing changed. The names of the Ku Klux Klan were published in the newspaper, and there was a big hoopla about it. There were a lot of angry letters to the editor—some defended the men, others expressed outrage—but ultimately the only thing that changed, as far as I could tell, was that Daddy lost the next election in a landslide victory for the other side.

Nana Trueluck and I are sitting in the kitchen when Mr. Chambers arrives. They have become great friends. They go to movies together and take walks along the Battery in the cool of the morning. He always kisses her on the cheek when he greets her, and today is no exception. Then he joins us at the kitchen table.

"I have some big news," he says to us.

Given I am fully immersed into the boredom of my summer, just hearing the words excite me.

"Tell us," Nana Trueluck says.

She always smiles whenever Mr. Chambers is around.

"I just got word that Martin Luther King Junior plans to visit Charleston tomorrow," he says.

I instantly think of Paris. The riots last week in Detroit, where he used to live, were reported to be the worst in a hundred years. That's a lot of rocks thrown through windows. Thankfully Paris' mother moved back to Charleston last year, but he still has cousins there and an aunt and uncle.

"I worry about Dr. King coming here," Nana Trueluck says. "I can't imagine that he's safe anywhere."

Mr. Chambers nods his agreement, his mustache downturned.

Nana Trueluck and I continue to watch Walter Cronkite every evening. Riots are taking place all over the country: Memphis, Durham, Illinois, Newark.

"When will he arrive?" I ask.

"One-thirty at the Charleston airport," Mr. Chambers says, turning toward me. "That's not all. I have a surprise," he continues. His mustache smiles again. "Dr. King wants to meet you."

"Me?" I say and wonder if Mr. Chambers is the type to pull someone's leg.

"Well, all of you," he says. "Paris, Vel, and even your grandmother." He gives Nana Trueluck a wink.

I pop up from the table so fast it makes them laugh. "Really?" I ask.

He nods again.

I telephone Paris and tell him the news and have to take the telephone away from my ear when he screams his excitement. Vel is less enthused, but gets off the telephone quickly to pick out something to wear.

The next day Paris and Vel and I pile into the backseat of Nana Trueluck's car with Mr. Chambers sitting in the front passenger side. Her driving was already slow, but now it reminds me of turtles. Ancient turtles. My right foot presses into the floorboard to speed things up, and I long for next year when I can finally get my driver's license.

For the outing, Nana Trueluck wears a thin scarf wrapped around her head and dark sunglasses. She looks like a much older version of Kim Novak in *North by Northwest*. Thankfully, we leave the house with an hour to get to North Charleston. Daddy and Mama promise to join us at the airport a little later.

Paris is much taller now and sits in the back seat with his knees practically in his face. When we feel courageous, we parade our friendship out in the open as a sign of peaceful protest. We always get stares. In the meantime, Vel has rejected perms and wears her hair long and straight, but she still wears pink more than any normal person should.

"I can't believe Dr. Martin Luther King Junior wants to meet us." Paris has already said this about a dozen times today.

Mr. Chambers turns to look at us in the back seat. "Dr. King is on a tight schedule," he says. "He only has a few minutes at the airport before he eats and cleans up at Septima Clark's home. After that he'll speak at County Hall."

"Can we go to that, too?" I ask Nana Trueluck.

"Your father thinks it might be too dangerous," she says.

I moan my disappointment.

Last night I overheard Daddy and Mama talking about the numerous death threats to Dr. King and about how the entire Charleston police department has been assigned to protect him. To make matters worse, the race riots up north have escalated things and they are afraid of riots right here in Charleston.

We pass through a police barricade, where Mr. Chambers tells an officer that we have been invited specifically by Dr. King. Then we park and go into the airport with thirty minutes to spare. With the exception of that day he ran around the rotunda in the State House carrying the rebel flag, Paris is more animated than I have ever seen him.

Large fans move the hot air around in the terminal, and a trickle of sweat slides down my back and stops at the elastic in my bra. For a second I wish I had my old Barbie watch so I could time it. But that watch now lives in the bottom of my jewelry box with other things I have outgrown.

No longer wearing her dark glasses and scarf, Nana Trueluck seems as excited as Paris is. Photographers are nearby, as well as a man with a news camera. The smell of floor cleaner mingles with the odor of overheated bodies.

After what feels like forever, a plane lands, and word passes through the crowd that he has arrived. Everyone stands straighter. The atmosphere in the airport feels like the charge left over after a lightning strike. Paris' Adams apple bobs to swallow his nervousness. Never without a book, Vel fans herself with a paperback copy of *To Kill a Mockingbird*. We read it in our high school English class last spring, and Vel has reread it twice since.

"Here he comes!" Paris says, seeing over the crowd.

Nana Trueluck squeezes my hand and whispers into my ear, "We're watching history take place."

In a city filled with history, this is saying something. Chill bumps crawl up my arms in the hot airport.

Half a dozen men travel with Dr. King and stay close by. Madison Chambers waves and they walk over. Handsome, with a wide serious face and dark eyes, Dr. King wears a black suit and tie on one of the hottest days of the year. I can only imagine his discomfort, but to my surprise, he doesn't look miserable at all. Only serious. And determined. Like he is on a mission and nothing can stop him from doing what he needs to do. Today, what he needs to do takes place in Charleston.

Mr. Chambers introduces Dr. King to Nana Trueluck. He shakes her hand and tells her to keep up the good work. Tears pool in her eyes. She apologizes for not doing more, and he tells her that whatever she can do is appreciated. Mr. Chambers then introduces me. Dr. King shakes my hand, too. A warm, firm shake. I am close enough to see the sweat soaked into the collar of his white shirt. When he shakes Vel's hand, she gives some kind of weird curtsy/bow combination.

Then he turns to Paris. "I heard about what you did at the State House," he says. Paris' smile is huge, and I worry that he might swoon like a southern belle from seeing his hero.

"Thank you, sir," he says. "Can I have your autograph?"

From his back pocket, Paris pulls out a copy of Dr. King's *Letter from a Birmingham Jail*. Dr. King takes a fountain pen from his jacket pocket and signs the book. The look on Paris' face is something I will remember for the rest of my life—a combination of awe and pride.

Someone tells Dr. King that they have to go, that people are waiting on them. He shakes our hands again and tells us to keep up the good work. We promise we will.

He exits the airport and gets into a waiting car. As the car drives away, I think about how, for a few brief seconds, I shook hands with history.

Chapter Thirty-Seven

Three Years Later
1970
Ida

Six years have passed since that fateful summer of 1964. Six years since Paris pulled Trudy out of the path of a Sunbeam Bread truck and saved her life. Six years since our unlikely band of rebels took down the Confederate flag at the State House in Columbia, and the Charleston newspaper released a list of names of the local Ku Klux Klan.

Last week the Trueluck family attended Trudy's high-school graduation. In the fall, she will study journalism at the College of Charleston. After that she wants to work for the newspaper and report stories that inspire people to act on what they believe in. She may even write a book someday.

Two days ago, Madison Chambers asked me to marry him. I haven't told anyone the news. Not even Trudy. We are taking everyone out to Henry's tonight to announce it, the same restaurant where Madison proposed.

My happiness with Madison is a different kind of contentment than I had with Ted Senior. Part of it is that love at my age is so unexpected. After Ted Senior died, I closed the door to romance, never dreaming I'd have a love life again. But *never say never*, as the old saying goes.

The telephone rings in the kitchen, and Abigail answers it. She practically coos when she announces that Madison wants to speak to me. Perhaps she is entertaining the thought of someday not having her mother-in-law living in the spare bedroom.

Abigail now co-owns Callie's Diner and does all her baking there, where her peach, apple, and lemon meringue pies are famous. She invested in Callie's after Ted Junior's literary agent in New York sold his first novel to Harper & Row. Meanwhile, my grandson Teddy, as an incoming freshman, has already been secured as a defensive tackle by the high-school football team.

Over the phone, Madison calls me *darling*. Even Ted Senior never called me *darling* or *sweetheart*, like Madison often does. To Ted Senior, I was always *honey*. Honey this and honey that. It was sweet to be someone's honey, and I miss him still.

I tell Madison I am almost ready, just in need of some finishing touches.

"I'll pick everyone up," he says.

We end our call, and I go upstairs.

Thirty minutes later I am dressed and take a look at myself in the full-length mirror. I wear a teal summer cotton dress with pearls along with my high-top sneakers. I suppose, there is still a bit of a rebel in me yet.

After a knock, I open my bedroom door and Madison is there.

"Oh my," he says, with a playful sigh. "I'm in love with the most beautiful girl in the room."

"The only girl in the room," I say with a short laugh.

He closes the door and pulls me into his arms like he is Rock Hudson in *Pillow Talk* and I am Doris Day. We kiss. Not a peck on the lips, mind you, but a long and passionate hello, guaranteed to make an old woman's knees a bit wobbly.

"Ready to shock the Truelucks?" he asks.

"As I'll ever be," I answer, getting my knees up under me again.

The entire Trueluck clan gets into Madison's car, and we head to the restaurant. After dessert, Madison clinks his butter knife against a water glass and the two of us stand, holding hands. I announce our plans to have a small wedding ceremony at Circular Church next Saturday. Followed by a honeymoon in Savannah. Then I will move into Madison's house on Tradd Street, where we will begin our life together at seventy-six years of age. We get a standing ovation. Not only from our family—with Abigail in tears and shouting the loudest hoorays—but from the entire restaurant, including servers and cooking staff.

I imagine we are considered brave to get married at our age, but I am no longer willing to waste a moment. After all, I am still making my own history.

Later that night, Trudy sits on the end of my bed. We are the night owls in the Trueluck family and have had some of our best conversations after midnight. I look at her and take a mental snapshot. My tomboy granddaughter has turned into a beautiful young woman.

"I'll miss you living here," she says.

"I'll miss you, too," I say. "But you'll be in college soon, and you can always visit me at Madison's. In fact, I'm counting on it."

We exchange a hug. Having these last six years together in the same house has made us close. I am her buffer from Abigail, as well as someone she can trust to love her as she is. Grandmothers are experts at unconditional love.

"What are Vel's plans now that she's graduated?" I ask.

"She's going to USC," Trudy says. "She wants to major in criminal justice and work at the State House someday."

So much has stemmed from that summer when we all came together.

According to Trudy, Vel still carries a book everywhere she goes, in a purse slung over one arm. After becoming totally boy crazy from the seventh grade on, Vel gave up Nancy Drew for romance novels. In the last year she has had a steady boyfriend named Mel, short for Melvin. Even though he hasn't asked her yet, she constantly plans every detail of their wedding. From the pink wedding gown, right down to *Mel and Vel* printed on their reception napkins. Trudy and I both roll our eyes at that one.

"Has Paris found a place to live yet?" I ask. With Madison's help, Paris was accepted to an acting school in New York City.

"He'll live with an aunt and uncle in Harlem at first," she says. "Then he and Hoot may get an apartment. Hoot has applied to three schools up there."

Hoot Mackelhaney's transformation is perhaps the most dramatic of any of us. Within a month of the newspaper releasing the Ku Klux Klan names from an anonymous source, Hoot's uncle figured out that he must have been involved. When Hoot confessed, every single member of his family disowned him. Since he had nowhere to stay, Miss Josie offered to let him live at her house. As a result, Paris' Uncle Freddie helped Hoot get back in school, and he recently graduated with honors. He outgrew his acne and plans to become a lawyer who represents Civil Rights cases. He and Trudy have become great friends, as have Miss Josie and I.

Looking back, the summer of 1964 turned out to be a pivotal time in my life. Everything changed after that—my small world got bigger. In some ways it seems like my life started over that summer. It was the summer I found my voice and learned to be bold.

Who knows what the history books will say about this time and this place. For many in our country it was a time of heartbreak. For others, it was a time of great change. It strikes me that life is full of mystery. In the midst of the darkest and

most tumultuous times, laughter can light the way to new beginnings and love can exist in profound proportions.

THE END

Thank you for reading!

Dear Reader,

I hope you enjoyed *Trueluck Summer*. I worked on this book on and off for over a decade. At first, this story was only from the children's point of view and never quite seemed to work. Something was missing. And so it sat, year after year, while I wrote other books.

Then, in June of 2015, a young white man opened fire during a prayer meeting in a historic black church in Charleston, South Carolina, killing nine people. As someone who lived in Charleston with my daughters for fourteen years, this was heartbreaking news. Then a month later, after 54 years, the confederate flag flying over the State House in Columbia was finally taken down. A decade before, I had imagined Paris Moses—with the help of Trudy and Vel—bringing about a similar change.

And so, in July of 2015, I pulled this story out of its retirement with the intention of breathing new life into it. It was then that I discovered Ida Trueluck. It was as if she had been waiting all these years for me to finally notice she was there. The story needed a grandmother. Someone who had witnessed the changing times and finally had the courage to act on what she believed in. The decision to have Ida share the storytelling with Trudy made perfect sense to me. Together they would tell a sort of coming-of-age tale. Ida coming into her old age with a new boldness, and Trudy coming into the beginnings of adulthood with her own bold passion. Finally, the story felt complete.

Thank you so much for reading. It has been an honor to share *Trueluck Summer* with you. You are the reason I write, so feel free to be in touch with me. Tell me what you liked, what you loved, even what you wish I'd done differently.

You can contact me via email at susan@susangabriel.com, on my website SusanGabriel.com or on facebook at SusanGabrielAuthor.

Finally, I need to ask a favor. If you are so inclined, please consider leaving a review at Amazon, Nook, iBooks, Goodreads, etc. Reviews help readers who aren't familiar with an author take a chance on their work. A review doesn't have to be long; it can be one or two heartfelt sentences. You can tell potential readers what you liked most about the book and what interested and surprised you.

In gratitude,
Susan Gabriel

P.S. I'm now working on Book Three of the Wildflower series (Books One and Two—*The Secret Sense of Wildflower* and *Lily's Song*—are already out). I will also be writing a sequel to my comic novel, *Temple Secrets*. If you would like to be notified about these and other future books, please sign up for my newsletter at www.susangabriel.com/new-books/.

P.S.

About the Author

Trivia from 1964

Other Books by Susan Gabriel

About the Author

Susan Gabriel is an acclaimed writer who lives in the mountains of North Carolina. Her novel, *The Secret Sense of Wildflower*, earned a starred review ("for books of remarkable merit") from Kirkus Reviews and was selected as one of their Best Books of 2012.

She is also the author of *Temple Secrets*, *Lily's Song*, *Grace, Grits and Ghosts: Southern Short Stories* and other novels. Discover more about Susan at SusanGabriel.com.

Trivia from 1964

Average Income per year: $6,000.00
Gas per Gallon: 30 cents
Average Cost of a new car: $3,500.00
Loaf of Sunbeam Bread: 21 cents
United States Postage Stamp: 5 cents
Average Monthly Rent: $115.00
Ticket to the movies: $1.25

From *American Experience* on PBS.org regarding 1964:

- Betty Friedan's *The Feminine Mystique* is released as a paperback, with its first printing selling 1.4 million copies. Friedan's book ushers in a transformative feminist movement as housewives across America come to identify with the "problem that has no name" and acknowledge dissatisfaction with their domestic roles.

- G.I. Joe makes his debut as an "action figure" toy in response to the popularity of Barbie dolls.

- The Beatles perform "Till There Was You" live on The Ed Sullivan Show to an audience full of screaming teenagers and a record-breaking 73 million television viewers. Though the group had been rapidly gaining popularity in America since the December 1963 release of "I Want to Hold Your Hand," their Ed Sullivan appearance confirms that Beatlemania is sweeping the country.

- In a surprise upset, Olympic gold medalist Cassius Clay beats Sonny Liston in Miami Beach, Florida, and is crowned heavyweight champion of the world. Just one day later, he announces that he has joined the Nation of Islam and is changing his name. For the remainder of the decade, Muhammad Ali becomes known outside the boxing ring for his socio-political beliefs—specifically on racial equality and the Vietnam War.

- In the United States' first-ever televised trial verdict, Jack Ruby is found guilty of murder and sentenced to death for fatally shooting Lee Harvey Oswald, the alleged assassin of President John F. Kennedy.

- The largest earthquake in U.S. history hits Alaska, registering a magnitude of 9.2.

- Jeopardy! premieres on NBC.

- At the 36th Annual Academy Awards ceremony, Sidney Poitier becomes the first black man to win a Best Actor Oscar for his role in "Lilies of the Field."

- In June, the first group of Freedom Summer volunteers gather for training in Oxford, Ohio. Of the nearly 1,000 participants working to educate and register African Americans to vote in Mississippi and across the South, the majority are white college students from the North.

- A day after the first group of Freedom Summer volunteers arrives in Mississippi, three civil rights workers set out to investigate a church bombing near Philadelphia, Mississippi. The three activists are arrested for a traffic violation and held for several hours. When they are released at 10:30pm, it is the last time they are seen alive.

- In July, President Johnson signs the Civil Rights Act of 1964 into law. The act prohibits discrimination on the basis of race, color, religion, sex or national origin in employment, ends segregation in public places. It outlaws segregation practices common in many southern businesses for decades.

- The Beach Boys' "I Get Around" begins a two-week stint at the top of the charts.

- In September, *Bewitched* premiers on ABC. The popular sitcom about a witch and her mortal husband subtly reflects changes to traditional domestic roles, as the leading woman, Samantha, has significantly more power than her non-magical husband, Darrin.

- In October, Dr. Martin Luther King, Jr. is awarded the Nobel Peace Prize for his nonviolent civil rights activism. At 35 years old, Dr. King is the youngest person ever to receive the prize.

- The popular children's book *Chitty Chitty Bang Bang* by Ian Fleming is published posthumously. The author, well known for his James Bond series, died August 12.

Most Popular Films of 1964:

1. The Carpetbaggers
2. It's a Mad, Mad, Mad, Mad World
3. The Unsinkable Molly Brown
4. My Fair Lady
5. Mary Poppins

The Number One Hits of 1964:

The Singing Nun - Dominique
Bobby Vinton - There! I've Said It Again
The Beatles - I Want to Hold Your Hand
The Beatles - She Loves You
The Beatles – Can't Buy Me Love
Louis Armstrong - Hello, Dolly!
Mary Wells - My Guy
The Beatles - Love Me Do
The Dixie Cups - Chapel of Love
Peter and Gordon - A World Without Love
The Beach Boys - I Get Around
The Four Seasons - Rag Doll
The Beatles - A Hard Day's Night
Dean Martin - Everybody Loves Somebody
The Supremes - Where Did Our Love Go
The Animals - The House of the Rising Sun
Roy Orbison - Oh, Pretty Woman

Manfred Mann - Do Wah Diddy Diddy
The Supremes - Baby Love
The Shangri-Las - Leader of the Pack
Lorne Greene - Ringo
Bobby Vinton - Mr. Lonely
The Supremes - Come See About Me
The Beatles - I Feel Fine

1964 Most Popular TV shows:

1. Bonanza
2. Bewitched
3. Gomer Pyle U.S.M.C.
4. The Andy Griffith Show
5. The Fugitive
6. The Red Skelton Show
7. The Dick Van Dyke Show
8. The Lucy Show
9. Peyton Place II
10. Combat

Most Popular Christmas gifts, toys and presents in 1964:

Easy Bake Oven
G.I. Joe
Rat Fink Collectible Hot Rod Figures
Password Game

Mighty Tonka Dump Truck (made popular due to the elephant stepping on it during a commercial)

Plastic Mr. Potato Head

Wham-O Professional Frisbees

Monster Magnet

Rube Goldberg's Animated Hobby Kit

Hand's Down game (with Slam-O-Matic)

Compiled from American Experience on PBS, Pop-Culture.us, and ThePeopleHistory.com.

Temple Secrets

A novel

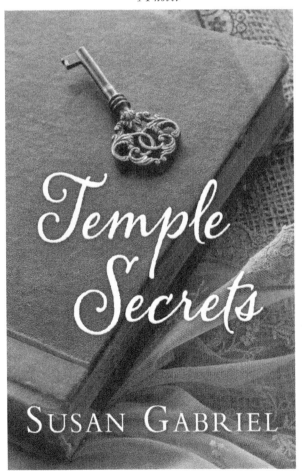

Fans of *The Help* and *Midnight in the Garden of Good and Evil* will delight in this comic novel of family secrets by acclaimed author, Susan Gabriel (*The Secret Sense of Wildflower*, a Kirkus Reviews Best Book of 2012 and an Amazon & Nook #1 Bestseller).

In Savannah, Georgia, one woman holds all the secrets. When she dies of a possible voodoo curse, the secrets start coming out. The ghosts are upset. And for the Temple family women, everything is about to change forever.

Aristocratic, 80-year-old Iris Temple has a fondness for exotic meats and her poison-pen Book of Secrets keeps her family and all of Savannah's elites in line. Shortly after Iris dies, compromising tidbits from the Book of Secrets are mysteriously published in the newspaper and the quiet lives of the Temple family women explode.

Iris's estranged daughter, Rose, escaped to Wyoming 20 years ago and married a cowboy. Will she accept the outrageous terms of the will?

Queenie, Iris's black half-sister, lives in the historic family mansion, suffering Iris's arrogant ways as her personal assistant. After all she's tolerated with Iris, will she inherit the mansion, as promised?

100-year-old Old Sally, who keeps the old Gullah traditions alive, is Queenie's mother by her white employer, Iris's father. For Rose, she is the mother Iris could never be. Did Old Sally put a voodoo curse on Iris?

When they discover who will inherit the historic family mansion and Iris's multi-million- dollar estate, the whole boisterous business of secrets forces the women into challenging – and sometimes hilarious – situations as they put the past to rest and forge a brighter future.

Temple Secrets is Southern gothic fiction at its best. If you like strong women, plots full of twists and turns, characters who are funny and unpredictable, and sibling rivalry of biblical proportions, you'll love Susan Gabriel's rollicking tale of the cost of keeping secrets, the healing that comes with their exposure and the bliss of coming home again.

Buy *Temple Secrets* and start unlocking the mysteries today!

Available in paperback, ebook and audiobook.

Praise for *Temple Secrets*

"*Temple Secrets* is a page-turner of a story that goes deeper than most on the subjects of equality, courage and dignity. There were five or six characters to love and a few to loathe. Gabriel draws Queenie, Violet, Spud and Rose precisely, with a narrative dexterity that is amazingly and perfectly sparse while achieving an impact of fullness and depth. Their interactions with the outside world and one another are priceless moments of hilarious asides, well-aimed snipes and a plethora of sarcasms.

"What happens when the inevitable inequities come about amongst the Haves, the Have Nots and the Damn-Right-I-Will-Have? When some people have far too much time, wealth and power and not enough humanness and courage? Oh, the answers Gabriel provides are as delicious as Violet's peach turnovers, and twice as addicting! I highly recommend this novel." – T.T. Thomas

"Susan Gabriel shines once again in this fascinating tale of a family's struggle to break free from their past. Filled with secrets, betrayals, and tragedy, the author weaves an intricate storyline that will keep you hooked." – R. Krug

"I loved this book! I literally couldn't put it down. The characters are fabulous and the story line has plenty of twists and turns making it a great read. I was born and raised in the south so I have an affinity for stories that are steeped in the southern culture. Temple Secrets nails it. All I needed was a glass of sweet tea to go with it." – Carol Clay

"The setting is rich and sensuous, and the secrets kept me reading with avid interest until most of them were revealed. I read the book in just a few days because I really didn't want to put it down. It is filled with characters who are funny, tragic, unpredictable and nuanced, and I must admit that I really came to know and love some of them by the end of the story." – Nancy Richards

"I was glued from the first moment that I began reading. The book accurately portrays many of the attitudes of the Old South including the intricate secrets and "skeletons in the closet" that people often wish to deny. Each character is fascinating and I loved watching each one evolve as the story unfolded. This was one of those books that I did not want to finish as it was so much fun to be involved in the action."
– Lisa Patty

"I just finished reading Temple Secrets today and I truly hated for it to end! Susan Gabriel writes with such warmth and humor, and this book is certainly no exception. I loved getting to know the characters and the story was full of humor and suspense." – Carolyn Tenn

The Secret Sense of Wildflower

"A quietly powerful story, at times harrowing,
but ultimately a joy to read."

—Kirkus Reviews, starred review
(for books of remarkable merit)

Named to Kirkus Reviews' Best Books of 2012.

Set in 1940s Appalachia, *The Secret Sense of Wildflower* tells the story of Louisa May "Wildflower" McAllister whose life has been shaped around the recent death of her beloved father in a sawmill accident. While her mother hardens in her grief, Wildflower and her three sisters must cope with their loss themselves, as well as with the demands of daily survival. Despite these hardships, Wildflower has a resilience that is forged with humor, a love of the land, and an endless supply of questions to God. When Johnny Monroe, the town's teenage ne'er-do-well, sets his sights on Wildflower, she must draw on the strength of her relations, both living and dead, to deal with his threat.

With prose as lush and colorful as the American South, *The Secret Sense of Wildflower* is a powerful and poignant southern novel, brimming with energy and angst, humor and hope.

Praise for *The Secret Sense of Wildflower*

"Louisa May immerses us in her world with astute observations and wonderfully turned phrases, with nary a cliché to be found. She could be an adolescent Scout Finch, had Scout's father died unexpectedly and her life taken a bad turn...By necessity, Louisa May grows up quickly, but by her secret sense, she also under-stands forgiveness. A quietly powerful story, at times harrowing but ultimately a joy to read." – Kirkus Reviews

"A soulful narrative to keep the reader emotionally charged and invested. *The Secret Sense of Wildflower* is eloquent and moving tale chock-filled with themes of inner strength, family and love." – Maya Fleischmann, indiereader.com

"I've never read a story as dramatically understated that sings so powerfully and honestly about the sense of life that stands in tribute to bravery as Susan Gabriel's *The Secret Sense of Wildflower*...When fiction sings, we must applaud." – T. T. Thomas, author of A Delicate Refusal

"The story is powerful, very powerful. Excellent visuals, good drama. I raced to get to the conclusion...but didn't really want to read the last few pages because then it would be over! I look forward to Gabriel's next offering." – Nancy Purcell, Author

"Just finished this with tears streaming down my face. Beautifully written with memorable characters who show resilience in the face of tragedy. I couldn't put this down and will seek Susan Gabriel's other works. This is truly one of the best books I've read in a very long time." – A.C.

"An interesting story enhanced by great writing, this book was a page turner. It captures life in the Tennessee mountains truthfully but not harshly. I would recommend this book to anyone who enjoys historical fiction." – E. Jones

"I don't even know how to tell you what I love about this book --- the incredible narrator? The heartbreaking and inspiring storyline? The messages about hope, wisdom, family and strength? All of those!! Everything about it!" – K. Peck

"Lovely, soul stirring novel. I absolutely could not put it down! Beautifully descriptive, evocative story told in the voice of Wildflower, a young girl of the mountains, set in a wild yet beautiful 1940's mountain town, holds you captive from the start. I had to wait to write my review, as I was crying too hard to see!" – V.C.

"I write novels, too, but this writer is fantastic. The story is authentic and gripping. Her voice through the child, Wildflower, is captivating. This story would make a great movie. I love stories that portray life changing tragedy and pain coupled with power of the human spirit to survive and continue to love and forgive. Bravo! Susan. Please write more and more." –Judi D.

"This is a wonderful story that will make you laugh, cry, and cheer." –T.B. Markinson

"I was pretty blown away by how good this book is. I didn't read it with any expectations, hadn't heard anything about it really, so when I read it, I realized from page one that it is a well written, powerful book." – Quixotic Magpie

"If you liked *Little Women* or if you love historical fiction and coming-of-age novels, this is the book for you. Definitely add The Secret Sense of Wildflower to your TBR pile; you won't regret it." – PandaReads

"Bottom line: A great story about a strong character!"
– Meg, A Bookish Affair

Available everywhere in print, ebook and audiobook.

Also by Susan Gabriel

Fiction

The Secret Sense of Wildflower
(a Best Book of 2012 – Kirkus Reviews)

Lily's Song
(sequel to *The Secret Sense of Wildflower*)

Temple Secrets

Grace, Grits and Ghosts:
Southern Short Stories

Seeking Sara Summers

Circle of the Ancestors

Quentin & the Cave Boy

Nonfiction
Fearless Writing for Women:
Extreme Encouragement & Writing Inspiration

Available at all booksellers
in print, ebook and audio formats.

CPSIA information can be obtained
at www.ICGtesting.com
Printed in the USA
BVOW08s1302200517
484646BV00002B/76/P